I0461079

THE
AMERICAN
WAY

THE AMERICAN WAY

Jomo Hendrickson

Pearl Olive Publishing, Los Angeles

This book is a work of fiction. Names, characters, places and incidents are products of the author's imagination or are used fictitiously. Any resemblance to actual events or locales or persons, living or dead, is entirely coincidental.

Copyright © 2016 by Jomo Hendrickson
All rights reserved. This book or any portion thereof
may not be reproduced or used in any manner whatsoever
without the express written permission of the publisher
except for the use of brief quotations in a book review.

Printed in the United States of America

First Printing, 2016

ISBN: 978-0-692-68713-0
eBook ISBN: 978-1-5323-0141-4

Pearl Olive Publishing

www.jomohendrickson.com

Cover illustration by Yohanes Haile

For the two who made me and those who inspire me

Chapter One

IT WAS ALWAYS LIKE THAT. Although I loved soccer, or football as we call it in my family, our relationship has always been bumpy. It all started with my first game, which was the last day I remember feeling like a regular kid.

I was ten years old. I remember my age very clearly because when Pops went to sign us up for the under eleven division of the Police Athletic League in Kokomo, Indiana, he was told there was no such age group.

I was there when the flustered young lady at the registration table said "There's not enough kids for a U-11. Nobody plays soccer here like that."

Her dismissive tone seemed to be more in reaction to Pops' accent than the actual question. Both of my parents were from St. Vincent, a small Caribbean island, and as such they apparently spoke with an accent.

I only knew they spoke differently because other kids

questioned me about it. "Are your parents from Africa or something? Why yo parents talk funny like that? Are your parents retarded?" I constantly had to explain where St. Vincent is and how to pronounce my name, Japeth Walker.

I spent so much time being defensive that I felt like I was always operating from a deficit. It's hard to build confidence in yourself when you feel that way, but football was one of the few areas that I actually felt like I had an advantage. Pops was one of the only parents in the area to have some experience with football. He grew up playing the game and he was happy that I was starting to play. He even signed waivers for me and my two best friends, Mike Wilson and Jack Johnson, to play in the U-12 league.

The morning of the first game I rushed through my breakfast and hurried to get myself ready. I was particularly proud of my Puma cleats. They were my first brand name shoes.

"What time are we leaving?"

"In due time," Pops answered with a smile.

"What time is the game?"

"Good time," Pops responded tapping me on the shoulder and sharing a laugh at my impatience with Moms.

"In the meantime, take those shoes off in the house. You're going to mess up the floor." He pointed behind me to reveal some black marks I had left on the cream colored tile.

I sat down to watch TV while I waited for my parents and little brother, Damian, to get ready. Finally, after an hour of waiting, they were ready to go.

We pulled up to the PAL fields and entered into a gravel parking lot. My eyes grew big as I looked out at the two lush green fields. Pops couldn't find a parking space so he dropped Moms and I off so that I could meet up with my team.

We stepped out of the car and I could smell the fresh cut grass mixed with the smell of popcorn and nacho cheese from the concessions stand. I searched for Jack and Mike but didn't see them anywhere.

I felt naked without them, especially Jack. We were both fast and could kick hard, which was all you needed to be a star at that recreational level. Mike liked to be the goalkeeper. I never understood his fascination with the position.

Moms stopped at a board with the schedule for the day. She looked at her watch, and then the whistles on both fields blew simultaneously marking the end of the previous games.

"Looks like you have about fifteen minutes to warm up. That's your team over there." She pointed to a group of kids with yellow t-shirts.

"Are you sure?"

"Yes."

I wasn't a big kid for my age and being younger than everyone suddenly made the experience very intimidating. Moms grabbed my hand and walked me in the direction of the team.

When we reached the coach, she first introduced herself as Elaine, my mother, then me. Coach Tina showed me a broad and anxious smile as her scraggly blonde hair blew to one side with the light wind.

She passed me a shirt and told me to join the team for warm ups. I checked my number. "Two? Do you have any other numbers left?"

"I have seven, but it's probably too—" Before she could finish, I grabbed the shirt, put it on, and was starting to run on the field when Moms grabbed my sleeve that hung down past my elbow and jerked me back towards her.

"Tuck your shirt in boy," she said as she straightened me up. "Have fun out there and be careful, okay?" She started bending and leaning in the direction to kiss me on my cheek but I moved quickly.

"Moms!" She laughed, then gave me a high five before I

ran to the field for my debut.

It seemed as if everyone on the team already knew each other, so at first no one paid me any attention. I knew they would notice me after they saw how many goals I scored, so I was not too bothered. Coach Tina huddled the team by our bench and called out her starting eleven.

My hands were sweating, hoping to hear my name. No such luck. I sat through the entire first half. At halftime, I looked across the field to see my Moms, Pops, and Damian sitting on the bleachers. I wanted to make sure they were watching for when I got in and scored my goals.

The second half came and went. No Jack or Mike and I didn't set foot on the field. I was pissed that neither of my friends showed up. I thought to myself that if they were sick, then they could have called me.

That was the only reason for their absence that made sense to me at that time. I would learn later there was a much more serious reason and that Jack had tried to call me, but that we had already left for the game.

I barely made it through the "good game" line before I darted over to my parents with tears in my eyes. Moms held me in her arms and told me it was okay. Pops comforted me for a short while right outside of the sideline before we left the grounds.

"If you want to play football, this will be the first of many obstacles, but if your heart is in it, you'll find a way through," he explained as we drove home. I got the logic of what he was saying but my ego took a blow that day.

When we arrived home I ran to the phone while Pops stood outside talking to one of our neighbors, Mr. Barney. Mr. Barney was usually a very lively character but on that day he looked more somber, more concentrated, more still. My calls to both Mike and Jack went unanswered. I went outside to tell Pops I was going to walk over to Mike's, who lived right behind our house.

"No. Go back inside and clean up."

"Go inside and clean up," I mocked Pops under my breath as I walked back inside. I grabbed my towel from my room then headed across the hall to the bathroom. I saw Moms at the front of the house, in the living room, peering out of the windows at Pops and Mr. Barney.

I showered and came out feeling a little better. I changed into some clean play clothes and was walking past the adjoining kitchen and dining room, when both of my parents stopped me. Moms wrapped her arm around my shoulder and said, "Sit down, son. We want to talk to you."

Chapter Two

WE ALL TOOK a seat at the dining room table as Moms squeezed a tissue in her hand. Pops sat at the head of the table, tapping his fingers on the surface. They were both silent. I reached my hand out and covered Pops' hand, putting a pause to his tapping.

"Hey, it's like you said, Pops, first of many obstacles, right?" Tears began to flow down Moms face and she launched herself up from her seat then disappeared into the bathroom. Pops palmed my fist, reversing my action.

His head bowed. "Mike's in the hospital."

"What?"

"Hold on son. Let me finish."

I sat waiting for him to continue. Moms appeared just outside the bathroom door wiping her face. Pops looked back at her and she gave him an approving nod. He nodded back, then turned to me.

"Seems like there was some issue between his mother and father—"

"What does that have to do with Mike?"

"Son."

"Okay." I replied.

"Katrina passed…they're not sure who did it."

"What do you mean they're not sure who did it?" Pops looked over at Moms, who was now sitting back in her seat. She shook her head no and kept her eyes down towards the table.

"What happened?!" I cried out loudly, for fear that the words wouldn't come out. Moms and Pops wrapped their arms around me and we all cried together as I asked what happened, uncontrollably over and over.

I caught a glimpse of Damian creeping slowly out into the hallway, but Pops waved his hand motioning for Damian to go back into his room.

THE STORY THAT I WAS ABLE to piece together over the course of the next week from overheard conversations and news reports was that Mike's father, Charles, had come home drunk and high early that morning from a night of partying at the local lodge. He raped Katrina and Mike.

Katrina was found lying on the cushy white carpet in the living room, soaked red with her blood. Her body was punctuated with several knife holes, while Mike was found naked in the same pool of blood, unconscious and barely hanging on for his life.

It took me back to a conversation that we had two weeks prior while Jack was shopping in Indianapolis with his grandmother. Mike and I were in my room playing video games. We were having a good time when Pops came in with stern words because he was upset that I hadn't taken out the trash.

I got up and did as I was told, then I settled back down into my bean bag next to Mike and started to play again.

"He's gonna beat you when I leave huh?"

I laughed. "Nah, man, I run things around here."

He paused the game of *Double Dribble*. His sad eyes locked in on mine. "Nah, man, for real. I'll stay the night if that would help."

"I'm not going to get a whopping tonight. It's done. He was just mad I'm sitting here playing video games and ain take out the trash yet. Why you acting so scared, dog?"

Mike's chin dropped into his chest and his eyes diverted away from mine. "Nothing. Forget about it."

"What is it man? What's going on?"

"Naw, man. It's alright. Let's play." He unpaused the game.

I paused the game again. "Quit bullshitting."

His chin tucked back into his chest. "Charles always beating on me. He usually sounds like your dad did just a minute ago, before he does, so I thought…"

I didn't know what to say, so I just bowed my head and allowed the silence to be. The quiet was broken by a sniffle that sounded like Mike was crying, but when I looked up there were no trace of tears.

"Man, it's like they always fighting and after he get done beating up Mama then he just kind of… come after me. I try to help Mama but…."

I stared at him blankly. When I realized I was staring I turned and peered out of the window that overlooked our backyard. I looked across the alley into the back of his home and tried to visualize Charles abusing Mike.

I was having a hard time matching the Charles I knew to the person that Mike was telling me about. He was always the life of the party. He was loud, but funny and charming.

"There are times, man…." I looked back at him as he choked up and swallowed hard. "Times when he makes me play with his dick man… After he makes me finish him off he says, 'Don't you ever forget who's the man of this house.'"

My heart dropped as though I had just come down from the highest point of a rollercoaster. The picture he painted was so clear now that my stomach turned and felt as though everything in it would come up. I tried not to let any of that internal confusion and sickness show because I knew he just needed a sounding board and not necessarily any sympathy.

He wiped the snot from his nose and cleared the tears from his face. "I'ma kill his ass one day. I swear to God, I'ma kill his ass."

"I got your back, dog." Tears now coming from my eyes. "Anything you need. A place to stay or help killing that mutha fucka. I got you... Aight?"

"Thanks, dog. Nice to know I'm not alone in this shit, ya know?"

"Yea, I'm here, dog. Why don't you tell Katrina?" I rubbed the tears away from my face.

"Shiiiiitt. She can't do nothing and even if she could, I'm not sure that she would."

We hugged and cried on each others shoulders for a few minutes until Mike felt he was alright. He unpaused the game again and we continued playing *Double Dribble* in a blue silence.

On our way to the hospital, I kept thinking about how I acted as if that situation didn't exist after he told me about it. I just took his cry for help and did nothing with it. It's my biggest regret in life. We stayed at the hospital the rest of the day, leaving when visiting hours were over at nine. Mike died a few hours after.

I heard the news early the next morning and for the next few days I stewed in guilt and sorrow. I couldn't bring myself to smile and I couldn't laugh. I was a ten year old zombie, void of emotion on the outside but full of inexpressible feelings on the inside.

I only said a few words to the cops who came by to ask me

questions about Charles. They asked in a roundabout way, never directly saying what happened.

I did not tell them about my talk with Mike. He was already dead, plus they hadn't even found Charles yet, so it didn't seem like that information would help at all.

After the funeral the following Saturday, Jack and I were finally able to chat. I told him about my conversation with Mike and we cried together.

A dark cloud hung over us as we cried together. Moms was the first to come over and hug us, then others followed. Neither Jack nor I knew how to deal with our mixed up emotions. I think the adults also struggled with coping so we were a whole community trying to figure it out.

When I went to bed that night I tried not to think of Mike, but his memory was unavoidable. I tried to fall asleep in every position, but ended up on my back staring at the ceiling. My heart was pounding with adrenaline.

I told myself to think of happier things like when I first met Jack and Mike at school. Before meeting them I didn't have any friends and kids at school made fun of my name. I hoped that happier thoughts would have calmed me down, and they did, but I still couldn't sleep.

I got up from my bed, walked into the dark living room and put in Pops' football highlight tape. It was a tape that Uncle Jimmy, Moms' uncle, had brought for him that had highlight segments covering some of the greatest players in the game: Pele, Johan Cruyff, Beckenbauer, George Best, and Diego Maradona.

I sat alone looking at video of the legends. It was inspiring and for the first time that tape took on a different significance for me.

Watching the brilliance of Pele brought to mind how happy Pops, Uncle Jimmy, and even Moms were watching him in action. It was as if his mere presence brought smiles to their faces.

I sat mesmerized as I watched the way Pele ran around the field, delighting the crowd with his brilliant touches and fancy dribbling. He didn't have to say or do anything to let you know he was the best. If he was just standing still, there was something about him that oozed greatness.

I wanted to feel like that. I needed a way to express myself and there was something magnetic about football. It was the only means that I had to honor Mike's death. The only way I knew to make sure that the world never forgot about Mike was through becoming the best footballer in the world and so that's what I set out to be.

Chapter Three

I WANTED TO PLAY all the time, but nobody around me played football. All the kids who played lived in the more financially established areas of the city. Pops worked during the afternoon and evening, so playing with him was not an option.

It wasn't until during one of our family dinners that I told my family I wanted to be the best footballer in the world. There was a glow that beamed in Pops' eyes. I'd never seen him so enamored with me and something I wanted to do.

The next day before he went to work, he took me out to the backyard and showed me a few drills that I could do on my own to build my skills. He gave me a set of cones and a ball. Over the period of a few months he also gave me two videos: "Pele: The Master and His Method" and "Soccer on the Attack – Dribbling," an instructional video done by the Busch Soccer club in St Louis.

Once I had those tools to get better, I spent hour after hour by myself working on drills to improve my ball control and dribbling. When I was able to get some time to play with Pops, he focused on showing me how to shoot and pass the ball. "Focus on striking the ball properly, then the power will come. You want to hit the ball in that sweet spot," he would say to me.

Over that fall and winter I grew more comfortable dribbling and passing. I studied games from the Mexican League that Pops had his friend record from the Univision channel in Indianapolis. I recorded any game that came on TV. I studied the movements of the players and the different styles of each player and team. I was a football sponge.

Entering my second season of PAL soccer I had two goals: I wanted to be the best player on the team and then the best player in PAL U-12. "Big goals are made up of many small ones," Moms always told me, so I figured those were good, achievable small goals.

Before the start of our first game in season two, Coach Tina huddled us up and announced the starting eleven. The last name called was, "Japeth. Right forward." My heart felt as though it was vibrating in my t-shirt as I stood at the halfway line waiting for the referee. Then the whistle blew. Five minutes into the game, one of our defenders cleared the ball from our defensive end and over their last line of defense. I burst past the last defender. It was me and the keeper one on one with plenty of green in between us.

The sun seemed to focus all of its intensity on me. The cheers from the crowd reduced to a faint muffle in the background. Before I knew it, I was eighteen yards away from the goal and the keeper was rushing out at me.

I pushed the ball to the side, moving away from him, then slotted it into the back of the net. I ran off the field to my parents who were cheering very spiritedly on the bleachers for my first goal, even Damian was celebrating. I spent the rest of that first half scoring the goals I thought I was going to score a year earlier.

I sat out most of the second half, while some of the players of lesser quality got more playing time. We won the game 15-2. With my ending goal total being thirteen.

My parents' pride after that game was a feeling that I never wanted to let go. I felt destined to have a chapter in the history of football.

Many years later I told my younger brother Damian about this moment and he mentioned that he had a similar feeling at his very first basketball game. He was two years younger than me, but his talent for basketball was greater than I'd seen in anyone for any sport at that time.

The rest of the second season followed a pattern of blowout wins led by my double digit scoring feats. I was the star of the team and U-12 group. The players and parents from the older age groups and other teams would come early or stay late after their game to watch me play. My first taste of success showed me at an early age that hard work pays off. It gave me the confidence to believe.

At the end of that season a group of U-13 parents formed a U-13 all-star team to enter into the White River State Games. I was asked to be on the team and I accepted.

"This will be a good test for you and the team. The best teams in the state compete in this," Pops explained. In the weeks prior to the tournament, the U-13 PAL All-Star team was assembled and we practiced three days a week.

During our practices the game moved faster and was more controlled, which meant there were less mistakes to capitalize on. I worked hard in and out of practices, and quickly established myself as one of the best players on the team and had hopes of being of the best at the tournament.

Walter Hernandez, another strong player on the team, was the most complete player I had actually seen at that point in my life. He made good decisions and could hold onto the ball under pressure. He also understood the game way better than any of us.

Our first game was against a team from Logansport, a small town about twenty minutes north of Kokomo. I could see from their warm ups that they were more polished as a team.

They were running back and forth across the field, alternating between exercises I had never seen before. My team was lining up across the eighteen-yard line and shooting at the goal. The game followed the same pattern.

The Logansport team passed the ball around us effortlessly and dribbled through our entire defense. We barely got across the halfway line. The final score was an embarrassing 12-0. I overheard a conversation between two of the Kokomo parents as Damian and I walked back to the car.

"I thought for sure we were better than that," one parent said.

"Yeah, and Japeth didn't do much of anything. Guess he's not *that* good. Those guys owned us," the other responded.

"Maybe they just need better coaching."

"12-0? We could bring in Red Auerbach and I don't think it would change a thing. Those kids are just better."

"I don't know. I think our kids just need some more practice."

When I heard that, I felt a small pang of discouragement. I didn't know how I was going to practice more than I already was, unless my parents allowed me to quit school, and that was definitely not going to happen. Never the less, I wanted a second chance at that Logansport team and any team like it. I thought I would have to wait a whole year, but opportunity knocked sooner than I expected.

A few weeks passed and one of the parents called Pops to let him know that he was putting together a traveling U-13 club team and he wanted me to be a part of it. The Kokomo Renegades opened up a whole new world of football for me, full of levels and tournaments.

That fall we started in one of the lowest league levels, level B. The team was basically the same U-13 All Star team with the addition of a defensive player or two.

Our coach, Saheed, was from South Africa and was new to Kokomo, having just started an engineering job at Delco.

He was part of a wave of highly educated internationals the company and the other factories in Kokomo were hiring. Since Pops didn't even have his Associate's degree, it put the brakes on his chances to get into one of the factories, so he continued to work at a meat processing plant just outside of Kokomo.

My mom was lucky that her Uncle Jimmy had already paved the way for her family to come to the USA. He moved up to the States, from St. Vincent, ten years before and traveled around the country. In those years he worked odd jobs here and there.

An orange picker in Florida, a farmer in Mississippi in the Jim Crow south, then a quick stop in New York before making his way to Indiana.

Once he was settled, he invited my mom and her brothers and sisters up for their shot at the American Dream. Pops followed Moms to the States a year or two after she arrived.

The factory job situation in Kokomo at that time often made him reminisce about his earlier days in Kokomo. "Three factories in this town: Chrysler, Delco, and Haynes International." His fingers always flipped in the rhythm of one, two, three as he rang off the factories.

"Straight out a high school, some not even that, and get jobs making good, good money. Not to mention that some of dem would hop around either quitting or getting fired from one factory one week and be working at another factory the next week. I bet these sab suckas wish they had dem days back," my Uncle Jimmy would say.

Several of the parents on the youth team worked at Delco

THE AMERICAN WAY **21**

with Coach Saheed, so I assume that one of them brought him in.
He had a thorough understanding of the game.

With him as our coach, we spent several hours learning
how to run with the ball, different dribbling moves and several
different types of passes. My desire for revenge against that
Logansport team was like a wind to my already burning brush fire
determination. Every single day I pushed myself to be better. I had
to get better.

When we had our first game against Noblesville we were
prepared and battled our way to a 2 – 1 victory. We all improved
under Coach Saheed's guidance and finished that season with a
respectable 6-4 record.

I once overheard Coach Saheed telling Pops, "Sonny, he's
got real talent and potential. Unlike a lot of the other kids, I never
have to get on him about his effort. He pushes himself harder than
I ever could." It was reassuring to hear because Walter was getting a
lot of praise for being the best player on the team and I felt I
deserved more recognition.

Walter was even invited to tryout for a AA premier team,
the highest level in youth football. He made the team and was set to
begin playing with Indianapolis United the following spring.

I was happy for Walter, but again I couldn't help but
wonder why Indy United didn't want me too. I was the leading
scorer on the team. I would learn later that Pops had also been
approached about me playing for Indy United, but the offer came
at a difficult time for the family.

Chapter Four

I WANTED THE OPPORTUNITY to play at the highest level once I heard about Walter's news. I begged and pleaded for weeks. Finally, Pops and Moms sat us down for a family discussion. Moms hands wrung themselves around each other as she sat on the couch across from me. Damian ran into the living room, kicked my foot, then jumped on the couch next to me as he laughed. He was sweaty from playing basketball on his breakaway basketball hoop that hung over his bedroom door.

"Japeth. Damian. I have to go back to St. Vincent for a little bit." Pops said to Damian and me.

"Why?" I asked.

"Do you remember when you were learning about US citizenship and immigration in Social Studies class?"

"Yeah…"

"Well… the time on my Visa will be expiring soon, so I have to go back to St. Vincent for a bit while I sort out my green card situation."

"You've been here for so long. Why now?"

I'm filing for my papers through your mother, which is usually fast, but I guess there's an influx of people coming into the country and it's taking longer than usual. So I have to go back home while everything gets taken care of in the system. I don't know when I'm going to leave yet, but I'm going to stay here as long as I can."

I looked at Moms. She tried hard not to blink. Damian blurted out, "Moms, are you leaving too? Can I go with you?!"

Pops looked across the room at me and answered in a low tone, "No, Moms is staying here. You and your brother stay here and take care of her okay?" Pops wrapped his arm around Moms.

"Can I still play football?"

Damian quickly added on, "What about basketball?"

Pops squinted his eyes at us. "I'm leaving and all you two care about are some damn games?" He took a deep breath, then exhaled loudly while he shook his head.

"Look, guys, we have to cut back and save some money so Damian, you can play basketball at the local community center. No YMCA this year." I looked at Damian. He seemed content with that. The better players were at the local community center anyway. Pops set his eyes on me.

"I looked into those AA premier clubs, son, and that is some serious money. They travel out of state on the weekends. Then you've got the hotels, uniforms and gas to get to and from practice and games. And I haven't talked about the club fees yet. I mean it really adds up to thousands of dollars, son." He shook his head slowly. "We just don't have that kind of money right now."

I knew that if there was anything that Pops could have done to avoid having to make that decision, he would have done it. It didn't take away from the disappointment that I was feeling. I felt betrayed. I had been the butt of jokes for my cheap wardrobe, but as he explained it, we all had to make sacrifices in order to achieve our dreams.

I thought I was sacrificing brand name clothes for a shot at my dream, but there we were, with all of my sacrifice given and I was still at zero. I couldn't figure out how this American dream thing worked, but I knew I was going to have to go about it in a different way.

In my room I watched A Different World and The Cosby Show, and I'm sure everyone else did as well. Usually we'd watch those shows as a family, but I think everyone just needed their space that night.

The main topic on both episodes centered around the more pampered characters getting part time jobs. I realized money was central to my need as well, but I had never thought of trying to earn it myself.

The antics of Theo and Dwayne Wayne helped lift my spirits a bit, but I was still wrestling with all of the information unloaded on me that evening. I looked up to Pops and relied heavily on him for my picture of manhood. He and moms were a team, with him being the iron fist and Moms being the heartbeat of our household.

I couldn't imagine life with only one of them. I thought more about life that day than I had ever before. I thought so much I tired myself out and fell asleep early that night. The next day at school, I didn't tell Jack about the situation with Pops but I did express my desire to start earning money.

"Yeah man, me too. How we gonna do that though? You gotta be fifteen to get a worker's permit."

"Yeah, I think I'm going to start shoveling snow, probably pick up a paper route, thinking bout detassling some corn too."

"I'll shovel with you, but you gotta get up too damn early to do a paper route. And detassling?!! Forget about that shit, dog. Ole boy Harry, the white boy with the Dyno bike, he be detassling in the summer and his arms be cut–the-fuck-up. I ain messing with that shit."

I laughed, but I *had* to play football. I was possessed by this vision of myself as the best player in the world. Honoring Mike's death was my main motivation.

It certainly didn't hurt that Pops was also at his happiest when I was on the field. He was proud when Damian was the best on the basketball court, but he grew up playing football so the game's connection to him was more intimate.

During recess I waived Harry over to me as I stood off to the side of the general playground area. "Harry. Come here a minute."

"Hey Japeth." There was a tentative tremor in his voice.

"What's up Harry? You detassel corn in the summer right?"

Harry responded with a drawn out, "Yeeeaaaa."

"Can you tell me a little bit about it?"

"Sure. I mean, what do you want to know?"

"Well, I'm thinking bout doing it. I heard it's good money but I have no idea what it is."

Harry moved his long, stringy brown hair that had blown into his face with the cold wind that December day. It was only then that I realized that Harry had a huge gap in his front bottom teeth, which was odd because I saw Harry everyday in class.

In his southern drawl he started, "Wellll…it's definitely good money, but it's some hard work."

"Okay. How much we talking?"

"Hmm. Last year I made about $1400. The year before, that was my first year and I made about a grand."

"Wow. How long do you work?"

"You get to the fields about 7am. Work until about 6pm. Usually Monday through Friday for about three weeks in July."

"Where are the fields?"

"The ones I work at are in Tipton. If you want to, I'll let you know when I'm signing up again and you can sign up with me.

I'll talk to Bob, the guy who runs the farm, and put in a good word for you."

"Yeah, do that. Thanks man!"

"No problem."

We shook hands and went in different directions within the general playground area. I walked toward the basketball courts to meet Jack. "Where you been?" he asked. "I'm over here all by myself and shit."

"Sorry dog. I was talking to Harry about detassling."

"What'd he say?"

"Said he'd hook me up."

Jack shook his head. "You really going to do this, huh? What you trying to do…Finally get some shell toes?" he laughed, then slowly stopped when he saw that I wasn't laughing. "Joke's not the same without Mike here," he said with sadness deepening his voice.

"I miss that dude so much."

"Me too." I added. For the first time since his death we stood there during recess and laughed about old times with Mike. It felt good to remember everything that was funny about him. In our laughter it actually felt like he was present. We thought it would be just us two forever. We would have never imagined who would become a part of our circle next.

Chapter Five

AT THE TIME WE DIDN'T notice it, but Darrell Brown—DBrown for short—had just gotten his shot swatted on the basketball court. He was part of a local gang called the Capones, made up of middle school aged kids like us. Darrell, was big with a thick muscular body and fiery eyes.

"Fuck yall laughing at?!"

Jack was first to see that DBrown was talking to us since I had my back to the court. Before I knew it, DBrown was standing over me so close that his black and yellow Starter pull over was brushing against my light brown generic winter coat that Moms had gotten from Hills, a local department store.

I started to explain that our laughter had nothing to do with him, but he snatched my Charlotte Hornets winter hat off my head and threw it on the ground before I could finish.

I could hear the snickers and laughs from his friends. "Some shit was funny to you little punk!" The glare of his stare forced me to keep my head down.

It felt like everyone on the playground was looking at us. DBrown's body flexed, and for a second I thought I was about to be hit so I flinched. I quickly regained my balance. When I looked up, I saw DBrown holding the side of his face. Jack was shaking his hand and wincing. He and I locked eyes.

Immediately, I heard voices shouting, "Fuck that shit! They jumping DBrown!" The last thing I wanted was for DBrown to be fully recovered and in the crowd that was about to beat our ass so I took two steps and swung the most powerful kick I could, landing it right in his balls.

He shrieked and squirmed on the cold ground and soon Jack and I were surrounded by flying fists, elbows, and feet. I lost Jack in the sea of black and yellow, but tried my best to fight back and use moves that I learned from karate movies and practiced in a game Mike, Jack, and I used to call Chop Chop. The melee probably only lasted about thirty seconds before the teachers broke it up.

It felt like it was about fifteen people we were fighting but when we ended up in the principal's office there were only eight Capones in there with us. I sat patiently, tasting the bitter, iron taste of blood from my busted lip. I looked over at Jack who was holding an ice bag against his right eye. He and I were bruised, but looking around the room I noticed that we had gotten a few of them pretty good too.

When it was my turn to go into the principal's office, I confidently said, "DBrown and I had a misunderstanding and ended up wrestling around a bit. That's all."

"Then why was everyone else fighting?" Mrs. Carter asked. Her hands balled into fist on the desk, her face tight with great intensity in her eyes. Tall with tanned white skin, she was attractive but she had these narrowing eyes that could make you pee your pants.

"I don't know what happened there. I can only tell you

what I know."

"Japeth, this isn't like you. You're a good student, even won the Good Citizen award for your class last year, right?"

"Yes, ma'am."

"Listen. Tell me what happened *now* or you'll have detention for a very long time."

Honestly, the threat of detention itself didn't scare me much. I didn't talk to many people at school anyhow. I didn't consider myself shy. I just liked to be around those with whom I was most comfortable, which was only Jack at that point. It was my parents reaction to what happened that scared me most.

"That's all I can tell you Mrs. Carter. That's all I know."

"Get out. I'll deal with you later."

After Mrs. Carter was done talking to everyone, her assistant, Miss Rhodes, an older, sweet lady that reminded me of Rose from the Golden Girls called our parents to pick us up. I was the third person to leave when Pops came.

Miss Rhodes explained, "Japeth was fighting today in school and we suspect he's not telling the truth about what happened so he'll be suspended for the remainder of this week and has detention for two weeks after that."

On the way home, Pops didn't show any signs of being upset. "So… what happened son?"

"Jack and I were joking around and I guess Darrell thought we were laughing at him. He came over to me and took my Hornet's hat off and threw it on the ground!"

"Uh huh"

"I was so mad, Pops, I was going to hit him, but then Jack beat me to it. I guess his friends thought we were jumping him, but we weren't."

"Why would they think that?"

"I don't know. Jack got him pretty good in the jaw and Darrell's a big guy. Maybe they figured both of us had to do it…

I don't know."

"So how did the brawl happen?"

"They all came rushing over! Jack and I just tried to defend ourselves. Next thing I knew the teachers were there."

We arrived home by that point and were getting out of the car. At the front door Pops asked, "What you just told me... Is that what you told Mrs. Carter?"

I unlocked the door and walked in. "No."

"Why?" Pops inquired.

"I didn't want everybody thinking I was a snitch. Plus, what was telling her going to do? The fight already happened."

Pops words became more stiff, "You might not have gotten suspended, that's what. I'm proud of you for standing up for yourself, but you gotta be careful with that shit. These things add up and next thing they gonna want to send you to boy school." The thought of boy school scared me a bit, but then I figured it was just Pops being overly paranoid about something he read or heard in the news.

Moms was really upset when she got home. As she nursed my busted lip she said, "I better not see no C's, D's, or F's come through this house or it's me and you! Hmmph!"

I usually had one or two C's on my report card. She knew that, so I felt that was an unfair request. As I look back on it now, the combination of bad grades and bad behavior must have signaled to her a slide in my overall progress towards her dream for me.

She encouraged my football dreams, but she was more obsessed with my education. "Never leave sure for unsure." That was one of her favorite sayings and to her, football was unsure.

She thought it was best that I became a doctor and tried to steer me in that direction, but I was becoming more stubborn in what I wanted to do. That stubborn attitude would prove to be both a good and a bad thing.

Chapter Six

I SPENT MY TWO DAYS at home working the house like I was an abused orphan – doing extra chores like polishing silverware amongst other things. Moms and Pops made sure that I had so much to do that I started at 7am and had to race to finish by 3pm.

My first Monday back at school, Jack and I talked for a few minutes before detention. It was the first time we'd had a chance to speak since the incident. I asked him if he told Mrs. Carter or Mrs. Johnson what happened.

"Hell naw, man! I told both of them that somebody hit me blindside but I didn't know who. DBrown was the closest so I thought it was him and I hit him back."

"Mrs. Johnson whopped that ass huh?"

"Naw, man. That crazy woman punched me!"

"Why?" I said as I restrained my laugh.

"Man, dog… She mad cause I got my ass whopped!" I couldn't hold my laughter anymore. Jack mocked his grandmother doing his best shrill, southern old lady voice and wagging his finger the way she did.

"Don't come back here with no ass whoppings cause if you do, I'ma whop yo ass again!" We both laughed. "Don't let my old age fool ya, boy. I'll beat the shit out of you!"

Mrs. Johnson was a real firecracker. I used to always wonder what she was like as a young girl in Alabama then as a young woman in St. Louis. We laughed about her threat, but it was real. She would beat his ass.

The school bell rang and we had to take our seats in the detention room. It felt like jail, or at least what I imagined jail would be like.

Our homework was delivered to us as a task list with little direction. Luckily, I was able to take my work home and have Moms help me, but this meant that I spent my evenings doing schoolwork instead of practicing football.

After two days of detention, I was telling Pops about how bored I was. "All I can do is stare at the wall. I can't do my work. AND we don't even get to eat lunch with everybody else! We eat by ourselves!"

He looked at me. "It's not supposed to be fun, Japeth. It's a punishment."

"I know! But I have to suffer through this for two weeks. Wouldn't be so bad if I could actually do my homework."

"You could practice your maths." He sensed my hesitation with that idea. "Hold on," he said as he got up and went into the bedroom.

When he returned he was holding a short, thick paperback book. "Here, read this." I took the black book and looked at the cover. "*The Autobiography of Malcolm X*? It's going to take me a year to read this!"

"Well, you've got plenty of time to start."

I used my only defense left, "Malcolm X? Isn't he the guy that wanted to kill all white people? Are you sure I should be reading this?"

"Now that you've asked that question, I've never been more sure that you should. Matter of fact, I want a book report when you're done with it. Son, don't look at this as a punishment. I think every young black man should read this book in his formative years, which you're coming into. Trust me it's going to be one of the most important books you'll ever read."

I held the book and suddenly felt a responsibility to read what Pops considered to be a rite of passage to black manhood. I studied the cover with the determined face of Malcolm X then looked at Pops and said "Okay."

The next morning in detention I did my History and English homework for two hours. Math was a particular struggle and usually had to wait until I got home.

When I was done with schoolwork, I daydreamed about being the best footballer in the world. I could hear the crowd roar and chant my name.

After some time lost in my own head, my attention shifted to the Malcolm X book in my book bag and I slipped it out. I caught Jack glancing over at me and laughing.

I couldn't risk falling asleep and getting more detention time, so I opened the book and began reading. The first few sentences sucked me in like a time machine with a tornado-like portal and I spent the next hour living in the 1920s and early 30's through the eyes of a young Malcolm Little before breaking for lunch.

"Who the hell is Malcom X?" Jack asked.

"You never heard of Malcolm X? You need to talk to your grandma. She'll tell you."

"Ah shit. I can't take that We Shall Over Come bullshit. Maybe that shit is important to an African booty scratcher like you, but I don't give a fuck. I'm here, that's all that matters."

This wasn't the first time that Jack called me an African

booty scratcher. It was another running joke between he and Mike. I never really fretted about the name before, but this time was different.

Maybe because I had just experienced the emotions of a young black boy being tortured by society. For whatever reason, I snapped at Jack, "Fuck that mean?"

"Sorry, didn't know you took your books so seriously." Jack raised his hands in defense.

"Sorry, dog. I don't know, being locked up in that detention room got me irritable or some shit, but the book is really a good book so far."

"Irritable?! You ain no professor. Mutha fucka read two sentences and start using big words like irritable. By the end of the book you going to be talking all nerdy and shit." He did his best impression of an awkward, nasally, nerdy person talking. "May I have a fry please?" We both laughed, relieving some tension.

"Naw but for real, dog, I can't read that type of shit. Makes me hate white people. When grandma be telling me stories of her days in Alabama, I be wanting to kill somebody."

"Yeah, it does kinda give you that feeling." I also struggled with those thoughts, but the sense of responsibility to honor those revolutionaries overcame those hateful emotions.

I spent the rest of that week at school and home with my nose in that book, until I finished it over the weekend. My view of Malcolm X was now completely changed and I had forever learned a very important lesson: Always seek to understand someone before you judge them. It's a lesson that I don't think a lot of people learn, based on my experiences later in life.

Instead of casting Malcolm X aside as a man full of hate, I now saw and still do see him as a man that was full of love and somebody that to this day I look up to and greatly admire.

It amazed me that this incredible man wasn't even covered in our school history books at the time. All we heard about was the great Dr. Martin Luther King Jr., as if he was the one and only person, along with Rosa Parks, to make things happen for black people.

My book report to Pops expressed these sentiments. "You read this Elaine?" Pops said to Moms as he waved my book report.

Moms rolled her eyes and said, "Uh huh."

"That's my boy right there."

"He sure is."

In the end, I was thankful for those two weeks in detention; without them I'm not sure I would have ever developed the thirst to know more about our history outside of what was taught in school. Ironically, some parts of my young life were beginning to mirror the early days of Malcolm Little.

Chapter Seven

THERE WERE ONLY FOUR of us left from the brawl in detention. DBrown, Dorian Pitt, Jack, and myself. One day, DBrown and Dorian cornered us after school. I was nervous and I could tell by the way Jack gripped his hands that he was uneasy as well.

Mrs. Glendale came over to us, noticing that the situation looked suspicious. DBrown spoke up first, "Mrs. Glendale, we've already squashed our troubles and we're friends now." She looked at Jack and I for a response.

"It's true. We're friends. It was just a misunderstanding." I wasn't sure what I was getting us into, but I was about to find out as Mrs. Glendale waddled away towards the departing buses.

DBrown looked at Dorian who was right next to him. "See, I told you they was down." He turned his attention to me, as he popped a few chips into his mouth.

"A dog. *Chomp chomp.* I thought yall was some nerds, but yall did alright for yourselves."

I was still leery about what was happening so I just nodded and kept myself guarded.

"Yall know we Capones, right?"

Jack responded snarkly, "Of course, yall only jumped our asses the other day. How can we not?" I shot Jack a stabbing look.

Dorian piped in excitedly, "That's right! And we'll do it again. Nobody fucks with Capones."

DBrown gave Dorian the same look I had given Jack. There was a brief moment of silence then he continued. "He ain lying. Nobody fucks with Capones. We run this shit, hands down. The way yall handled yourselves the other day was nice. Yall didn't back down on no pussy shit and didn't go running to the teachers like some punks. Yall carried yourselves like some Capones. If you want in, we'll count that beat down as your initiation." He paused for a second, glanced across to Jack, then Dorian, then back to me before asking, "Are yall in?"

"We're in," Jack answered before I could get a word out of my mouth. But I didn't speak up to correct him. I'm not sure why I didn't say anything, because I was uncomfortable with the idea of being in a gang. If my parents ever found out, I'd be in for a severe whopping.

On the other hand I was excited about the invitation to fit in somewhere outside of Jack and me. As a kid, all you want to do is fit in, or at least I did, and I certainly didn't fit in easily to the universe of Kokomo. In this world, a first generation Caribbean kid with a funny name was like a square peg in a round hole. It was the first time that peer pressure won over the fear of my parents, but it wouldn't be the last.

DBrown ended up being a cool guy. He was born in Kokomo and part of one of the other larger families in the area. DBrown's dad lived in Texas and he loved to talk about the summers he would spend down there.

It was one of those things that him, Dorian, and even Jack could bond over. "Man down in Alabama… down in Texas… down in Louisiana…." You could insert just about anything that was good after starting a sentence like that and it instantly made you sound cooler. At the time I couldn't talk about St. Vincent because for one, I hadn't been there yet and two, it would not have sounded cool in that circle.

Our first day back at school after being in detention for two weeks was completely different. It felt like a totally different school. It was a breath of fresh air to be seen, where I once felt invisible. Kids went out of their way to say hi to me and if they didn't do that, I could feel that they were too shy or didn't feel worthy to speak to me.

Jack and I spoke about our changed perception amongst our peers. He was enjoying the feeling of fame as well. He experienced the extra tangent of popularity with the girls immediately.

His hazel eyes, brown complexion, and athletic body attracted girls to him like bees to honey while I still repelled them like insect killer.

The Capones were fairly large, probably about a hundred kids, but my circle was tight. I really only hung with Dorian, DBrown, Jack and a guy who lived down the street from me named Landon. We were some of the most respected members of the whole gang for our fighting ability, loyalty, and hustler mentality.

Aside from the Capones, there was an older gang called the 8Ball Posse in Kokomo at that time. We looked up to those 8Ball guys. Guys like Tiny Man, Lenny, Thomas, and Quinton had an arrogance and style that we wanted to emulate. They had the highest level of respect, the girls, and wardrobe we wanted for ourselves. We all had our own way of trying to achieve these things.

Jack and I made about $600 that winter shoveling snow from sidewalks, walkways and driveways for people who either didn't feel like doing it or older people who simply could not. As the days of heavy snowfall tapered off, Moms was able to get me a paper route in my neighborhood that paid $250 every two weeks. I gave every cent that I earned to my parents, hoping I'd be able to pull together enough to play football that spring.

My love for football took priority over my desire to have the best clothes, shoes, and music like everyone else, but that didn't mean the desire for these things went away. I knew that I no longer simply wanted to sacrifice everything, so I found other ways to get what I wanted.

Chapter Eight

I WAS YOUNG. I was only twelve years old, but I'd already learned that if I wanted something I had to take it. I didn't expect anything to be given to me and I think all of my friends felt the same way.

We were entitled, but not the way our richer counterparts were. We knew we had the guts and know how to actually get anything we wanted by ourselves. Looking back, it's not surprising that our mentality first came to action through stealing.

My friends and I would walk into Musicland at the mall together, usually on a Friday or Saturday, and separate as we sorted through the tapes in the singles section. Our eyes always in constant motion trying to spot employees that were paying attention to us.

The lights above us showered down heat that always made me sweat a little under my coat and clothes. My heart would race in those moments, scared that I would miss an employee who was staring right at me or that the video cameras in the black bubbles on the ceiling were actually on.

We'd grab the tape we wanted as if we were reading what was on the cassette cover, have one last look around, then while holding the tape in the palm of our hand, we'd use our fingertips to push the tape up the sleeve of our coats. We usually ended up with about four or five singles in each arm sleeve.

The scariest part of it all was walking out of the store. Each step towards the open mall area would push my racing heart up into my throat. I would get so scared that I usually became dizzy and light headed.

The fear never left, but somehow we continued to get bolder. Bold enough to even steal the full album cassettes once we found out that the plastic security casing did not set off the alarm. DBrown's cousin, who also stole tapes, was the first to defunct that myth.

When it came to clothes, I only stole one or two Cross Colour shirts from department stores. The rest of the crew did more stealing from places like Lazarus and Elder-Berman. I thought it was too risky. Those stores didn't have as much traffic as Musicland and stealing required a bit more slickness.

Between DBrown and I, we amassed a huge collection of hip hop music. Our pool of music had artists like Eric B. and Rakim, Geto Boys, Kool G Rap, N.W.A, and Big Daddy Kane. We didn't have any hip hop stations in Kokomo so Yo! MTV Raps on Saturday mornings served as our window into the hip hop world.

Jack usually borrowed from our collections to record what he liked. I was making money on my paper route and also started selling mixtapes for $20, turning my stolen library into pure profit. On the weekends I mowed lawns. All together I was making about $800 every two weeks, which was enough to fund playing for a AA premier team.

Pops was able to arrange a special try out structure with the Fort Wayne Citadel club, where I could practice with them for a week. If they thought I was a good fit, they would take me. If not, I would not be invited back.

When we arrived for the first practice Pops said, "Just play the game like how you know to play it. Your abilities will show through. Play hard and have fun."

While putting on my shinguards Coach Andy came over, towering above me, and introduced himself. My first impression was that he looked more like a Ken doll than a coach. He split us up into different teams and had us running a drill in which we played quick transitional games of 3 vs. 2 or 2 vs. 1.

I was probably a little selfish on that first day but I had something to prove and I wasn't going to let anything stop me from reaching my goal, or at least that's what I thought.

The next week I got the news that I was selected to be on the team. The first tournament I played in was in Cincinnati, and our first game was against the Cincinnati United "B" team. Twenty minutes into the game, Billy Smith, the team's star central midfielder, slotted a pass between the left back and central defender.

I jetted in behind them and hit the ball one time into the far corner of the goal. The keeper didn't even get a chance to react. We won the game 1-0.

Afterwards Pops, Moms, Damian and I had lunch with the team. The guys were pretty cool but when they spoke of their trips to Disneyland and exotic islands, I had nothing to add to the conversation. After lunch, we went back to the hotel, took a nap, then returned to the field for the afternoon match.

Over the next two games I became part of the starting team and scored four goals. The final game for the championship was against a club from Detroit called Vardar.

The score was still 0-0 after overtime and that meant we had to go to penalty kicks to decide the winner. I was picked to be the fifth penalty kick taker over Meyer Bindman, the team's main forward before I arrived.

Billy was the first to take his penalty and scored. Over the next few kicks we missed one and right before my turn our keeper made an incredible save, leaving all the pressure on me to win the game.

I placed the ball on an elevated mound of grass. I walked back towards the 18-yard box line. I stopped and turned around. I knew I was going to make it. The referee blew the whistle.

I jogged up to the ball, not knowing which direction I was going to go. Midway to the ball, I decided I was going left. I struck it with my right foot across my body and into the lower left corner of the goal.

The team rushed me. It was the first tournament that I won. I was electrified having scored the game-winning goal. I was floating on a cloud, higher than any drug could ever take any human being.

I was emotionally spent and wanted to sleep on the three-hour drive home but instead I spent the majority of the time talking to Pops about the weekend. "That Billy kid has some good skills," he remarked.

I was more impressed with a winger from the Vardar team. I didn't know his name but he was tall, strong, and dangerous. Just about every opportunity they had came through him.

"You still lose the ball too much and they're knocking you off the ball too easy. It'll come though. Keep working." Pops said. It was frustrating to face the reality that my play was not on par with my teammates, but I was happy to still be scoring goals.

For the remainder of the summer if we didn't win, we usually were somewhere in the top three of our tournaments. I missed a lot of goal-scoring opportunities and even struggled to create them in the latter part of that summer.

Coach Andy moved me back to the right wing. I hated that position because I had to defend more than I attacked. I was frustrated with the situation and I started to feel like I was in a losing battle.

The Fort Wayne players had the opportunity to play in pick-up games with high school kids and college level players. I didn't have those same opportunities in Kokomo.

I realized that without the chance to actually play, I would not improve as fast as the other guys. I talked to Walter and he was having a similar experience with Indy United, although he seemed to be maintaining a higher level.

I made it known to Coach Andy that I wanted to get back in the line up as a forward, so he gave me a chance during the second to last tournament of the season. I wanted to prove that I deserved that position, but I only ended up scoring one goal in four games.

Despite not doing as well as I would've liked, I still wanted to be the best player in the world. I just wasn't sure I knew how to get there anymore.

I was having problems becoming the best player in Indiana, so the best player in the world was starting to feel unrealistic. As my faith in my dream began to fade, I seriously started to consider whether I was up for the journey.

Chapter Nine

MY WEEKENDS HANGING OUT at the mall were cut down to nearly zero after I started playing for Fort Wayne Citadel, but I was still able to hang out during the week. That summer, which was 1990, there was an influx of people to the black community in varying ages from Chicago, St. Louis, Cincinnati, and Louisville.

All the new faces and interactions raised the level of excitement. Every night the neighborhood park was packed with people hanging out. You wouldn't see many people there during the day because that summer was really hot and humid.

But once the sun started to set, the tricked out, old school short and long body Caddys, Caprices, and Chevys began to line up on the street that ran through the park and divided it from the single level housing projects. Ice Cube's "AmeriKKKa's Most Wanted" blared out of most cars driven by men. If I closed my eyes that summer and heard Candyman's "Knockin Boots", ninety-nine percent of the time I would be right in my guess that it was a car full of women.

The new faces brought with them different codes of conduct from their cities. It was the first time I ever heard about Bloods, Crips, Vice Lords, and Gangster Disciples. DBrown, Jack, Landon, and I were in youthful awe.

Once we got an understanding of signs, visual cues, and language that indicated membership to the gangs, it seemed as if everything around us became gang related. All of a sudden we'd hear the language of gang culture in our music and see it in the music videos, which led to arguments about what groups certain rappers represented.

"Geto Boys are GD! You see in the video Scarface had that blue rag?" I might have said. Then one of the other guys might have followed with something like, "He's always talking about the six, too."

Gang affiliation gave us some connection to these superstars who seemed distant otherwise. Over that summer the 8Ball Posse and Capones faded away and were replaced by Vice Lords and Gangster Disciples. Bloods and Crips were a far away thing having their base out in LA, but we assumed there was kinship there between red and blue nations.

I spent a lot of time down at Landon's that summer. Jack was still my best friend, but since Landon lived three houses down from me it was easier to just walk down there. I'm not sure why we didn't hang out before then. Perhaps it was his height and usual emotionless face, but those were like an optical illusion for his humor.

He used to always say stupid shit like, "That girl got a pooter on her." Whenever I left his house my stomach always felt like I had done a thousand crunches because it would be so tight from laughing.

I remember one time DBrown, Jack, and I were in Landon's living room watching TV. We were sitting in the cool, air – conditioned house eating pizza and a commercial came on where a bridge was part of the scene.

The image brought to mind a story of a young lady who was thrown off of a bridge in Texas when DBrown was visiting his father. We all started to let our imaginations go to work on what could have possibly driven someone to throw a woman off of a bridge. DBrown and Jack had exhausted their imagination, which wasn't much to begin with.

"Only thing was she had a gap in between her two front teeth," DBrown added at the end of his description of the young girl. Landon's long body livened up in the couch. "I'm telling yall, it's the curse of the mingy!"

"Ah shit... here he go with that," Jack said as he rose from the couch to get a pop from the nearby kitchen. DBrown rolled his eyes and focused his attention on the TV as he shook his head.

I began laughing and through my laughter asked, "What the hell is a mingy dog?"

"He ain never told you that dumb shit about the mingy?!" Jack yelled from the kitchen as he erected himself from his hunched position in front of the open refrigerator.

"Naw, man," I shouted back, then turned my eyes to Landon giving the go ahead to continue with the story. He calmed himself from laughing then continued as he held a smile on his face.

"The curse of the mingy man. It's this African curse from back in the day. When you have a gap between your teeth that meant you brought bad luck and shit. So what they used to do is, they would kick'em out the tribe right. Because they didn't want nothing bad happening. Because we don't do that, bad shit be happening. The curse of the mingy man. I'm telling you."

I erupted in laughter. "What?! When the hell, you make that one up?"

"Naw, man. This is for real. I saw it on that one channel." Jack had dropped back down on the couch with a cold pop in his hand. I continued to laugh hard, as did Landon, while Jack and DBrown tried to focus on the TV.

"Yall be laughing at some dumb shit," Jack said dryly. DBrown chimed in, "That mutha fucka watch too much damn TV."

I spent a lot of time at Jack's house over the years and as a result, had a great relationship with his grandmother. She even came to a few grandparents days at school for me in place of my own grandparents who were in St. Vincent.

That kind of connection was not the same with Landon's family. I rarely saw his mom. Never saw his dad. He didn't talk about them, so I didn't feel it was my place to bring them up. The only person he talked about was his brother who was away at boy school.

Landon's older cousin from Indianapolis, Choco, came down about midway through the summer and was staying at Landon's house. The way he smoked his cigarettes, talked, and wore his clothes, all of it was just cool.

He even made being slew footed look cool, with his sway back and forth as he walked. The scene of Malcolm X meeting and admiring the Harlem hustlers came to mind when I met Choco.

DBrown, Jack, and Landon had started to sell pieces of unscented soap that were held in tied off corners of sandwich bags. They did this for a few weeks before they had a close call with a pissed off crackhead.

From what I heard, they were walking to Landon's when a crackhead started chasing them. They took off running and laughing. All the laughs stopped once the sound of shots fired pierced the air.

"Gimme back my money! You little sons of bitches!" Those were the last words they heard as they broke off into different directions and cut between houses, luckily escaping unharmed.

Later that night at the park everybody was laughing about it and Choco heard about the incident. The next day he approached those three and cussed them out for fucking up business. When I returned home from my tournament that weekend my whole crew had little five and ten dollar pieces of real crack.

I chose not to get involved. Five and Ten dollar transactions didn't seem to be worth the risk. I had so much to lose if I got caught. I was only twelve, but I seriously thought about the fact that getting arrested for selling drugs would lessen, or kill off, my chances of being the best footballer in the world. I didn't want to do anything to jeopardize that goal, even though I was on the fence about whether I wanted to pursue it.

Chapter Ten

DBROWN, LANDON, CHOCO, AND I made an early trip to the barbershop on a Saturday morning. I didn't have a game that weekend, so I was free to hang out. The neighborhood talent show was that night and the wait to get a fresh cut was going to be long if we didn't get there early.

There were two barbers, Pearl and the youngest barber, Drico, that we all trusted to cut our hair. They were the only two who could do the high top fades, gumbys, and slope haircuts that we wanted to wear. Choco put lines in his eyebrows like Big Daddy Kane.

On our way back to Landon's house Choco rolled up a blunt. We walked down some lesser traveled streets and joked as we puffed.

A lot of the jokes were about how my Pops was going to kick my ass if he ever found out I was smoking weed. I was the only person who was on the receiving end of those jokes. I didn't want to show it, but I was scared smoking out in the open like we were. My high made me even more paranoid and I was constantly looking around to see who might be peaking out of a window.

We decided to go to a local convenience shop, Fernando's. We all grabbed something to drink and I bought a dollar's worth of sour gummy worms that fit in a small brown bag.

The back of our shirts looked like Rorschach tests with the spattering of sweat showing through. I started to feel dizzy and light headed, so I took a seat when we got back to Landon's shaded porch.

"What up Landon? Choco!" a voice shouted through the black steel and mesh front door.

The voice was followed by the appearance of a tall, slender, figure. Choco and Landon embraced the person with hugs. It took me a second but then I realized it was Landon's older brother, Zarez, who was returning home from boys school.

Landon and Choco finished welcoming Zarez. Then Zarez turned his attention to DBrown, Jack and I. "What up?"

He introduced himself to me last with a firm handshake. "Z."

"Japeth."

Z and Choco stood while the rest of us remained seated. Choco was very animated in the discussion, while Z seemed measured in every movement. I noticed that he had a great sense of style as he wore a full North Carolina basketball outfit.

The heat forced us inside to Landon's living room where we were watching Ricki Lake and out of nowhere I just started laughing. DBrown asked, "What's so funny, dog?" My response was more laughter. Landon started laughing at me. DBrown and Choco continued to watch Ricki Lake trying to ignore Landon and I, by turning up the volume of the TV.

"Choco, you can't let these mutha fuckas smoke no more,"

Z said in his laidback tone. For the next fifteen minutes or so Landon and I continued laughing for no reason at all. DBrown, Z, and Choco got tired of us and went to the patio outside.

I stayed by Landon's until the early evening to let my high wear off before I went home. Once home I went straight to my room and started looking through my closet. The talent show started at 7pm, which left me with an hour to get ready. Damian appeared behind me as I searched my clothes.

"Where you think you goin?" Damian asked as he searched through my newest tapes.

"Somewhere you not. They don't allow ugly people where I'm going."

"Then how you goin?"

I turned from my narrow closet and hit him in his chest.

"Ow punk!" he said after he caught himself from falling back. I turned my attention back to my closet, scooting through the colorful options.

"You going to that talent show huh? I don't know why you goin. You ain goin get no girls. I got more girls than you."

"You only got them girls cause you related to me. Little punk."

I felt a sharp jab in my back. I turned to hit him but only saw Damian's back zipping across the hallway toward his room. "Come here!" I said through gritted teeth as I took two quick steps before Damian slammed his door shut. Moms peaked her head out from the living room to see what was going on.

"Stop slamming that damn door!" she yelled. Not bothering to get off the couch, she continued, "Japeth! Leave your brother alone! Hmph."

I left it alone for the moment, but kept that jab from Damian in my memory bank. I decided on a set of short black overalls with a white Cross Colours T-shirt that I had gotten from the Bargain Center.

Any clothes I had that were name brand came from the Bargain Center, a local defect and secondhand store. Moms used to take me and Damian there and we'd look through the racks for the cool gems.

After we found something we liked, we made sure the tag wasn't marked with a D for defect. Sometimes the defect was simply an incorrect stitching or something that couldn't be seen by the average eye. Other times it was something clearly visible.

I ironed my clothes with starch to make sure they were extra crisp while listening to a mixtape with a few of my favorite songs at the time. I recited the raps to "Step Into the Arena" while I put my clothes on. "Once you step in the arena, Kita, Ya gonna be a-mazed…"

The confidence in those lyrics came through me, giving me a little bump in my step. I slapped on a black LA Raiders hat that I was borrowing from DBrown, turning it backwards and kicking it to the left.

With a spray from a tiny sample bottle of cologne, I was on my way out the door to meet up with Landon. "Be safe and I'll come pick you guys up at 11," Moms said as I left the house.

The best part of the talent show was the teen dance that followed. All the folding metal chairs were cleared out from the upstairs area, the adults went home, and the DJ began spinning songs like "Atomic Dog" and "Poison." The party was bumping, jam packed and full of colors with everyone wearing a mix of Afrocentric gear. Everybody was doing the running man, roger rabbit, snake, whop, or even moves they'd made up themselves.

It was a fun party, but when 11 o'clock came I was actually happy that Moms was coming to get me. Around 11:30, everyone would begin getting coupled up and there were no girls interested in me.

The dancing would become slower with flirtatious touches

and whispers to songs like "Piece of My Love" by Guy. Landon and Jack seemed to be making some good progress with two different girls when Moms came to pick us up from the party and decided to stay longer, risking being caught out past curfew.

I got home and Damian was up watching his Michael Jordan highlight video for the millionth time in the living room. Moms went into her room and I joined Damian on the couch in the living room.

"Did you get any numbers?"

"Yeah, man. I had girls all over me. I took a few numbers but then I lost them. I think they fell out of my pocket when I grabbed my key or something."

He just nodded his head and said, "That's unlucky. You'll get'em again."

I looked at Damian. He was tall, light skinned, and had wavy hair. It's an odd thing to be jealous of your little brother, but I was. I sat and stewed, watching the highlight video while my buried feelings brewed and began to manifest.

Chapter Eleven

A FEW DAYS PASSED and the hot topic between DBrown, Landon, Jack, Dorian, and I was around getting initiated. We were no longer content with just being "down." We wanted to be "in." I'm not sure how everyone else chose their side, but for us Choco was the main reason most of us wanted to be Vice Lords.

We saw him snatch gold chains right off the chest of guys that towered above him and they did nothing. He essentially became our guiding light on how to be men in the streets. It just felt natural for most of us to follow his footsteps and officially become a part of his family. Dorian was the only one who decided to join the Gangster Disciples.

He was hanging around us less and less and was spending more time around his cousin Eric. Eric was a Gangster Disciple from Chicago who was somewhat similar to Choco in demeanor. The difference between the two was that Eric would provoke trouble.

He was the kind of guy to pinch your girlfriend's butt in

front of you just so he could fight, stab, or shoot. I never felt safe around Eric. Choco, on the other hand, only went there if he had to, but he wasn't afraid to fight, stab, or shoot either.

DBrown, Landon, Jack, and I made our decision and told Choco we were ready to be initiated.

"Yall know this ain no game, right? This is serious shit. This is family. Once you in, the only way out is death."

"We know that and we want in," DBrown replied, speaking on behalf of all of us.

Choco took a pull off his cigarette as he sat in a chair on Landon's porch. He exhaled, releasing a cloud of smoke, and stared off into the distance. He flicked some ashes on the porch floor then turned his attention to us.

"Yall little niggas really think yall ready?"

"Yeah," we said in unison.

"I was probably about yall age when I got jumped in too. I love yall little niggas. Yall got heart. Yall are already my family. Anybody who fuck with yall got a problem with me. You don't have to do this shit."

It was my turn to speak for the group. "We already running around here claiming it. People see us as Vice Lords. We want to be official. We want to be family."

"And what about you, man? You playing that soccer shit. This ain for you, man."

"Fuck that shit man. I'm thinking about dropping that anyway. Shits going nowhere."

"You quit soccer I'm going to beat yo ass personally, nigga."

"Cuz, you going to do this or not? Landon chimed in. Choco looked around at each of us then off into the distance again as he took another pull.

"Yeah, man. I got yall. Yall come up to the meeting on Wednesday at four o'clock."

"Thanks cuz." Landon slapped hands with Choco then the rest of us followed showing our gratitude.

Three days later on an overcast afternoon, each of us endured an initiation beat down for fifty seconds by three Vice Lord members.

People always think it's just about getting beat up, but for us it was much more. We learned the principles, meanings behind our signs, learned history, and took an oath. The beat down seemed to be more a test of will and courage.

Chapter Twelve

LATER THAT SUMMER, Harry stuck to his word and hooked me up with a job detassling corn. In the nights leading up to my first day I began to fixate on the work. The night before, I decided I wanted out but Moms and Pops made me honor my commitment.

We started the Tuesday after the 4th of July weekend. Pops woke up before the sun rose to drop me off at the bus that took us to Tipton. I found Harry and sat next to him. He introduced me to a few guys on the bus as his classmate. The vibe from some of them was good, a few not so good. As the bus pulled away, I looked around. I was the only black person on the bus.

It was already hot and muggy that morning when we arrived. An older gentleman took us through a tutorial on how to do the job, then we were on our way. Out in the field the work was tough and I was glad I took Harry's advice on wearing long sleeves and pants. The tassels were reaching right through my shirt and scratching me.

I must have sweat off fifteen pounds of water weight

before our first break. At lunch we sat at a picnic table that was in the shadow of a large storage barn.

It was only about five degrees cooler in the shade but it helped. Harry and I had begun to strike up a pretty good friendship, talking while we worked and then again at lunch.

We spoke about how his dad had moved out when he was young and now he lived in a trailer park community on the north edge of the city. His mom had a boyfriend who lived with them in their trailer who was a drunk and would beat her. I thought about Mike, but there was a difference in the way Harry talked about the issue. He was more matter of fact, as though he assumed his situation was normal.

While talking to Harry at lunch, I felt a tap on my shoulder. I turned to see a tall, thick necked redhead boy peering down at me.

"Get up. I want to sit here."

I laughed thinking it was a joke, but the boy's face remained still. "No. I'm sitting here man. Go sit with the other guys in the grass."

"I don't want to sit on the grass, BOY. I want to sit here. Now move!"

"I don't have to do shit. AND who you calling boy?"

He slammed his brown bag down on the table. "Nigger. You need to learn your place!"

I looked across at Harry. He turned away from me.

"You hear me, BOY!?"

I leapt up and wrapped my hands around his neck, squeezing as tight as I could. I felt hands clawing at me. I wrestled my way free quickly then "POP!!!" I hit one guy in the nose and he fell to the ground.

Possessed by anger and survival I won over three guys. Within three minutes all the guys attacking me were on the ground knocked out or groaning in pain. I felt a strong hand sharply grab the collar of my shirt.

"Aye nigger!" I looked up to see the owner's brother staring down at me.

"I told my brother not to hire any niggers. Yall ain't nothing but trouble. Harry! Ain't this your friend here?" I felt like I was in the movie *Roots* and was about to get lynched.

"No. Ain no friend of mine. Thought he might do some good work around here. That's all."

I was determined to not let them see me cry. The redheaded boy had recovered and was coming for revenge.

"Nigger, I'm gonna kill you!" He began rushing towards me but was halted. "Come on, Bob, let me get a piece of him!"

Bob let go of his shirt and said "No! Don't want no problems around here." Bob turned his attention to me.

"Now I suggest you get on that bus and take your ass back home if you know what's best for you."

I rushed to the bus, stopping at the door. The bus driver was white and I suddenly had visions of him driving me somewhere and hanging me.

I started running again and kept running for about two miles, hoping that I didn't come across any stray dogs or Klansmen, before I got to the highway that lead back to Kokomo. When I reached it, I hitch hiked for about ten minutes before an older black lady stopped and offered me a ride. I accepted and got into her car.

"What are you doing out here by yourself? Is everything okay?"

"No. It's not. Worst day of my life."

"What happened, baby? Are you hurt?" She examined me for any signs of damage.

"I was working in the corn fields and…." I broke down crying.

"Aww it's okay, baby. Tell me what happened." She reached out and rubbed the back of my head gently.

"Thank you, ma'am. I don't mean to be rude but can you drive?"

"Sure, baby. Where ya going?"

"Kokomo."

"Oh that's right on the way. I'm heading up to Gary." We drove for about fifteen minutes with no words exchanged between us.

"Ya hungry?"

"No ma'am. Thank you."

"Alright darling. Look, you are going to have to tell me something about why a little boy like you is on the side of the road by yourself."

"I got in a fight at work and they fired me."

"What was the fight about?"

"White boy called me a nigger."

"Oh, baby. I can't believe after all that we've been through, all the progress we've made and sacrifices, yall *still* have to go through this craziness. Did they hurt you?"

"No. I'm fine ma'am."

She looked at me and smiled. "Did you get a good lick in?"

"I got a few good licks in."

She laughed. "Good."

The ride felt shorter going home than going to the fields. When we pulled up in front of my house Moms was sitting on the porch. I thanked the kind woman and ran up the stairs towards Moms. We hugged and she asked, "Where have you been? Where have you been, Japeth?!"

"I'm okay Moms." She gathered herself then walked over to the car and thanked the woman for giving me a ride.

They had a short conversation then Moms handed her some money. Inside Moms told me that Bob had called her and told her what happened.

She was furious about the situation and regretted sending me into that area. She heard rumors of Tipton being a racist town, but she thought it was a reputation left over from the past. I told her my version of what happened and she cried even harder than before.

Pops went in early to get some overtime hours, but he called to make sure I was okay. Damian was at basketball camp, so it was just me and Moms in the house for the afternoon until Damian returned in the evening.

We both took a nap, weighed down by the events of the day. I didn't sleep well with nightmares of my body hanging from a tree. When I awoke, I joined Moms in the living room and we watched *Wheel of Fortune* together.

"The newspaper called," she said during one of the commercial breaks.

"Yeah, what did they want?"

"They said they were consolidating paper routes and that they wouldn't need you anymore."

I was hurt and I wanted to cry, but I don't think I had anymore tears left in me that day. It was the feeling of being rejected that really upset me.

Between the incident at the cornfield, getting fired, and not doing well in football I was really questioning where I fit in life. I thought about it for awhile and I felt a little less shitty once I realized I was leaning toward giving up on football anyway.

That would at least free me up to start exploring other things that I could realistically be good at. "Are you okay?" Moms rubbed the back of my head.

"Yeah. I just never heard of a kid getting laid off." For the first time since I'd gotten home Moms smiled and cuddled with me on the couch for the rest of the evening until dinner.

Chapter Thirteen

THE REGIONAL TOURNAMENT took place around the middle of July. It was the last tournament of the summer. I was not going to be heartbroken if I couldn't make it to the regional tournament. The only reason I stuck it out and helped pull together money was because I didn't want to embarrass my parents anymore.

I felt I was already embarrassing them by being demoted from the starting team. I could not stand to let them down again. Without the paper route, I had to find a quick way to bring in some cash.

The fastest way I could think of was to join my crew in selling crack. As shocking as it may be, the decision was that simple. In my mind, I figured I would only do it for a few weeks and move on unscathed but that world has a funny way of pushing you into weird situations.

Between Moms shaving the grocery list down amongst other things and my money from crack sales, which was hidden under the category of "cutting grass," we had barely enough to make the trip.

At the tournament my play was uninspired, coming in as a substitute in the right wing position. Most of my time on the field, I was under attack from other players who had actually gotten better throughout season. I was chastised on the field.

"Damn. One touch Jay! That's why it's called a one-two," one teammate scowled at me.

"Get him off the field!" Billy shouted to the coach during one game. Five minutes later I was headed toward the bench.

I wanted to yell back, but I didn't feel worthy of being on the field with them. They had parents that could afford to send them to Europe for football camps or hire personal trainers. I only had two videotapes.

The games were somewhat competitive but the other teams were simply better than us, so we lost all three of our matches. It was a four-hour trip from Minnesota. I tried to sleep, but my thoughts kept me awake.

I thought about how hard I worked just to be able to play AA premier. I felt like the sacrifices I made would go to waste if I were to quit.

I also thought about how heartbroken Pops would be, but then considered that perhaps me continuing to deplete in my status was the real torture for him. His eyes no longer had a spark when we talked about the games, if we talked about them at all.

When we arrived home, I decided that I was going to quit football but I didn't tell my parents that yet. The game required too much of me.

I was fine with dedicating my life to the craft, but I needed to feel like it was going to be worth my effort. At that time, I didn't have that feeling. This period of my life ended up only being a break from the game and not a full stop as I thought it was going to be.

LATER THAT WEEK I was with Jack hanging out on Trish Beverly's porch on another hot afternoon. Jack had many girlfriends over the past few months, but Trish stood above them all.

She was full of curves even at an early age, had a pretty face, and was a year older than us. She was one of the 'it' girls in the neighborhood. Jack made an extra effort to make her feel special. With her, it wasn't about getting her to buy him clothes, music, or shoes. He seemed to really like her, but they were off and on again in those middle school years.

I was always cool with Jack's girls, some of them even knew me first before meeting Jack. Once they met Jack that was who they wanted.

Although it upset me, I learned to deal with it and never let my disappointment show. I was no different than the other guys, I was attracted to Trish too but I knew there was no chance I could get a girl like Trish.

I was used to girls laughing at me and saying that I looked like an ant, or Kunta Kinte, or a burnt piece of meat. There were times that I remember being laughed away from hang outs because girls were dissing me so hard. Jack would try to stand up for me but sometimes it wasn't enough. I never had quick enough wit to be good at talking about people so I just walked away.

Trish actually ended up being the first girl, outside of Moms, to shower me with attention. She would say "Jay, you are so sexy with yo chocolate ass." She said these things right in front of Jack. She made me feel like I inhaled happy gas.

She also had a younger sister, Kim. The first time I saw her, Landon, Jack, and I were hanging out on the porch with Trish when Kim returned from summer school. I was struck by her beauty.

Her face was small, and her eyes were beady but bold.

Her short haircut sat in rippling waves on top of her head, with wavy strands extending on each side the length of her ears. When we went over their house she would answer the door. She was often in her short shorts and a tank top, accentuating her small but, curvy body.

The berry scent of her body spray greeted my nose before she would say, "What's up, Japeth?" I loved the way the "th" drew her tongue up to her two front teeth.

We'd all hang out at her house watching TV until Kim's mom was on her way home later in the afternoon. Sometimes Jack and Trish would go to Trish's room to fool around. I was still only twelve, but I felt my life was lacking because I was still a virgin. I had not even kissed a girl yet.

Jack and I would usually meet up with Landon and DBrown after hanging out at Trish and Kim's house. We all would head to the park and sell crack. Selling crack was much easier than the hustles I was doing before and I was making about the same amount, and sometimes more.

The downside was seeing what that drug did to people in a very close way. Over a period as short as week or two, I witnessed people go from casual use to desperate addict. I watched as men let good paying factory jobs slip right through their fingers because of failed drug tests. I saw addicted women do sexual acts they usually would not do, and it was with one of these women that I saw my first vagina.

Chapter Fourteen

MISS KLINE WAS HER NAME. I went to school with her son, but he was more of an acquaintance. Miss Kline was a regular customer and she didn't look the part of a strung out crackhead.

She was normal looking and still had a nice body. One day she was a little short on cash and asked what she could do to make up for the rest.

"Fuck that bitch! Ain't no favors around here. Go get some money, then come back and see us," DBrown shouted at her from a few feet behind.

"Who you calling a bitch? You need to learn some respect with yo little bad ass. AND I ain't even talking to you. I'm talking to Jay. So shut yo ass up." DBrown started to respond when Jack grabbed his arm.

"Hold up, man. Hold up. You gonna fuck up good business." Jack walked over to where I was standing with Miss Kline.

"Katrina. I'll tell you what. You suck all of our dicks and that will make up for it."

Miss Kline twisted her neck and looked at me. I looked back at her. "Well? What are you going to do?"

"Jay. I expect that from these little shits. I don't expect that from you. Come on. You really gonna make me do this for five dollars?"

"We're one crew and we don't break that shit for no one." I scratched the back of my head, not quite feeling comfortable with the situation.

Miss Kline huffed and looked around. She started bouncing on one leg and biting her lip. "Fine."

Jack smiled then said, "I'm first," and began to walk with her toward her car.

"Why you get to go first? It's my sale," I shouted after him.

"Yeah, but it was my idea, Jay. You can go next," Jack yelled back to me as they got closer to the car.

When it was my turn I walked towards the car where Miss Kline was gargling Listerine. Apparently, she always kept a small bottle in her car. She said she used it for post lunch rinses, but I wondered if she had done this kind of arrangement before. I entered the car and she drove two minutes into a nearby alley.

"You know I actually don't mind with you, Jay. It's just that little bitch DBrown but I still can't believe you gonna make me do this."

I unzipped my pants, but still had not pulled out my member. I placed my gun on the floor. I started carrying a 380 that Choco gave me once I started dealing crack. He suggested that I have it on me whenever I was working for protection. "Let me see your tits."

She straightened herself and looked at me quizzically. Then she raised her shirt and bra up and revealed two big, golden brown breasts with erect nipples that sat above a small pouch of a stomach. I was throbbing in my pants. "Let me see your pussy."

"Little boy! You are just asking too much now."

"Come on. Let me see it."

"I'm not sucking your dick if I show it to you."

"Okay."

She furrowed her eyebrows. "Yo ass aint never seen no pussy, huh? You a virgin, ain't you?"

"Nah! I done had plenty pussy. I just want to see yours."

"Uh huh."

"You gonna let me see it or not?"

She pulled down her shorts, twisted around so that she was out from under the steering wheel and spread her legs. The hairy mound stared at me. It had a little shine. I could definitely see a hole and the skin looked like a raisin. "You wanna touch it?"

"Yeah. Let me see what yours working with." I ran my hand over the slimy skin, massaging the outside.

"Put your finger in it." I did, and the warm hole grabbed a hold of my finger. I quickly removed it and jumped back. Miss Kline smiled.

"Alright. Happy now?"

"Yeah."

"How does mine compare to the others you've had?"

"It's cool. Not the best, not the worst. Ya know?"

"Uh huh." She looked down at my hard on. "I can't let you go back to them like that. Come here." She reached over and exposed me before I could stop her. For the first time my erect penis stood naked in front of a woman.

"How old are you again?"

"Twelve," I said apprehensively.

"Wow. So big for a twelve year old."

I felt like the earth had just rolled right off of my back. I happily laid back and enjoyed her massage. I never expected my first sexual experience to be like that. I also didn't have any expectations of what it would be. I was just happy that it happened. A few weeks after that, I would encounter another surprise, but this one wouldn't be as pleasant.

Chapter Fifteen

ONE SUNDAY AFTER MASS, I changed my clothes and went in the backyard with Pops to knock the ball around. Pops never played for the St. Vincent national team or anything but according to Uncle Jimmy he was a solid defensive back.

Pops and I juggled the ball together and played a little one on one in which he always beat me. His solid 6'2 frame and speed made him a very challenging opponent. When we came in from playing, Moms said that Jack was on the phone.

I grabbed the phone from its resting position. "What's up?"

"Yo, They got Jared and his girl last night." Jared was a fellow Vice Lord who was close to our age.

"What? What you mean? What happened?"

"They were at the mall last night and they got jumped by some Disciples. They beat them up pretty good. They in the hospital now." I kept my voice quiet. I didn't want my parents to overhear my conversation.

They had no idea I was in a gang. They didn't know or

socialize with too many people in Kokomo, so they weren't to in tune with what was happening in the streets. I heard some noise in the background on the other end of the line.

"Where are you?"

"Down by Landon's. Me and DBrown down here. Choco and Z in there playing Big Whiz with Dave's crew." Dave was a senior ranking Vice Lord from Chicago and the major cocaine connection in Kokomo.

Later that night Choco and Dave found out who it was that jumped Jared and delivered justice. In the weeks following the mall incident there were a lot of shootings and beatings, each violent act trying to avenge the one prior.

The increased presence of cops in the neighborhood couldn't stop us from firing shots at each other or fighting in school and all throughout the neighborhood. The north side of the city, where most of the color in Kokomo resided, became entrenched in the back and forth of the war.

We were so caught up in defending our honor that the thought of death didn't cross our minds, much like a country boy thinks nothing of mudding or making pipe bombs for fun.

We didn't feel as though we would die; it was like another badge of manhood to be able to stand your own in gun battles. It was scary, but it was also exciting. The feel of the gun pushing back on my wrist as I pulled the trigger. The power I felt in knowing that if I needed to shoot someone, I could.

The war was still active when Labor Day arrived. On that day Landon, Jack, DBrown, and I were hanging out at my house. Pops was bar-b-queing while we played some video games inside and waited for him to finish.

Damian was being his bothersome little self and buzzing around us as we played. The enticing smoky smell wafted into my room from my window and my mouth watered with anticipation. We took turns harassing Pops. "Is it done yet?"

"Mr. Walker, is it done yet?"

We went to the backyard and sat around a temporary outdoor table. The early afternoon sunshine was blazing hot, but our tent cover kept it from baking into our skin. Moms brought out containers of baked beans, potato salad, and corn on the cob.

She laid them down in the middle of the table next to the large aluminum container full of barbeque chicken, burgers, and hot dogs. The last item Moms placed on the table was a jar of ice cold, sweet, homemade iced tea.

"Ask me if I'm a car," Landon said to me after taking a gulp of iced tea. I was confused like everyone else at the table, but I asked anyway.

"Are you a car?"

"No." I answered then remained silent for a second. I was confused, but looking at Landon's smirk, I began to find it funny. A long second passed and I erupted in laughter joining Landon. Tears came from our eyes we were laughing so hard.

Jack and DBrown shook their heads and smirked. Continuing to shake his head Jack spoke, "Mrs. Walker, that's your son."

"I know. He's a weirdo, but that's still my baby."

"What a dork," Damian chimed in.

A light, warm wind blew Pops' napkin off the table. He sucked his fingers clean from the chicken. "Elaine, where's the king fish and ground provision?"

"It deh where it deh."

"Ah ha. You gonna have me getting fat like these yankees."

"That's okay, I'll still love you. I just might have to find a second man."

We laughed at their banter. "Mr. Walker, why you call Americans yankees?" Landon asked.

"That's what we call you guys back home in St. Vincent."

"Oh. Never heard that before. What's it like in St. Vincent? Is it like Africa, where you live in huts and stuff?" Landon asked then filled his mouth with baked beans.

"Ummm. Not really. I grew up in a house that's about the size of this house. Actually, probably a little bigger." Moms jumped in, "Landon, it's a beautiful country. It's small, but we're very self-sufficient. We caught our own fish and grew a lot of our food. We swam in the ocean everyday, we played like you guys play when were younger. It's home."

She paused and took a drink before she continued, "There are poorer areas, but that's not the whole country. It's like up here. There's places like Louisiana, where there are sharecroppers living in huts, places like here and others like Beverly Hills. It's the same in St. Vincent."

"Hmmm. Interesting. Every time they show stuff on TV about Africa or the Caribbean, it's always poor people." Landon answered.

Pops was quick to jump back in. "I know. That's how they like to have us looking. Every time we heard about black America it was about the ghetto with pimps and prostitutes. Look, this system don't want you to see yourself in a positive light, so those are the images they show you."

There was a thoughtful silence and it slowed the pace of the conversation for the remainder of the lunch. We all took in more than our share of food and dispersed from the table. Me and my boys laid out in the living room watching a kung fu movie before we all fell asleep. It was only about an hour before DBrown was tapping me on my shoulder.

"Let's go over by my house," he said softly as he put his pinched index finger and thumb to his lips. I nodded my head in agreement. We nudged the other two awake and slowly rose to our feet. Every time that day crosses my mind, I wish that we would have stayed at my house.

Chapter Sixteen

I KNOCKED ON MY PARENT'S DOOR and told them I was going to DBrown's house. Pops' groggy voice shouted back that I needed to be back by five o'clock.

"That's only a couple of hours."

"We going down by Uncle Jimmy later," Moms answered.

"Okay."

Halfway down the block we saw some of our friends riding their bikes towards the park. They changed their direction to come talk to us.

"What yall getting into?" one of them asked, as we showed each other some love.

"Heading over this dude's crib," Jack said, nodding his head in DBrown's direction.

"Ah. Okay. Shiiit. We heading down to the park. Everybody's out today."

Jack posed the question. "Yall wanna go?"

"Let's go dog" Landon replied. The four of us hopped on

the handlebars and mags of the bikes and started on our way.

We turned onto the street that lead to the park. We picked up some good speed and were cruising and cracking jokes about one of the guys having girl troubles.

Our bellies were full and I could see that the park was packed with people playing basketball and hanging around. Even from blocks away the smell of weed and the basslines of the latest hip hop songs reached us. The snapshot of that moment lives with me forever. It was when Kokomo became home for me.

Just then, an old school blue Cadillac flew across our path, blowing past a stop sign that was about 800 feet away. POW! POW! POW! POW! I flew off the back of the bike I was on. The shots kept ringing out as I ducked behind a big metal dumpster that was nearby.

I grabbed my 380, looked up and saw the blue Cadillac stopped in the middle of the intersection. The doors flew open and guys with blue bandanas covering the lower portion of their faces were firing shots. I recognized one of them as Dorian. His round body shape was one of a kind.

I fired back from behind the dumpster. I heard one of them scream out "Shit! I'm hit!" I ducked back down behind the dumpster away from their view. More shots rang out and pinged against the metal, then I heard the doors shut and the sound of rubber peeling out.

I peeked my head out slowly and saw that they were gone and the crowds from the park were heading in our direction. I rushed out to the street and immediately recognized one of the bodies on the ground as Landon. He lay there trembling. I dropped to my knees next to him and screamed for help. His chest and stomach were fully ripped open from the shots. His blood was pumping out onto the concrete.

I couldn't stop crying. I just held him and kept screaming for help. I looked up and saw that some of the crowd from the park was gathering around the scene. Then sirens pierced my eardrum, followed by the sound of doors opening and closing.

I locked eyes with Landon and his face shivered. He stared back into mine and gave a faint smile. He squeezed my shirt and took a breath. His head relaxed and his body went limp. His chest now laid still. I froze, not wanting to believe it. I felt myself taking deep, heaving breaths but the rest of me was numb. Then I entered a dark state.

The next thing I knew I woke up in an ambulance on my way to the hospital. I heard a voice shout, "This one isn't shot." Another one responded saying, "Probably just fainted. Check for signs of shock." Then one noticed I was waking up and began asking me questions.

When I got to the hospital, my parents, Damian, and Jack were there waiting for me. The doctors recommended to my parents that I stay in the hospital for a few days. They wanted to keep me under close supervision and make sure that I was mentally stable after such an event.

That night, any time I closed my eyes I saw Landon's insides pump his blood into the street and so I didn't sleep much that night.

The next day the story was on the front page of the local newspaper. Three kids shot and killed. The police came by that day as well. There were two officers. Pops was the only one there with me because Moms had to go back to work. They asked about what happened the day before. I told them everything, leaving out the part about when I shot back and any gang affiliation. At the time I didn't know what happened to my gun, but I later learned that Jack took it and hid it.

"Did you ever know Landon to be involved in gangs?" One of the officers asked.

"What kind of question is that? Because they're little black boys they're gang affiliated?" Pops' eyes narrowed in on the officers.

"No sir. There has been a lot of violent activity over the past few months and we're starting to see a thread of gang retaliation."

"Well you can cut that short right there. My son isn't in a gang and I'm pretty sure that Landon wasn't in a gang. These are just kids who like to hang out together. That's it. Move onto the next question." The speaking officer looked at his partner. His partner gave an approving look and they continued inquiring about the day before for another fifteen minutes. The cops were just the beginning of a long line of questioning.

I stayed at the hospital for a few days meeting with psychologists and doing tests. I answered a lot of questions. They kept asking me "how I was feeling?" After being asked that question for the thousandth time I answered truthfully.

"I'm pissed off that yall keep asking me the same damn question!"

The psychologist, a middle aged woman, jotted a word or two on her yellow legal pad. "Good. Good. And what makes you so angry about us asking you this question?"

"Oh shit. Forget about it." She again jotted a few words. That was all those doctors did. Write notes and say "Hmmm." I don't remember one of them trying to comfort me. If they would have been genuine and sympathetic then I might have told them that I was angry and sad all at once. I might have told them that I had begun to truly feel mortal where I didn't before.

The only thing I definitely would not have told them was how badly I wanted to get out of that hospital so that I could avenge Landon's death.

When I finally got home, all I wanted to do was sleep and eat some decent food. I didn't feel like talking, so I didn't. It would be several months before I got back to appearing to be normal and many years before I dealt with the feelings I kept inside.

The next morning Pops came into my room and let me

know that he booked us a flight to New York, leaving in two weeks.

"What? What do you mean New York?"

"I know son listen. That could have been you instead of Landon. I can't...we can't afford to lose you. The doctors advised us to get you into a new environment as soon as we could to help with any trauma you may be going through. My visa expires in three months anyway, so your mother and I figured that it would be best to get you out of here now. We'll spend a little time in New York then we'll go down to St. Vincent until my green card is sorted out."

"But I don't want to go to St. Vincent. I want to stay here."

Pops stayed silent and shook his head slowly. "We can't do that son. You have to come with me. It will be good for you. You'll see." He put one arm around me, a huge emotional gesture from a man who doesn't hug, kiss, or say I love you to his kids. America, the land my parents thought had streets paved with gold, continued to disappoint. I could see it in Pops' eyes, so I accepted my fate begrudgingly but I cried myself to sleep for several days.

I READ IN THE PAPER that Dorian's body had washed up on one of the banks of Wildcat Creek, which ran through Kokomo's north end. He was missing for two days before he surfaced.

I was happy to see that Dorian got what he deserved and was certain that DBrown and Jack killed him. Over the next few days the news was full of deaths from the war. At the time, I was hesitant to read or listen to the news because I feared that DBrown or Jack would be on the list of the deceased.

The phone rang early one morning. I would have usually let someone else answer it, but for some reason I flung my arm over the edge of the bed and picked up the receiver. It was Jack.

"You hear or see yet?"

"Hear or see what? What you talking bout, man?"

"This morning police was all over the place. I heard sirens like crazy so I woke up. Looked out the window and I saw a guy hanging from the light pole."

He paused as if he was trying erase the memory then it spewed out. "Dude's whole chest was split down the middle! Couldn't tell who it was though. Looked down the street and saw a few other light poles with bodies hanging and blood dripping from them."

"Quit bullshitting man. What the hell you talking about?"

"Jay! I put that on the five my dude. On everything I love. Shit went down last night. Turn on the news and see for yourself. It's all Donuts too. Ten and counting."

I searched for the remote frantically then turned on the TV. The pictures were as Jack said. A local news anchor was on Taylor Street talking and searching for details about the massacre. Jack sat in silence on the phone as we both watched and listened.

I repeated to myself what the reporter just said. "Had to call in ambulances from Peru, Logansport, and Greentown?" Jack and I continued to stare at the images of the blood pouring into the street gutters on Taylor Street. I broke the silence.

"All donuts huh? You think…...?"

"Yep. I'm pretty sure it was." We both heard stories of Dave's past. He was known to be one of the most gruesome and violent killers in the Westside neighborhoods of Chicago. The stories always seemed to be exaggerated, but the massacre reflected the style of killing that we heard about. Dave made Vice Lords proud, but pride was only one part of the emotional tornado I was experiencing.

I remember lying in bed and thinking how much things had changed over the past year. Jack and I had gone from being outsiders to gang members. We went from mimicking karate movies to shooting real guns. I carried this ugly feeling about giving up on my dream of being the best footballer in the world and that haunted me because I felt like a failure.

Without football, I couldn't do anything about Mike's death. I had vivid nightmares about Landon dying in my arms and I was scared I was going to lose DBrown and Jack.

On top of all that, I was leaving home and going to a foreign land. The thoughts became too much to handle. I rolled over and threw a few punches at my pillow. Then I squeezed it and fell into it sobbing.

Those minutes of sobbing were the only time I actually hated my parents. I couldn't understand why they thought this move was going to help me, but it turned out that they were right.

Chapter Seventeen

I REMAINED SILENT for most of the flight to New York. It was just Pops and I. Moms had to stay and work so that we could keep our house. She kept Damian with her because she said that she couldn't let go of both of her babies. I didn't hate my dad then, but I still wasn't happy with him. The only time we talked to each other was when he nudged me with his elbow and asked "Son, are you involved in this gang stuff I've been hearing about?"

It was odd that he picked a public space like an airplane to ask me that question, so I couldn't tell him the truth even if I wanted to. "No." He looked me in my eyes, looking for truth. I returned his stare. We remained like this for a few long seconds then he said "Okay son." Years later he brought this moment up and said that he almost broke down when he looked at me that day. He said that my eyes carried the sadness of a widowed wife. I tried my best to be fine on the outside, but inside I was a mess.

The flashes of Landon's heart stopping, the look of death in his eyes, or the sound of his last breath haunted me. We landed at JFK airport in the evening. The airport was full of hustle and bustle with nearly everyone wearing black and blue business suits while carrying briefcases. The music coming from nearby stores were sounds I only heard at home or at Uncle Jimmy's.

When we exited the skybridge a woman ran towards Pops and gave him a hug. He kissed her on the cheek.

"It's been too long."

"I know!" Pops responded.

"I missed you, boy. You looking good."

"Thank you. You too, Evelyn."

"Japeth. This is your Auntie Evelyn." I smiled at the tall, fair skinned, heavyset woman and she gave me a hug.

"Nice to finally meet you, Japeth. You don't remember me, do you? I used to change your diapers when you were just a tiny little thing." I gave her a faint smile. It was all that I could muster. She looked at Pops. I pretended to not notice him mouth "he's still not there yet."

A blue Lincoln town car picked us up about fifteen minutes after we got our luggage and took us to the Crown Heights section of Brooklyn where Auntie Evelyn lived.

The buildings in her area were all about five stories high with little room between them. People were going in and out of the local stores for the needs of the night. Reggae and soca music blared from the corner store nearby as we unloaded our luggage from the trunk.

I struggled to catch my breath after walking up the four steep flights of stairs to Auntie Evelyn's apartment. "I have to leave here early for work tomorrow, boys, so I'm going to shower and get to bed. I fixed up some ox tail with rice and peas there in the kitchen. Help yourself."

Pops and I prepared heaping plates for ourselves and ate in the living room while watching TV. We watched a show on general sea life then the New York City news before shutting our eyes. It was another sleepless night for me. Once again, I saw the images of Landon's heart stopping .

The next day Pops and I rode the graffiti ridden trains and walked the trash heavy streets of Brooklyn. We hung out on stoops all day as Pops and his friends drank beer and talked about old times.

When it started getting dark, Pops hailed one of the blue Lincoln town cars, heeding his friends advice to stay off the trains. It was interesting to hear Pops and his friends tell stories about everything ranging from football to the night before in a seamless rhythm.

I remember hearing about past famous Vincentian footballers. Some names were new to me, but I heard about some of them from previous discussions with Pops. What was most interesting to me was the back and forth about the players abilities and who was better and why.

They were talking about football with the same passion that people talked about basketball in Indiana. I loved it and for the first time in months, I felt my fire for the game beginning to rekindle. I soaked up every word that day and allowed myself to daydream about my name being in those discussions.

A week passed and Pops and I settled into a rhythm in Brooklyn. We usually left the building around nine and would visit some of the landmark locations, have lunch, then usually ended up by a family member's apartment. I was still being very quiet and rarely said anything more than hi and bye. I answered specific questions, but I gave the most minimalistic answer that I could. That's why when I met G Man it was such a shock to my father.

Every time we left the building this boy would be there on the stairs outside with his pen and paper. I always wondered about him, so one day while leaving with Pops I stopped and introduced myself. I asked him what he was doing.

"Writing rhymes."

"What's your name?"

"G Man."

"We'll be back later. I want to hear some of those rhymes when I get back." I don't know why I felt so comfortable talking to him.

After a sleepless Friday night, I looked out the window early Saturday morning and saw G Man on the step. I got dressed and ran into Auntie Evelyn, who was on her way to the kitchen to cook breakfast. I asked her if it was okay for me to go down to the stoop to hang out with G Man. "Oh rapper man Greg? He's a good kid. Gwan."

I went downstairs and heard G Man mumbling words that were only slightly audible.

"Mind if I sit?"

"Naw." I sat down staring out into the street waiting for G Man to finish mumbling. The place always seemed dusty and unkept.

He finished reading from the page in the notebook. "You rhyme?"

"Naw. Those are your lyrics? I pointed to the composition notebook that he held. He nodded.

"Can I hear what you have?" He seemed hesitant but flipped to the previous page in the notebook and started rapping for about three minutes before he was finished. G Man's demeanor was similar to mine at the time, quiet and reserved, but when he started rhyming he lit up. He turned into a pint sized superstar, like a mini version of Big Daddy Kane.

After his last bar, the quiet and measured G Man returned instantly and asked me "What do you think?"

"It's dope."

"Thanks." We both sat on the steps and looked out into the street without saying any words. I didn't know it at the time, but G Man's mother was killed a couple months before I met him. G Man would tell me months later that she was killed by a stray bullet while leaving the grocery store.

"Who's your favorite rapper?" I asked breaking the silence.

"Uhh…, Kane or G Rap."

"Why them?"

G Man gave me a look of disgust. "Where you from?"

"Indiana."

"Oh a country boy huh? That's why you ask dumb questions like that. You ever heard Kane or G Rap?"

I returned his look of disgust. "Kane is one of my favorites too, but I gotta go with Rakim and Scarface as my others. Haven't listened to much of G Rap."

"G Rap is dope as shit country boy. Who's Scarface though?"

"You never heard of Scarface? The Geto Boys?" He shook his head no.

"Face is dope. You gotta listen to the Geto Boys."

We sat on the step for about thirty minutes going back and forth about who was better than who. Minutes before ten I invited G Man to watch Yo! MTV Raps in Auntie Evelyn's apartment. We raced upstairs and I checked with Auntie Evelyn to see if G Man could come in and she grudgingly said yes, but pulled me aside and told me that she doesn't like people outside her circle in her place.

"Next thing you know they see you have something they want and rob you. Understand? This isn't Indiana." I shook my head yes and returned to the living room where G Man was watching the first rap video.

Despite her discomfort, Auntie Evelyn put together two egg and sausage sandwiches for us while we watched the week's top 10 videos, not saying much to each other. Over the next few weeks, Greg and I became good friends although I was careful not to get too close because I knew I was leaving soon. We grew close enough that we built the base from which our friendship would grow for the years to follow.

My last night in the city was full of people drinking Canadian Mist, eating ox tail with rice, goat head soup and engaging in lively discussions. In the middle of it all I got a call from Moms as I did every night. She always called to see how I was doing and how the day had gone. I remained silent about my feelings. She always said, "Boy, you gonna make yourself sick."

We talked for about ten minutes. It was hard to hear her over all the voices in the background, but we both said we loved each other and she wished me a safe trip before talking to Pops. I could hear Damian in the background asking to talk to me, but there wasn't much time left on the phone card.

Boarding the plane early that next morning, thoughts of home were swirling in my mind. I missed Jack. I missed Landon. I missed Mike. I missed that familiar world. The hang outs at the park. My friends and I riding bikes and mobbing through the streets of Kokomo. Most of all I missed Moms, home, football, and Damian.

But it was time to leave all that behind, except for football. While in New York, I decided I would start playing again when I arrived in St. Vincent. The plane ascended and I was on my way to a new country, St. Vincent and the Grenadines.

Chapter Eighteen

OUR FLIGHT WAS FAIRLY UNEVENTFUL; the most torturous part was our layover in Trinidad. We spent the whole day waiting in the airport, our flight was not scheduled to leave until 10pm.

Once we finally boarded, the flight felt like it was five minutes before we landed on the strip at the small airport in St. Vincent. When we got inside we were greeted by a man who looked like Pops, only he was a little shorter. My Uncle Ruben, otherwise known as Eat'em, came over to me and shook my hand saying, "You know me, bwoy?" I answered yes and he laughed.

I was sleepy so I gave in as soon as we got into Eat'ems jeep. The car slowing down awoke me and I looked out into the darkness to see that we arrived at what I assumed was my Granny's house.

I exited the jeep and noticed there were no sidewalks and the streets were narrow. We grabbed our luggage. I looked up and down the street again and decided there was no way that two cars could pass on it, given its width. We walked up to the gate and heard a familiar voice shout, "Ya finally reach?! Welcome to Layou!"

I knew that voice from several phone conversations over the years. I looked up to see a beautiful, short woman with dark skin, her small eyes glittering under the porch light. I heard the sound of a chain moving on concrete and little feet rapidly hitting the pavement. "Woooff! Wooof!" I dropped my luggage and started to run before Pops stopped me.

"You fraid dog?" Granny asked.

"Yes Granny." She told me that I didn't have to worry about her dogs because she always kept them chained up.

"There's that one and another one in di back. No need to bother yourself" she said as she gave me a big hug. I could feel her love permeate through me like ink to water.

"Where's the old man?" Pops asked.

"He gone up di road. You'll see him tomorrow." We all went inside and Granny took me to my new room.

It was small and simple, but comfortable. I had a window that faced towards the street. Below that window was part of the dogs roaming territory.

Granny offered me some callaloo soup that she prepared for dinner, which was one of Pops' favorite meals. I declined and told her I was ready to go to bed. She gave me a hug and kiss then sent me to brush my teeth.

For the first time in a while, I didn't have trouble falling asleep that night. The next morning, I woke up to the smell of breadfruit and salt fish. I went into the kitchen and met Pops and Eat'em sitting with Granny. The radio played in the background. Granny prepared me a plate along with some hot tea sweetened with condensed milk. We all went on the porch and they continued their conversation.

Eat'em and Granny were catching Pops up on all the things going on around the area. We were on the porch for about ten minutes when Grandpa approached the gate and entered.

"Mister Japeth! You sleep long bwoy! Half di day done gone already!"

"I was tired." He came up to the porch and moved Pops out of his seat by raising his hand as if he was going to give him a clout accompanied with a "Bwoy move ya ass." I smiled as I thought back to a time when Pops stomped on Damian's foot for being in his favorite spot on the couch.

Pops offered to take me into Kingstown, so I threw on some more decent looking clothes. Pops was entering the house from the porch when he saw one of his old buddies from school passing in the street and stopped to catch up on old times.

While they talked, Grandpa and I sat on the porch. He started talking about cricket and his favorite player of all time, Sonny Ramadhin. His energy became like that of a young school boy and he went on and on about how there will never be another batsman like Sonny.

"I named your father after him." He paused, smiled to himself, and continued to look towards the clear sky. "First child and it was a boy. One of the best moments in my life." He turned and looked at me.

"You just like he, you know? That boy love ah football. He and Eat'em used to get plenty licks for sneaking off to play football instead of taking care of me goats." He laughed out loud before rising up from his seat. I smiled and nodded.

"Well, Japeth, it don't look like you going nowhere today." He said to me, but really sending a message to Pops. A few minutes passed, then Pops finished his conversation. We walked out the gate and down the street.

"Just down here by the corner we're going catch the van to Town." Pops said as we neared the pick up area. A few vans passed, but Pops was waiting on a special one that an old friend of his drove. After a fifteen-minute wait, a royal blue van pulled up.

It had "Trust Me" spray painted onto the side in a very colorful, graffiti style.

"Sticks!? Long time me nah see you man!" the driver shouted back to us as we entered the packed vehicle and made our way to an open spot in the second row of bench style seats.

Pops shouted back, "Yea dred! We catch up some time soon, eh?"

I was impressed with the driver's ability to control the vehicle around the many potholes and blind ascending corners. The day was hot but there was a cool breeze passing through the van. We could hear music from the various types of houses we passed along the road matching the sounds in the van from Nice FM.

I recognized one of the songs that played as we got closer to Town. A few people around me sang along with the lyrics: "Come inside the people fete....Dance all night until we wet..." More people joined in for the chorus, "Gal you ain nothing but a teaser!"

We got to the main bus drop off, which I later learned was called Little Tokyo, the official bus stop in Kingstown, and we filed out of the van. Some people were rushing off to work, others leisurely walking to the market for dinner items that night, and some that seemed to not be doing much at all. We took an escape from the heat under the shelter of a store.

It was small in comparison to what I was used to seeing in the States, but it was one of the bigger stores in the capital city of Kingstown. Pops roamed around looking for something while I spotted a black and white, octagon-paneled ball. I grabbed it and Pops was happy to buy it for me. It was the ball I used to train with in St. Vincent. I would have kept that ball had I known what it was going to be the start of.

Chapter Nineteen

I WAS ANXIOUS to kick the ball around on the sand, the only thing which I was excited about in weeks. Pops told me so many stories about playing there, that I was ready to experience it myself. Unfortunately, we were short on time as the evening was quickly approaching, so Pops promised to take me the following morning.

The night passed at a tortuously slow pace before the morning appeared and we went down to the beach. The sand was hot under my feet, but got cooler the closer we got to the water. I noticed a small game going on towards the high cliffs that created a border on the right side of the beach.

Pops and I started passing the ball back and forth. The sun was beating down and drew out a nice sweat from both of us as we trained, while the cool breeze that slid off the sea helped make the heat bearable.

We ran through a series of drills working on my left foot, volleying the ball back and forth, various dribbling exercises and overall ball control. I enjoyed dribbling the most, even though it was the most draining activity, it was the most direct way for me to express myself.

I struggled with my movement in the grainy sand for the first week. It was like playing with fifteen-pound weights around my ankles and I would tire quickly under the sand's strain.

I would go up against Pops one on one in dribbling, but he tackled hard and used his size against me. That first week I could barely push the ball one step before he would nab it from me.

"Damn boy, you ever going to get over here? You weak, shouldn't even be out here with me," he taunted.

"That's cause you're older and bigger! If I was your size, I'd be past you all day!" I finally responded after a week of taunting. It was perhaps the most words I had put together for anyone outside of G Man since Landon's death.

Pops punched me in the chest, knocking me into the sand. He snatched me back up to my feet grabbing me by my thin arms and squatted so that he was face to face with me.

"Don't you ever give up son! You hear me? You gonna have to toughen up to play down here. You see them boys over there? They will eat you alive, not because you don't have the skills or the talent but because you don't have 'it' up here." He released one arm to tap his temple.

"You heard of the 'it' factor? All the greats have 'it' but nobody bothers to tell you what the damn 'it' is. Well I'm telling you son. 'It' is here." Again, he released one arm but this time his finger tapped my forehead.

"If 'it' is here, then here will follow." His finger now tapped at my heart and I was lost in his words as if God himself was talking to me. He paused for a moment, gripping my arm again with an eased tension.

"That's all it is son. You think this is bad. This world will shred you and tear your heart out if you let it...but perhaps you already know that."

He softened a bit coming back to a calmer version of himself. "I don't like having to do this, but you have too much talent to let these boys—anybody down here or anywhere—break you. Learn to deal with it. Life isn't easy son. It's full of disappointments, set backs and heart aches. Learn to make it your fuel. If you can find out how to do that, trust me, you will never run out of gas. AND another thing…"

He began to rise in anger again before tightening his grip on my arms. "I don't ever want to hear you complain about somebody being bigger, faster, or anything more than you. You got gifts. Use them!"

"You're smaller than me right?" I nodded. He stood up straight and pulled me so that I was standing side by side with him. I could feel how he would topple or halt if I were to wedge my body against his body.

"Change up your direction and get me off balance. You hear me?" I nodded again.

"Go swim," he said as he released his grip on me. Much like his advice after my very first game when I was disappointed from not playing, the words made logical sense but I wondered if I had it in me to apply his advice to my life.

I ran into the sea and splashed my way out to where my feet could no longer touch. Pops joined me and we wrestled in the water and swam around for about an hour.

Leaving the beach my eyes burned from the salty water. We walked a few short feet to Mama's house, who we tried to visit before we went to the beach but no one was home. Mama was my Moms mother. "Sticks!" I heard a voice call out. I noticed that the voice came from an older woman sitting on a bench in the shade of her driveway.

He shouted back "Hey, Mama!"

"Sticks, that's my boy Japeth?"

"Yep. The one and only." Pops said as we continued to walk closer.

"You gettin' tall bwoy." Mama rose from her seat and hugged me. Her love was palpable in her touch like Granny's.

A few of my cousins trickled out of the house wearing school uniforms and eating homemade bread. Pops explained that we had stopped by earlier before going to the beach.

"I just get back from getting dem kids from school." Although Mama and I talked frequently on the phone, it was always in short intervals so it was actually a little awkward meeting her in person. I noticed that my other cousins and neighbors were calling her Miss Ting. I felt so formal for calling her Mama, but I didn't feel comfortable enough to call her Miss Ting.

I followed my cousins back inside the house. They all sat around a table breaking off pieces from a loaf of homemade bread. The girl, Jessica, waved me over.

She got up and grabbed a small plate from the cupboard in the nearby kitchen, placed a piece of bread on it and handed it to me. Her long, toned legs were silky and shiny. She flipped her long hair back over her shoulder before returning to her seat at the table "Man, if she wasn't my cousin…" I thought to myself.

The boys had not said a word to me at that point. Only a nod of "what's up?" The youngest one, Kendall, finished his bread and reached across to Ramel's plate. He quickly snatched Ramel's last piece and took off from the table. Ramel jumped up chasing Kendall outside catching him before he could get out of the driveway, but it was too late. Kendall had stuffed the whole piece of bread in his mouth by the time Ramel caught him. Jessy and I peeked outside the door to see what was going to happen.

I glanced back at her and she was only half way interested. Her face looked more fed up than anything. I was curious to see what would happen. Kendall's mouth was so full he couldn't talk or chew properly. Mama had the same look on her face as Jessy did.

Kendall struggled to enjoy the bread, but what was unmistakable was that he enjoyed annoying Ramel more than anything. The more Ramel saw him trying to chew the bread the more upset he got and he gave Kendall a good clout. The half chewed bread came flying out of Kendall's mouth, through the doorway to the inside of the house.

"Hulk! Bwoy! I done tell you about cloutin up your brother like dat!" Mama shouted as she rose up from the small bench.

"But Miss Ting Smally take me bread," Ramel, or Hulk as he was called, responded.

"I don't care what he did, I say stop, you stop. Understand?" Kendall—Smally—was inside the house out of the sight of Mama and was now taunting Hulk, laughing at him quietly but animated, as he was being rebuked by Mama.

"Yes, Miss Ting."

The boys went upstairs to change. They were going to play football in the open lot across the street. I wanted to play but Pops said we had to leave to meet up with some more family later that afternoon.

We stayed long enough to see the beginning of the pick up game. In the short bit I did see, I understood exactly what Pops was talking about. Every touch the boys took, every run they made, and every dribble was criticized by somebody.

It was like a team full of coaches. Not only did the criticism come from players on the field, but also by the rum drinkers who hung around the area and stopped to watch the game.

The players were good and had that special silky touch that only came from hours and hours of playing with the ball. I'd heard one of the announcers during the 1990 World Cup say that the people in Cameroon had a saying, "touch of the toes," and I wondered if this was the touch they meant.

I had put in my fair share of practice but my touch had not

reached that level, nor had any American footballer I had seen. I was happy that we had family to visit later that afternoon, potentially saving me from an embarrassing moment.

Chapter Twenty

THE FIRST FEW WEEKS in St. Vincent, life was deceptively fast between meeting dozens of family members, practicing football, and exploring the island. The island was beautiful, with its bountiful green mountainous terrain and sandy beaches ranging from brightly white to darkest black. There were times when I was out in the sea that I felt like I could reach out and touch the sky.

The air was crisp and clean. I would pass houses on the road and smell the delicious meals being prepared during the early evening hours. Even on days when it was rainy and overcast, the island still seemed to have the sun smiling down on it.

The rhythms of soca, reggae, and dancehall music drove the movement of the people, always playing in the background providing a soundtrack to their lives.

It was against this backdrop that I had begun to recover from my internal wounds in Kokomo. I still had nightmares about Landon, thought about Mike and worried about Jack, DBrown and Choco. I got my first letter from Jack about a month after being in St. Vincent. Granny gave me the package and I hurried to the room to open the small box. Inside I found a few blank tapes with labels that read Tribe Called Quest, EPMD, and 8Ball and MJG.

I opened the three-page letter and read it intently. I felt as though I could hear his voice speaking the words on the page. I could see his facial expressions and the actions that accompanied each word. Pieces of that letter still stick with me today the way the words of your favorite childhood songs stay in your mind.

"Shit is crazy around here. You lucky you got to leave my dude. Po-po came through and arrested bout twenty people for that massacre shit. They got Choco too, saying they got evidence against him. Nobody sentenced yet, but it ain't looking good. DBrown been kinda bugged out since that shit my dude. He ain't been the same. Been straight snappin on mutha fuckas.

The other day at school, this skinhead dude looked at him wrong, D ran up on him, grabbed him by his shirt and his belt buckle, lifted him up and drove his head into the ground. Police came and all that shit. I put it on the five my dude. Enough about the bullshit though, we miss you over here my dude. When you coming back?"

In those words, I could sense a sort of desperation growing within Jack. Dreams giving way to a false sense of reality. A complacency settling into his bones and wondered to myself if he would be alive when I returned. I didn't know when that would be but I hoped it was soon.

It was March by the time all my paperwork for school was finally completed. I just recently turned thirteen years old on February 17th. Based on my age, I was enrolled at Barrouille Secondary School in a neighboring village that most just called Bagga.

"You remember the talk we had awhile back on the beach

about challenges?" Pops asked me the night before my first day of school.

"Yeah."

"Well, it's going to apply to your schooling too. Form 1 is the equivalent to the ninth grade in the States. The school system here doesn't have what you know as middle school. We start high school at thirteen down here, so it's not going to be easy and you are going to have to be strong and determined to do well. I know you can do it, though." I had struggled to keep C's off of my seventh grade report cards. I thought there was no way that I'd be able to keep up, but I ended up doing okay.

The next morning, I woke up early and put on my new uniform of freshly pressed gray slacks, short sleeve white button up shirt, with a brown and white tie. I ate some tri tri cakes and bread washed down with tea, then headed out to catch the van. When I got in the van, it was full mostly with kids. The boys were dressed just as I was and the girls wore brown skirts with white button up shirts.

We were soon in Barrouaille and stopped at a big lime green building with large overlooking trees that ascended up into the mountain behind it. It looked as if it the school was built into the hill on which it stood.

There were several conversations being held around me, but I participated in none of them. I walked through the doors of Barrouallie Secondary School for the first time nervous about how I would fit in. I stopped the first adult I saw and asked them where I could find Mrs. Douglas's class. The middle-aged woman looked at me strangely.

"What's your name, young man? I've never seen you here before."

"Japeth Walker, ma'am." She reviewed my features closely. Her face lit up as if she'd found the answer.

"Wait…. you for dem Walker's up First River in Layou?"

"Yes mam. My dad is Sonny Walker."

"Well, look at that! Sticks bwoy ah come Barrouallie Secondary. It must be cause you come from America. Your dad was one of the brightest in his class at Grammar School, you know? Come, let me know show you where Mrs. Douglas is."

She guided me up a set of stairs, then down towards the end of a hallway. Before we got to the classroom she asked me if Elaine was my mother. I replied yes and somehow her bright smile dampened just a bit. She then escorted me into the classroom and introduced me to Mrs. Douglas.

Mrs. Douglas seemed like a very nice woman, probably around the same age as the lady who escorted me in. She was fairly attractive with long, pressed black hair. Before my escort left, she asked me to tell Pops that "Miss Jen Harper" said hello then Mrs. Douglas assigned me a seat in the back row.

The school bell rang and Mrs. Douglas asked me to stand. She told everyone my name and mentioned that I would be joining the class. I was amazed to find no one laughed at my name and she actually pronounced it right.

She started class and went through the lessons, randomly asking questions of the students to make sure we were paying attention. One of the guys in class got caught talking during her lecture and she called his name sharply. She walked over to him holding a wispy looking ruler in her hand.

When she arrived at his desk, he held out his hand feebly. Thwack!! He quickly withdrew his hand and shook it up and down as if he could shake the pain off like water.

She turned and went back to teaching her lesson. I looked around to see the reactions of the other students.

Most had no reaction at all and others, mostly boys, were trying to restrain their laughter. I closed my eyes for a few seconds and said a prayer asking for protection and that my father's green card issues got sorted out quickly.

Despite my efforts to hide, Mrs. Douglas asked me to answer a geometry problem. My eyes widened. I could not form a word in response to the gibberish she wrote on the blackboard.

"Well it seems, we need to go back to the English lesson for Japeth." She moved on from me, but held me back from the first ten minutes of recess.

"I know your mother and father want you to be at this level, but I just don't know if it is the best thing for you. Do you think you can make it in this class or do you want to try Junior 5 first?"

I knew Moms and Pops would be disappointed in me if I tried to take the easy way, but I was definitely considering it. I knew I wasn't ready for the class that I was in, but I had to at least try for Moms and Pops.

Chapter Twenty-One

I STEPPED OUT to the dusty area where all the kids were running around and playing during recess. I felt drawn to the football pick up game. I had managed to dodge playing football with anybody outside of Pops up to that point. In that short span of time, my dribbling became smoother, my ball control was tighter, and my confidence soaring again.

During our one on one battles, Pops kicked me down, tripped, pushed, and tugged at me as if he was playing for the World Cup championship. He'd criticize me just for the sake of it. I had no complaints. I practiced mentally figuring out ways to deal with the pressure and creatively finding a way to win.

I couldn't tell you what it was that drew me to that particular game that day. It could have been the need to prove something after that embarrassing moment in class or maybe I was just ready to put my skills to the test. I stood watching the game.

"You play?" a taller dark guy asked.

"Yeah, I play." I heard a few laughs from the group.

"Well, come run wid we next. We need ah next man."

One of the guys sitting on the ground shouted out, "You da man who can't talk?"

I wasn't sure if I heard him properly. "What?"

"Oh, ya can't hear either." He sucked his teeth and said in the direction of the taller guy standing. "John, he can't talk, can't hear. What's he go do pon di field?"

The group started laughing. I understood everything he was saying now.

"Fuck you laughing at bitch. I can talk and I heard every—" Before I could finish the group started laughing harder as Justin continued in a high pitched voice, "O God! Di man retarded! You hear he?!" I started to dive after Justin only to be held back from behind.

"Let'um go Cam so I can bust he ass!"

With a strong hold on me Cam said, "Calm down bredda. We don't deal like that around here. A man give you jokes and you ready to beat him? That make any sense?"

"I'm alright." Cam's grip softened and just then we were called in from recess. Cam and I walked back into the building and he invited me to play after school by a park in Bagga.

"Thanks, but I didn't bring any extra clothes to play in. Maybe tomorrow."

"Okay. We play everyday after school, so whenever you ready."

The rest of the day passed and I felt uneasy the entire time. It felt like everyone was laughing at me. The embarrassment was heightened by the presence of Renell, the prettiest girl in our class. Her skin was a silky, radiant caramel brown and she was curvy but had a small frame. Her teeth were perfectly white, straight, and had no gaps.

I tried not to look at her, but found myself glancing in her direction frequently. She seemed to be pretty popular, judging by how many people interacted with her. I never would have imagined that one day she would become a part of my life.

That afternoon, I decided I was finally ready to go play with Hulk, Smally, and their friends down by Jackson Bay, which was the beach in Layou.

I started the game with a few bad touches and the drunks watching started in on me. "Don't let that yankee boy touch di ball man! He salting up di game!" The players on the field echoed what was being said outside of the pitch. Soon, they were not passing the ball to me and I was starting to let the negative energy get under my skin. It wasn't that I was beaten down by the commentary. I was unfairly singled out. Some of the other guys were playing much worse than I was, but when they made a mistake the words in their direction were kinder.

I kept playing and eventually the numbers dwindled down to a comfortable six versus six game. I was starting to find my rhythm amongst the boys, but unfortunately the crowds were gone. Dusk had just started to set in as three of the guys, Blue, Front Seat, and Cat eye came over to Mama's after we finished playing to hangout with Hulk, Smally, and I.

We ate a loaf of bread before Jessy came down from the second floor. "Aye! You fellas think that bread just for you!" She pointed at Blue, Cat Eye, and Front Seat. "You don't even live here! Yo nah shame?!.... Eating up people bread."

We all finished what we already had in our hands then went outside to the driveway and talked about football. Blue, Cat Eye, and Front Seat first struggled with my accent. "I can't understand him either. It's the most I've heard him say since he come." Hulk responded to their requests to translate.

After a few minutes, they were able to piece together what I was saying and we found that we were all obsessed with football. That lead to an automatic connection between us. We grew to be very tight and eventually practiced together several times everyday.

The energy between us reminded me of how Mike, Jack and I used to be a few years before. It was hypnotic, but also going against what I planned for myself.

I didn't want to get to close to anyone or used to the lifestyle in St. Vincent because as soon as Pops' green card was arranged we would return to Kokomo. We didn't know when that would be so I think both of us tried to enjoy the time as much as we could without becoming attached.

While we were there, Pops became instrumental in setting me on my path for greatness. He was the voice in my head that always urged me forward no matter how much I achieved. The memory of Mike and Landon were the pulse that kept me moving. Between Pops and the memories of my best friends, my dream felt reachable and my new friendships became very critical.

Everyday Hulk, Blue, Cat eye, Front Seat and I would compete amongst ourselves playing games and doing the most difficult drills faster and better. My favorite game used to be one versus four keep away.

We'd square off a ten by fifteen yard area and see who could hold the ball the longest against the other three players. It helped develop extremely close ball control and anticipation of the next defender.

My game had blossomed over a matter of months. I became one of the top players on the Barrouille Secondary school team that I had joined. There were two other players from Bagga on that team that were really good, Cam and Markee.

Eventually both of them would join Hulk, Blue, Cat Eye, Front Seat and I in our intense training sessions. We formed what became later known as the Wicked 7, a collection of footballers that would shake up the nation.

Chapter Twenty-Two

THE NAME WICKED 7 came from Otis. He was a drunk that used to hang around Layou. His nickname came about because of his love for Otis Redding, which you could sometimes hear him bellowing out on quiet Layou nights.

Otis would see us playing small four on three games anywhere we could, whether it was a beach, park, or open lot and would provide the commentary similar to what you would hear at Rucker Park in Harlem. He was so impressed with the level of our skills that anytime he would see us in a regular pick up, school team, or club team game, he would say to others that we were from the Wicked 7. I thought nothing of it at first, but then it started to catch on and that name began to mean something.

There was a responsibility to be the best on the field at any moment. The way we competed against each other everyday made our standard for play very high. We cracked jokes and talked shit amongst each other, but there was a common love there that made it okay. Nobody had to explain that we were trying to make each other better, we just knew that was the purpose behind everything we did.

I began to loosen up and it felt good. Pops and my family were happy to see my personality come alive again. Even Pops, who was reserved and guarded in Kokomo, was more social and humorous. He was always like that in the house with us, but in Brooklyn and St. Vincent was the first time I knew him to show that side of himself to the outside world.

I still had the nightmares, but the dark cloud of emotions that consumed me seemed to be floating away. At the time, I thought that cloud would leave completely but it always lingered within my emotional atmosphere. I would say that I was always overcast at best and a stormy tornado at worst. That stormy tornado definitely passed through in a few seasons of my life. My friendship with the Wicked 7 grew past football, but that was still ninety percent of what we talked about.

There were several nights that the seven of us would be hanging out in Barrouaille at the post office debating who was the best team or players in the game. Some of the older guys around Bagga used to be hanging out around the post office and join the heated debates. At times the passion in our voices could be mistaken for the beginnings of a fight depending on who was involved.

The older guys would be present at one moment and the next they'd slip off into the darkness of the night only to reappear an hour or two later, satisfied from their secret lady company. Eventually, our actions would mimic theirs as our popularity grew.

For the first time in my life, I was a wanted man. The girls were flocking to me in St. Vincent, which boosted my already rising ego. I had my choice of any girl I wanted on the island, but Renell still held my attention.

Over the past few months Renell and I had become friends. Unaware of the "friend" boat, I thought I was making some good progress with her. That was until one day when I was about to walk with Renell to the shop before playing with the guys.

"Bird! Let she go with she girl friend them nah man!" Bird was a nickname that I picked up for my scrawny size and also for how fast I could run.

"Renell, what you give that man to make him act so?" Blue shouted, joining in on the jokes.

"He ain getting nothing from me! Is his choice!" The emotion and heat in which she served the words made me think that all the work I thought I was doing was for nothing.

I walked with Renell to the shop then I jetted off to play with the guys at the park. I passed two women at the van stop discussing what they would be wearing to the Carnival launch party in Kingstown the following weekend.

Carnival created an energy that buzzed in the humidity of the air. The old and new sounds of the summer thumped in speakers everywhere. Touch's new song, "Move Yo Front," was getting a lot of play on the radio and predicted to be the Road March Winner. It seemed as though the whole island worked and lived for that time of year so I was anxious to see if it was as fun as everybody hyped it up to be.

The weeks passed and I could see why everyone was so excited about carnival. There were parties every night that seemed to take on an escalated energy that lead up to J'ouvert, an early morning street party that kicked off the actual carnival festival. Out of seven guys, nobody bothered to warn me that I needed to wear clothes that I was comfortable messing up to J'ouvert.

"Where you goin in them good clothes? People don't wear good stuff to J'ouvert. You have to wear something to mash up." Granny laughed to herself as she helped me get my clothes together and I was glad that she caught me before I walked out of the door.

J'ouvert was the wildest experience that I had up until that point. People were throwing powder and paint everywhere. The crowd moved up, down, and around to the rhythms the DJ blared out the speakers. It was like the talent show parties in Kokomo on speed.

The girls in Kokomo could dance, but these girls were on a different level. Their waist moved effortlessly, swaying whether fast or slow, as if it had no attachment to the rest of their body. I was mesmerized by the beauty of how their behinds would roll or bounce back and forth, tick tocking like a pendulum. My admiration also held me paralyzed by the fear of not knowing what to do with it.

I saw Renell after the J'ouvert jump up and she asked me if I would walk her home. I was hesitant after the way she played me a few weeks prior, but I walked with her anyway.

We walked up through gutter, a short cut up the hill in Bagga, and she asked why I had been so cold to her recently. I told her that she pissed me off with the way she acted before.

She apologized, saying that she meant nothing by it. "It's because they were being so loud. I guess I just didn't want people to go back and talk. Sorry I vex you so. I do like you though." She paused for a few seconds. "Do you like me?" I tried hard not to look at her keeping my face down to the road.

"Yeah."

"So why you nah say something. How was I supposed to know that?" I didn't answer, as I suddenly felt immature in her presence. As we reached her house at the top of the hill she continued, "So what now darling?" I shrugged my shoulders.

She rolled her eyes and her face went from happy to fed up. "See how you hardheaded! What do you want to do?! You want to be with me or what?"

I looked up to notice the expression on her face begging for an answer and for the first time I noticed that she was a little scared I may say no.

"Yes."

Renell's face spread into a smile and we stood there facing each other on her porch overlooking the village below leading out into the sea. She stepped closer, pressed her body against mine, and kissed me. My head was dizzy with excitement as our lips interlocked.

I caught the next van that would drop me off in Layou, with a Kool-Aid smile on my face. The smile and good feeling continued to fill me as I got home. "What happen… some girl out a road kiss you up bwoy?" Grandpa joked as I joined him, Pops and a few of Pops' friends on the porch.

"Must be that girl Renell me see him with," Pops chimed in.

"Leave the boy alone." Granny jumped in. "If di boy is in love, di boy is in love. You want something to eat Japeth?"

"Nah, I'm not hungry."

"Di man full off ah love." Grandpa began cracking up at his own joke with the rest of the group. Granny laughed along as she hit Grandpa playfully before asking Pops, his friends and I to pose for some pictures.

"I have to send Elaine some pictures of this." We all posed with our powdered and messy bodies. We took a few pictures all as one group then Granny told the rest of them to move so that I could take one by myself.

"My bwoy Japeth's first J'ouvert," she said to herself as she snapped a few images.

"Take one of the my J'ouvert crew too mommy!" Pops shouted out.

Granny finished up taking pictures then hosed me off before I went inside to take a proper shower. After my shower, I began to feel hungry and fixed myself a plate of peleau that Granny had prepared. I was shoving loaded spoonfuls into my mouth when the phone rang. Granny answered. "Yes he is, may I ask who's calling? Renell? Okay hold on."

I rushed to the phone. "Hello?"

"Hey babes, what time you going Town?"

"Supposed to meet up with Cam and them in the next hour or so."

"They meeting you on Bagga side or Layou?"

"Layou."

"Okay darling. We leaving here soon, so I guess I'll see you around down there."

I nervously looked up at my surroundings, wishing I had some privacy. I wanted to return all the love I was receiving. "Well, wait, how you gonna know where I'm at?"

"Cuteness don't pass the eye easy babes." My body tingled with a buzz of electricity and that Kool-Aid smile returned as I hung up the phone.

"Eh eh! Look at teeth!" Grandpa shouted as he peeked around into the living room from the porch.

"What are you talking about?" I walked out towards the porch.

"Uh huh." Grandpa acknowledged my poorly feigned ignorance.

"That's Renell for Charlie Kennedy, right?" Pops asked.

"Yeah."

One of his friends chimed in with filler information, "Charlie can play some serious bass, ya know."

Another stretched his fist out to me as I reached the porch. "A nice looking girl dat my youth."

I met his fist with mine. "Thanks."

While we waited for the bus, I told all the fellas that Renell and I were a couple now.

"Come on… nah man! You know Renell don't like you like that." Cat Eye rebuked. Hulk and Smally, my own cousins, were even doubting me. It seemed like a complete waste of time to tell them about the kiss, so I didn't.

When we got to Town the place was crazy. The same energy as J'ouvert, except there were colorful costumes, half-naked people, and some people dancing around on really tall stilts. I was amazed with how the guys moved as if the stilts were non- existent. They jumped, whined, and carried on just like the rest of us in the wild street parade.

Through the day we were splitting off here and there, but always seemed to meet back up somehow. Cat Eye was with me when Renell and I met. Renell greeted me with a kiss on the cheek and a hug.

I looked over at Cat Eye after we kissed and the expression on his face only added to my victorious feeling. Renell and I were dancing together as Hulk, Smally, and Cat Eye linked in with her friends. We all followed and danced behind the massive truck with the band Touch. I was shouting out with the rest of the crowd "Moooooooove Yo Front!" when I felt a tap on my shoulder.

I turned around to see Pops dancing and having a good time. There was a lady behind him that I remember him introducing me to in those first few weeks on the island, but I couldn't remember her name.

"You having a good time?!" he yelled to overcome the mixture of music, pulsing whistles and chanting crowds.

"Yeah! Pops, this is Renell!" Renell stretched her arm out towards Pops and they shook hands.

"This is my friend, Tanya," Pops said extending his arm around her shoulder. Pops took a swig of his Hairoun beer, "Alright, well have fun!" He leaned over and said into my ear, "It's great to see you enjoying yourself son. Didn't I tell you this would be good for you?"

"Yea, you were right. Thank you." My words were gratuitous, but inside I was wondering about Tanya. I watched them as the bounced away, but they did nothing to indicate that they were a couple.

I never asked Pops about Tanya and I never told Moms about her. I figured it was better to keep things as calm as possible. I was in a better space and I selfishly didn't want to disrupt that.

We continued to party the whole day, with Renell and I slipping off every now and then to sneak in a kiss or rest our feet. I laid in bed that night and wondered if Renell and I were real. The whole day felt like a dream that I didn't want to wake up from and the best part was yet to come.

Chapter Twenty-Three

IN THE DARKNESS of my mind I could hear the loud crack of gun shots. My mind flashed to the image of Landon's insides. Blood pumping straight from his heart out onto the pavement, some of it splattering on the ground, some of it oozing. Just then an unknown face appeared at my side with a gun to my head about to pull the trigger. I dug deep and screamed as loud as I could, only to find myself in the darkness of my room.

Grandpa and Granny rushed to my room, asking me if I was okay. I fell into Grandpa's arms with tears flowing down my face.

"Landon again?"

"Yeah," I sobbed. A minute or two passed and my fear turned to embarrassment.

Granny whispered something to Grandpa. Then she said "Come, Japeth. You gonna sleep with me tonight." She extended her hand and even though this only added to my embarrassment, the concern and pain in her eyes wouldn't let me say no. I got up and followed Granny into her room as Grandpa situated himself on my bed.

I thought about Landon and the good times in Kokomo as I lay there in Granny's bed. My mind drifted to the letters I was getting from Jack, every one guaranteed a new person or group of people that were going to jail for murder, drug possession, or found dead.

I AWOKE TO THE SIZZLE and crackle of Granny frying fish in the kitchen. I rolled over and looked at the time. I was going to be late in meeting up with my friends. I rushed out of bed, said good morning to Granny and Grandpa before going into my room to put on my play clothes.

I was about to step through the front door when the phone rang. "Japeth, get the phone nah man!" shouted Grandpa from the bathroom.

"Hello, good morning."

I could hear muffled laughter in the phone. "Hello," I said again.

The laughter became unmuffled and the voice mockingly said "'Hello, good morning.' You're such *dork,* dude"

"Shut up, Damian! You wasting up good minutes punk. What's up?"

"Nothing. I hadn't talked to you in awhile, so I asked Moms if I could call." The few minutes that we talked I felt like I was chatting with a buddy of mine instead of my annoying little brother.

He was still excelling in basketball and was named the MVP of the Kokomo High School basketball camp for twelve year olds. Towards the end of our conversation I could hear Moms tell Damian to pass her the phone.

"What's up, boy?"

"Hey, Moms!"

"So I hear you been carrying on for carnival."

"Who told you that? Pops?"

"Don't concern yourself with that. So who's this girlfriend you have?"

"Huh?"

"Don't huh me boy, who's the chick?"

"Renell."

"What's her last name?"

"Kennedy."

"Oh, that must be Esther and Charlie's girl."

"Yeah, that's her. You know them?"

"Yeah, we used to all lime together over Bambarow every now and then." Bambarow was a secluded beach between Bagga and Layou.

"Oh. Okay. Moms, can I call you guys back later? I'm bout to go play football."

"Yeah, that's fine. We just wanted to call and check in on you. Make sure you're alright. Still studying your school work this summer?"

I grudgingly said yes. I hated having to study with Pops and Jessy during the summer break, but I had to do it. I worked extremely hard during that school year to catch up and I even passed my Common Entrance Exam Test that allowed me move on to Form 2. I barely passed the exam, so I was going to have to work extra hard so that I wouldn't fall behind.

I hung up the phone and told Granny and Grandpa that Damian and Moms said to tell them hello. I grabbed a piece of bread and left to play football.

Over the months I had played so much that I had achieved that silky touch I wanted. The touch of the toes. I was the youngest, but I had become one of the most exciting players in the Wicked 7. I had become a terror for defenders in one on one situations, twisting them up and able to explode past them with a new found lightening speed.

I can't pinpoint when that speed kicked in. All I know is that I woke up one day and I was extremely fast. I was fast before, but now I was in a class by myself.

I was also comfortable having multiple players around me trying to take the ball. I had a variety of ways to shield it and a ton of tricky moves to get past one or more players that enabled me to get shots off in almost any situation around the box.

A year and some passed and my club team, Lucky Stars, was going to play against the number one team from Town. My performances and reputation had earned me a starting spot on the U-17 team even though I was only fourteen. Lucky Stars was based out of Layou, but Cam and Markee joined us from Bagga. In generations before me there was usually a strong tension and rivalry between the neighboring areas of Barroullie and Layou.

The Wicked 7 helped bridge that gap tremendously, even though there was still talk of whether the "Baga man" and "Layou man" out of the Wicked 7 were the best. We didn't pay much attention to it. For us, it was all about football and if anything, it was part of the jokes we had with each other but nothing further than us calling them "Black fish" and them joking about how Layou only had one street.

Our team was the most popular team in the country. We packed the Layou park every Sunday, with many people coming from other areas just to see us play. The Town team, Kingstown Bullets, were undefeated and most of the team were on the youth national teams ranging from U-17 – U-23s.

The anticipated crowd for the game was so big that it was going to be held at Victoria Park, where the men's national team played their home games. The impact of the game really hit me one day when I was walking to the shop for Mama with Hulk and Smally. All over we could hear the conversations about the upcoming game on porches, corners, and in households.

When I got home that evening Pops and Grandpa's friends

were on the porch talking and drinking beer. I made my way through the crowded porch, saying hello to everyone. I could smell the boiline soup that Granny was preparing. I was getting hungry, smelling the savory flavors of dumplings, vegetables and fish all stirring together in a perfect mixture.

"Japeth!" I went inside to answer Granny's call. I entered the kitchen and could hear the sound of the large bubbling pot. She placed few dollar bills and coins in my palm.

"Go up di road and grab me some bread and sugar please."

"Okay Granny."

"Five loafs and a pound of sugar!" she yelled out to me as I left the kitchen. I heard Pops and his friends on the porch talking about the game.

"Nobody produce like Layou man," somebody said and there was a collective agreement that I could feel without seeing or hearing an actual reaction. I parted the long hanging beads in the doorway and stepped out onto the porch.

"Trust me dred, nobody can take Japeth ball. Georgie *cyan* stop Japeth," Pops said referring to the captain and star defensive back of the Kingstown Bullets and national U-23 team.

I smiled as I jogged down the clear path on the steps between the bodies. It was getting late so I had to race down to the shop before they closed at seven. The store clerk, Mrs. Melbourne was an old lady who looked to be around Granny's age.

She grew up in Layou but spent most of her adult life in England before returning to St. Vincent in retirement. She told me on occasion that she ran the shop to have something to do.

"You get bored in old age, you know?' she would say in her mixed English and Vincy accent. When I arrived at the door she shouted to me, "John Barnes!" She said John Barnes was the best player she had seen in England. She spoke so highly of him, but I'd seen footage of him from the 1986 World Cup and I wasn't that impressed with him. Maybe I caught him in old age.

"Good evening, Mrs. Melbourne. Sorry to catch you so late. How was the day today?"

"Well, John Barnes, it was a regular day. Few people here, few people there." I stood at the counter admiring the brightly colored walls in the small shop. The local evening news was on the radio and the announcer was starting the sports portion.

"Well, we have to start with the elephant in the room," the announcer began. I looked over at Mrs. Melbourne who was sitting on her wooden stool in a long flowery dress.

She smiled at me and I must have blocked out the first few words from the announcer because I caught him mid-sentence.

"......well look, the Layou team is a very strong team. One of the strongest I've seen in years, but I think the Bullets are just too powerful. Layou massive doh bother me! We going see tomorrow eh! Victoria Park! 3pm! Trust me folks. You don't want to miss this game!"

Mrs. Melbourne raised her head from looking at the ground and looked at me. "You in this game?" She slowly rose from the wooden stool.

"Yes ma'am."

"You know in England they have a real professional league. They would never be promoting such a game amongst boys. I'm sure you boys are good, but how can you compare that to the likes of seeing John Barnes." She shook her head as she sauntered over in front of me, while staying behind the counter.

"This island really have nothing more to do than to bother themselves up with boys playing football." If I wasn't taught to respect the elderly, I would have let my feelings spill out in a series of bad words, but instead I simply said, "Five loaves of bread and a pound of sugar please."

Chapter Twenty-Four

THE SHARED PRESSURE we all felt was more than just representing Layou and Bagga. We represented those from Sion Hill, country, and all places that were considered to be "less than" those in Town on that Sunday. While warming up for the game before the crowded stadium, I repeated to myself, "I am the best. I can't be stopped."

That Sunday, the Wicked 7 walked out onto the field with four others in a single file line beside the Bullets, paid our respect to the country with the national anthem, and moved into our starting positions. I took my usual forward position and Cam positioned himself as the central attacking midfielder with Hulk cleaning up behind him. Front Seat and Markee took their places on the wings and Cat Eye anchored the defense from the center, while Blue took his place as a left wing back. There were violent tackles from both sides and the ball never settled in the first few minutes. On my first touch of the ball, I barely dodged a tackle that would have ended my career.

I didn't scare easily, but the thought of that tackle caused me to hold back during the first half. Cat Eye and Hulk were delivering most of the crunching tackles from our team in revenge. Both of them were monsters and you didn't want to get on their bad side. The quickest way to get there was to harm any of their teammates, especially Cam or I.

Cam was only two years older than me but his maturity on the pitch was way beyond his sixteen years. He had a deceptive pigeon toed walk that made him look awkward but with a ball at his feet he became smooth and graceful.

He was usually able to control the game with his vision and airtight ball control, but during that first half he struggled to make a meaningful impact. With only a few minutes left in the first half, Cam miss-hit a pass and a Bullets' forward made good use of the opportunity. The Bullets were up 1-0 at half time.

In the locker room, Coach Dopwell was not shy about sharing his displeasure with our timid performance. He honed in on Cam and I specifically before he kicked one of the lockers causing a loud bang in the otherwise silent room. He was a little man, probably not taller than five feet four inches, but he intimidated men twice his size and half his age.

"Get your damn heads in the game!" He screamed before walking out of the room.

"He's right, fellas. We a play soft and let dem Town man run all of over we."

"But Cat Eye, they're trying to break my legs! And the ref is just letting it go on!" I responded.

"And you think he ever gonna call anything?! The fuckin ref is a Town man!"

"Alright guys, calm down. Look. We are the better team. We all know this. We have to keep the ball moving and when we get in front that goal we have to shoot." Cam looked over at me as he took a pause.

"Bird. If you frighten then come off the pitch. This is no

time to be scared. There's too much on the line here."

"The same goes for you bro." I said staring right at him. Cam cut his eyes at me, but said nothing.

The whistle blew again signaling the end of the half time period. Our locker room remained quiet. I looked around the room. Everyone's eyes were possessed and their faces held no smiles.

Cam was the first to get up and walk towards the tunnel. He didn't say anything, but we all followed. We remained silent as the crowd either cheered or jeered at us. We took our positions on the field. There was a collective heartbeat, pulsing with a need to prove ourselves. The whistle blew and it might as well have been a match igniting a stick of dynamite.

Within five minutes, I got a pass from Cam about thirty yards away from goal. I dribbled past two defenders then released a shot that flew past the keeper and into the top corner of the goal. The Bagga and Layou section of the crowd exploded.

For the remainder of the first half, we embarrassed their defenders at will, negating their wild tackles and even slipping in a sneaky elbow or punch here or there. Our tackles were harder and our competitive spirit was unmatched as the Bullets wilted under the pressure. We won the game 5-1. Cam and I scored two goals each and Markee added the fifth.

After the game the crowds, DJs and cooks set up at Bambarow beach. The cooks fed the hungry crowds chicken straight from a makeshift grill, while they fixed huge pots of soup and rice.

I was hugging Mama before she left the party that evening when I looked over and saw Coach Ranks, the U-23 national team coach, talking to Cam. A few minutes later Cam told me that he was selected to be a member of the U-23 team for the upcoming game against Trinidad. I was a little jealous, but I was mostly happy for him.

We didn't talk long about it because he was soon chasing after a girl who caught his eye. While the guys flirted and tried to get as many girls as possible, I gave all of my attention to Renell.

It was strange that I finally had the opportunity to have many girls, like I thought I wanted, but Renell just consumed me. That day, I started to think that what I was feeling for Renell was love.

As the thought of love passed through my mind, she leaned over and whispered in my ear. "You're a big star here now. Are you still going to go back to the States?" I looked into her eyes. She met my gaze for a brief second before looking away. I didn't know how to answer because I had let myself forget about the possibility of leaving. Her question was very timely. The looming date of departure was closer than either of us could have expected.

Chapter Twenty-Five

GRANNY AND I were sitting on the porch on a rainy Saturday morning eating some mangoes. As we talked, we stumbled onto the topic of girls and relationships.

"Women only take money. They never add to it. You just keep practicing and stay focused on your game. Women are always goin' to be there. Enjoy them, treat them right, love them, but most importantly love them for who they are." I stared out at the raindrops falling and disappearing into the ground as she spoke. I absorbed her words like the earth took in the rain.

Looking into the rain I also thought about how lucky I was to be alive. I flirted with death many times in Kokomo, whether it was gun shots that barely missed me or side stepping a knife aimed for my chest. I was happy to be in St. Vincent and I started to think about whether I wanted to return to Kokomo.

I hung out with the guys that afternoon and when I returned home, Granny said that Coach Ranks called and left a number for me to call him back. I raced to the phone and quickly dialed the number. "Hello, good afternoon," a deep voice answered.

"Good afternoon, sir. This is Japeth Walker returning your call."

"Well, how do you do, Mr. Walker?"

"I'm well, sir."

"Well, let me get to the point. I'm sure your grandmother has a nice dinner prepared for you tonight. I was at the game against the Bullets a few weeks back and that was some performance you had. I've had a couple injuries come up in the U-23 team and I still haven't found a replacement for Dready. I want to give you a shot at the spot. What do you think about that?"

From what I heard around Layou and Bagga, Dready was a real football star. The efficient and simple goal scorer was the pride of Layou at that time. Before I had arrived on the island, his father arranged for Dready to live with him in Ohio so I never got a chance to see him play in St. Vincent, but we would run into each other later in life.

All we knew back then was that he was doing really well in the States and was planning to attend one of the top Division I programs in the country, Indiana University. "Those are some big shoes to fill."

"Oh, I'm sure you can find a way to fit them."

"I can definitely give it a shot. Yes, of course I'll join the team."

"Good to hear. I talked to Wendell, but I'm waiting for him to call me back with a decision. First training will be in two days on Tuesday at three o'clock sharp. You know the field. I'll see you there. Have a good evening."

"Same to you."

I hung up the phone and called Wendell, or as we called him, Blue. "Coach Ranks said he already talked to you about the U-23 team?"

"Man…me tell him I have to think bout it. Me nah like being second fiddle. "

I walked the phone into my room extending the extra long connection cord. "Blue. What the hell are you talking about?"

"Dread....me nah go on no team to sit on no bench. I's ah boss on the field and I need to play. You already know how them Town man stop."

His words did have some truth to them. I heard stories of players from areas outside of Town that were selected to the national team only to be benched.

Luckily, I was able to convince Blue that it was a great chance to prove himself, so he called Coach Ranks back and accepted the opportunity.

The U-23 team was a team of men. I was fourteen and anybody who saw me amongst those guys would have thought that I was a little brother or son of one of the players. I didn't let their overpowering presence intimidate me. I could hear Pops' voice urging me to use my gifts and I did. Over the next two weeks I played well enough to earn a starting position up front for the game against Trinidad.

On our trip to Trinidad, I heard some of the players on the plane talking about which Trini players were playing in England and which already played on the full national side. There were even jokes about past games which we lost badly. Those conversations angered me and fueled my fire.

Despite a dazzling display of composure, vision, and field control from Cam and some exciting play from Blue on the wing, we lost the game 2-1. I scored the only goal off of an incredible piece of work in which I moved through and around three defenders before blasting home a goal from the top of the eighteen-yard box.

Anybody who saw the game knew that the best players on the field that day were not wearing red, white, and black. I've since heard that the legend of that game spread around Trinidad. People didn't believe there was ever such a boy named "Bird" who made the best in Trinidad look like school boys. I knew we put up a good fight but my spirit was bruised from the loss.

A week or two passed and I was still feeling the disappointment of the loss. Certain mistakes I made during the match crept into my mind frequently. I remember laying in bed one night trying to block some of those thoughts by listening to music. The lyrics brung about happy thoughts of Kokomo. I missed home, but I had decided that I didn't want to return.

Chapter Twenty-Six

I LOVED LIFE in St. Vincent. It was much simpler, I had a security blanket of family, and I loved playing and hanging out with the Wicked 7. I was unwilling to go back to Kokomo to let my talent dry up again. I felt that Kokomo had served its purpose in my life.

I would miss my family and friends, but perhaps Moms and Damian could either move or visit frequently. I planned on proposing my thoughts to Pops the next morning over breakfast. I figured if I could mention it when Granny was around, that she might back me up.

The next morning was a Sunday. I walked out of my room into the living room where gospel hymns were playing on a small radio. Granny and Pops were in the kitchen and looked to be debating something at the kitchen table, but abruptly stopped when they saw me. Both seemed to be a little sad.

"Where's Grandpa?" I asked them.

"Sit down son." I forgot all about my plan and became concerned about what was coming my way. I sat slowly, remembering the moment when I found out Mike was in the hospital.

"Just got my green card for the States," Pops said, pointing to a large envelope on the table.

"Oh yea?"

"Yep. We're going home son." His face remained expressionless and Granny dodged eye contact with me by keeping busy in the kitchen.

"No." Granny turned sharply. She looked at me then at Pops.

"What was that?" Pops said.

"I said no. I don't want to go back to Kokomo. I want to stay here. I'm not going back." I was surprised that I had gotten away with saying so much. Talking back to Pops was usually not an option. I think somewhere in my mind I thought he wouldn't react because Granny was there. In hindsight, he probably was trying to be sympathetic.

"You remember you didn't even want to come down here, now you don't want to go back. I thought you would have been happy."

"Yea. Maybe last year, but this feels like home now Pops."

He stared at the wall and his face remained expressionless. "Your mom would kill me if I let you stay down here. You don't see it now but you'll have more opportunities in the States to do more things." He paused for a short moment and shook his head. "We have to go back."

"Can't she come back down here?"

"Son, we've got to go back. The time down here has been good and you've grown and made some great friendships. I'm very happy to see that, but our home is in Kokomo." There was a pause, then Pops got up and walked out of the kitchen.

After going to church with Granny, I told Renell that I would be leaving. I can remember the tears running down her face. It was as if I watched her heart break and I felt responsible for it. We sat on the beach, and she nuzzled under my arm while the sound of the waves splashing comforted us.

In the days that followed I told my friends and they were mad at me even though they tried not to show it. The following Saturday, I was playing football in the morning with the guys at the park in Bagga. While playing, I spotted Renell walking down to the beach with her scraggly friend, Joanne, for an early morning swim.

Renell always loved to swim by herself in the morning. She said that was the only time she could be free and not worry about anyone bothering her, so I was surprised to see Joanne with her on this particular morning. I took a break from the game and met with her right outside of the field.

"Hey Joanne, hey babes." I kissed Renell on the cheek.

"Eh, eh, look at sweetness." Joanne chided.

"Gal. Mind your business," Renell said before turning to me. "Getting a good sweat?"

"Yeah. It's hot this morning."

"I know. That's why we going to go down here to swim. That water gonna feel nice."

"Yeah. I bet it is."

"You fellas coming down after you done playing?"

"I am. I don't know about them."

"Oh. I have a secret for you babes." Renell stood on her tip toes and whispered into my ear. "Mommy going to choir practice this evening."

She stepped back away from me and looked into my eyes. Our eyes didn't leave each other for a long few seconds, then she turned and continued to walk towards the beach with Joanne.

"Bye, Bird!"

"Later, Joanne."

───────────

LATER THAT EVENING, Renell called and said, "Babes. She just left. You coming over?"

"Yep." I told Granny I was headed to practice but skipped training that day and went to Renell's.

I walked through gutter towards her house under the darker tones of the evening. I snaked my way up the winding set of stairs, keeping my body low. Once inside, she grabbed my hand and led me to the downstairs guest bedroom.

I turned around to find Renell in my face and soon after we were kissing. My body was electrified and tingling, so much so that I grew a little lightheaded before I was pushed onto to the bed. Renell stood in front of me, quickly removing all her clothes. I had enough of a mind to remove mine as well.

Renell jumped on me. Our first adventure into the world of intercourse must have lasted about twenty minutes before my body released and caved in under the pleasure.

I removed the used condom and laid in bed naked next to Renell, admiring her beautiful body with its sweaty glaze in the first slow moment since I'd entered the house. The moment only lasted a few seconds before she was putting her clothes back on as quickly as she had taken them off.

She rushed upstairs and returned with a box of matches. She lit one and blew it out, walked it around the room, then opened up the only window.

"Hurry up put ya clothes on babes." She gave me a kiss on the lips then pulled herself back.

I felt as though I had just scored the game-winning goal in the World Cup final. I slinked my way out of the house the same way I came in, down to the bus stop, then back to Layou.

As far as I was concerned, I had become a man over the past few weeks. I stood up to Pops, even though I didn't win, and I lost my virginity.

On our last day in St. Vincent, the Wicked 7, Smally, Jessy, and Renell came up to First River to see us off. Granny and Mama fixed up some Callilou soup, rice and peas, and goat meat for the occasion. A lot of Pops' friends also came over and it turned into an impromptu party. The latest reggae and soca songs blasted from the radio as we all joked and laughed together.

I didn't know what to make of my conflicting emotions that night. The wonder of whether the promises to stay in touch would be true. I was also concerned with leaving the best route to achieving my dream of being the world's best footballer. I was apprehensive and tender footed about facing gang life in Kokomo again.

There were no words to express this hodge podge of emotion, so tears fell in their place before I fell asleep. When I awoke, we were leaving under the same early morning darkness in which we first arrived and dark clouds were already beginning to hover above me.

Chapter Twenty-Seven

WE MADE IT TO INDIANA a few hours late because of a delay at the airport in Barbados. Moms picked us up at baggage claim and noticed that we only had our carry on luggage with us. She shook her head as she said, "Siot?" referencing the airline that we flew.

"Yep." Pops replied as they embraced in a long hug. I looked away before they kissed. I gave Damian a pound with my fist.

"What's up bro, welcome back to civilization."

"It was civilized down there. Much more than it is up here." I replied.

"Yeah, but you happy to be home though, right?"

"I am actually, especially after that trip." I couldn't bring myself to tell him that I actually wasn't happy to be back.

Stepping outside, the brisk cold November day slapped me in the face, causing my body to stiffen under the wind's grip. We rushed to the car in the parking garage, then started our journey back to Kokomo.

"Japeth, you've really gotten tall. Good thing you didn't

take after my side of the family."

"He's not that tall yet. Still a bit of a midget like you." Pops took his right hand from the steering wheel and slapped Moms thigh.

"Oh shush, Sonny."

When I left I was just at the beginning stages of puberty, noticing the first hairs in my manly region and the occasional crackle in my voice. Over time I eased into my new young man's body, standing at about five feet seven inches and weighing about 120 pounds at the age of fourteen.

"Now my boy Damian back there. *He* looks like he takes after my side." Pops was right, Damian was almost as tall as me and he was two years younger. I looked at him and I wondered how he got so lucky to get all of the good genes.

Our conversation evolved and moved into life in St. Vincent, adding color and details to the letters and short conversations. Pops beamed as he talked about the goals I scored and my popularity in St. Vincent. I added onto Pops' stories that covered the close to two years that we spent on the island.

The greyness of the early evening had casted itself down on the Kokomo landscape as I peered into the streets from the backseat. There was an edgy feeling that came over me as my mind flashed with memories of shootouts and fights triggered by seeing some of the locations where it all happened. I looked down the street where I almost got jumped when I was on my way to DBrown's house before Jack and DBrown luckily came to my rescue.

The winter streets were seemingly quiet. There was no soundtrack playing in the background. No drunken laughter of people passing in the streets or sitting on their porches. There was only the whistle of the cold wind with the sprinkled wetness of the dusty snow that had begun falling.

As I looked out the window of the car, I could feel the threat of death around me. It was a feeling that I had not felt since

I left a couple years before. It was something that I wanted to forget, but one that I could never sweep away.

Even on my happiest days in St. Vincent, in the warm and loving sun playing football and drinking coconut water straight from the coconut, I couldn't' shake the habit of looking over my shoulder. If St. Vincent were simply another city in the USA, I think I would have run away that day.

The memories of Mike and Landon were more vivid and I could see the ghosts of our former selves in areas around the neighborhood where we once were. Once home, we hurried to get inside our warm house. We put our suitcases in our rooms, not bothering to unpack them, while Moms ordered a pizza.

I looked around for any differences that had taken place in my absence. There was a new TV in the living room that was only a slight upgrade from the first one. Everything else seemed untouched by time. I didn't bother to wait for the pizza.

I wanted to sleep, so that I could get away from my own thoughts. Since I wasn't tired, I knew I was going to need some help. I remembered that there was a cold medicine that Moms used to keep in the medicine cabinet that made me drowsy. I checked and she still kept a bottle. I took a dose and went to sleep.

THE NEXT DAY I woke up early to the sounds of Damian playing his music while he got ready to go to school. I tried to go back to sleep but could only squeeze out another hour. I spent the day getting caught up on TV, watching daytime talk shows, game shows, and news. I didn't plan on calling Jack or DBrown for three or four days when I returned. I needed some time to acclimate myself with the world of Kokomo.

I knew from Jack's letters that not much had changed aside from the frequency of killings. There were still sporadic acts of violence between Vice Lords and Gangster Disciples. During those days by myself, I tried to refresh the rules and codes of being a Vice Lord in my mind.

I did all of this with a heavy heart. Before St. Vincent, it was glamorous and fun. When I returned, it was an obligation. I'm not sure if it was that I matured over those couple of years in St. Vincent or if my excitement for gang life was a phase.

At night, I continued to drink the cold medicine and sometimes even during the day for a nap. It became my escape from the reality of being in Kokomo. I thought my life as a footballer was over, and I was still dealing with the death of my two friends.

I finished half of the bottle that was in the medicine cabinet and figured I better buy my own bottles so that my parents wouldn't find out. I got some money from Moms, went to the local pharmacy and bought two bottles that I stashed under my bed. My parents didn't think much of me sleeping all the time. They figured that I was growing, which was valid assumption for a fourteen-year-old boy. I was in a sleepy fog and before I knew it two weeks had passed and I still hadn't called Jack or DBrown.

It was the week of Thanksgiving when I called Jack first. Initially, he was happy then I had to force the conversation for a few minutes, before he ended our short chat.

"I'll be over tomorrow after school," Jack said. I hung up the phone and picked up my report on *The Autobiography of Malcolm X* and smiled to myself. I thought about how the racist white teacher told Malcolm he shouldn't try to be a lawyer.

I had a similar feeling of rejection with football. Although, I didn't have a person telling me, I felt like I had a mountain of a system not wanting me to succeed.

I called DBrown, but his mom said he wasn't home. She welcomed me back home before she returned to what sounded like a party at her house with Zapp and Roger blasting in the background.

She said that she would tell DBrown that I was back.

The next afternoon Jack knocked on the door when I was on the couch in the living room watching re-runs of Saved by the Bell. After showing each other some love, he asked if we could take a walk.

"It's cold out there."

"I know man, but come on." I paused for a minute and searched Jack's face before deciding it would be best if I braved the weather. I bundled up in one of Pops' older coats and threw on a winter hat and scarf.

"Dude. It's not that serious. It's like 35 degrees."

"Yeah dread. That *is* cold."

"Dread? What the hell is that?"

"Nothing. Don't worry about it," I said as we walked out of the front door. We walked a few feet before Jack started talking.

"Man, yesterday was shitty. I'm still fucked up now but I had to come holla at you my dude. "

A strong wind blew and caused me to stop walking. "Hold that thought, man. Let's go back to my house for real. It's cold as shit out here. Remember I haven't felt anything colder than 80 degrees for nearly two years. This shit ain't for me right now. Cool?" He agreed and we walked back to my house.

We walked into my room and closed the door. "So what happened now?"

"They killed him."

"Who killed who? DBrown?"

"No. They killed him man, FUCK." I didn't bother to ask again. "My dad. They killed my dad."

"Ah shit. What happened? Last letter I got from you, he was thinking about coming here to live. I figured he was already here by now."

"Nope. He was doing good, you know. He got off that shit and had a job working at one of the grocery stores there in St. Louis."

He took a deep breath. "I don't know why, but I guess he got back into shooting that shit."

"Damn. He OD'd?" He started crying, then he was interrupted by a knock on my bedroom door.

"Everything okay in there?"

"Yes, Pops. We're good." Jack was hurriedly wiping the tears from his face. We could hear Pops walk away from the door and towards the living room.

"So what happened?"

"I guess he got some bad stuff but lived through it. He went to check the dude he got it from and they ended up fighting." He started to cry again.

"Dude shot him six times. I ain't never gonna see him again man. Shit is fucked up!"

"I know. I know. I'm sorry dude. This beyond sucks."

"We were just getting good again and now this shit." Jack eyes searched my room.

"I know. It sounded like it was going well when you wrote me, but look man, you know he loved you."

"Not enough! If he loved me, he would have stayed off that needle. That's all he fucking really cared about was that needle. That fucking idiot." He got up and grabbed a tissue from my dresser and wiped his nose.

"I'm so sick of this shit man. It feels like every week is either a funeral or someone going to jail. And going to jail might as well be death. Shit. I can't take this shit no more, Jay. I can't."

I wasn't sure that I could either. I was sad for Jack's loss, but I also feared for my own sanity. I had a glimpse of what a relatively worry free life as a kid was like in St. Vincent and I wanted it back.

Chapter Twenty-Eight

I HEARD THE HEAVY BRASS doorknocker pound on the front door. Thump, thump, thump. I got up and opened my bedroom door to see that Damian had already let DBrown in. I looked back at Jack who was drying his tears. "It's DBrown. You want me to have him come back?"

"Naw, man. It's cool."

DBrown was still unlacing his boots when I approached him. We showed each other some love then he followed me back to my room where the sadness was thick and hung around like a blinding fog.

"My dad died," Jack answered to DBrown's questioning face.

"Ah shit dog, sorry to hear that." I held my head low while Jack relayed the cold facts to DBrown. When he finished, DBrown shook his head and said "We need to put one in the air for this one. I gotta dime on me. Jay, you gotta blunt?"

"Naw, man."

"Nigga, yo ass come back from Jamaica. Don't got no

bud or no blunts." DBrown shook his head again. Jack looked over at me expecting to hear me correct DBrown on the name of the county, but I held tight. DBrown continued, "Man, come on yall, let's go grab a blunt, hit some blocks and put one in the air."

"You gotta car?"

"Yep. Parked right outside."

"But you don't have a license dude. How are you going to drive?" I asked.

"Fuck a license. I got these keys though."

Jack chuckled. "Yeah, Jay. Has it been that long? Mutha fuckas drive without licenses all the time. It ain't shit."

I looked at both of them and sighed. "Yall mutha fuckas really want me to get out in this damn cold. What happen, yall don't like heat?"

"Haha. Oh shit. This nigga talking that Jamaican shit. Irie nigga. Irie." DBrown waited for Jack and I to put our coats on. "Hurry up niggas. Day light come and me want to go smoke."

"Something is wrong with you man. You know that?" I said.

DBrown looked at me with a blank face and folded his hands in front of his chest. He recited the speech that Tupac's character, Bishop, said to Q in the movie *Juice* where he referenced that he was crazy and that he didn't give a fuck. At the end of his speech, he started laughing.

At the time, I hadn't seen the movie so I asked "What the hell was that?"

"Oh shit. You haven't seen *Juice*? Ah man. You gotta see that shit. Jack, you still got my bootleg?" DBrown asked.

"Yep."

"We gotta watch that shit today, my nigga."

"Aight, but man, you gotta stop with that nigga shit in my crib. Unless you want my Moms in that ass."

"Aight almighty."

I told my parents I was leaving and we went to DBrown's

car. We situated ourselves on the burgundy seats of the old white Caprice, with Jack up front, me in the back and DBrown behind the wheel. There wasn't much conversation on the way to the store, just the bump of the bass massaging my back.

At the convenience store, Jack bought a small cigar and a few bottles of fruit punch. He removed the tobacco from the cigar, replaced it with green leaves and licked it before torching the length of the blunt with a lighter. We drove around our neighborhood for about ten minutes smoking the blunt.

"Shit. You good, my nigga?"

"Yeah. I'm straight, man." Jack responded to DBrown. "I needed that. Good looking out."

"Ain't shit, man. You like my brother. Anything you need holla at me."

"Cool. Oh. Jay, how was St. Vincent?" Jack finally asked.

"It was cool. A lot warmer than up here. Had these beautiful beaches..."

"You mean beautiful bitches? Nigga, I want to hear about the pussy you was getting down in that mutha fucka. Don't tell me no shit about no beaches. Tell me about the bitches, nigga."

"Shit. I got a girl down there."

"What? Wait. Yo ass went down to Jamaica and shit. All that Pantra pussy and you went and got yo self a girlfriend?"

DBrown paused and let two seconds pass. "Shit. That lets me know you aint do shit worthwhile down there. Jack, your grandma home?"

"Yeah."

"Aight. Let's go get that movie from yo house and then watch it over by me."

We watched the movie, but I never really got a chance to elaborate on how great St. Vincent was for me. The more I thought about it, I felt guilty about sharing my time in St. Vincent. How could I expect them to take joy in the happiest point of my life, when at that same time they were experiencing their worst? So I kept my answers brief, even when they did ask me about it. The only person I shared my happy memories with, was Kim.

Chapter Twenty-Nine

SINCE I CAME BACK SO LATE in the first semester, my parents and the school authorities thought it would be best if I start during the second semester in January. The first day back at school I noticed that the undeveloped girls turned into developed young women; even Kim added some curves to her small body. When I saw her in my History class I think I blushed through my dark skin.

She jumped up and gave me a big hug before I could put my butt in the open desk next to her. "Japeth!" Her arms wrapped around me tightly. She had this bright smile and little glints of excitement reflecting in her eyes.

We talked for two minutes before the bell rang, then continued our conversation through the notes we passed back and forth during class and exchanged in the hallways for the remainder of the day.

The weeks passed and I grew more accustomed to the crowded school with its worn carpeted hallways spanning three floors. Everyday I saw Kim in school and talked to her on the phone. There were some nights that we talked on the phone well into the wee hours of the morning in our hushed tones so we wouldn't get caught.

Our conversations weren't about much many times when we had those late talks, but every now and then we really learned a lot about each other. I remember one night I was telling Kim about where I stood with football.

"Oh, so what were you saying about soccer earlier, or *football* as you call it?" Kim asked.

I laughed. "That's right. You're learning."

"Whatever. This is America boy. It's called soccer."

"Yeah. Anyway, what I was saying earlier was that they already had tryouts so I'm not sure I can get on one of the teams. Plus, I don't even know if we have the money for me to play. Pops still looking for a job, so it's only Moms making any money and it's four of us, ya know? I miss how easy it was to play in St. Vincent. It takes so much to play up here."

"Are you gonna start doing what you were doing before?"

"I really don't want to, but I might have to."

"I hope not. It's too crazy out there to be playing around. Anyway, so with this soccer you still stuck on trying to play with older people?"

"Yep. They have to play me at least a couple age groups higher." I answered.

"Oh, you that dope huh?"

"Hell yeah. I told you how I was getting down in St. Vincent."

"Yeah, yeah. The Wicked 7. I know."

"We were so dope. My game was so on point there. I'm trying my best to keep sharp here, just doing drills and stuff in the basement or on the porch but it's hard to stay fit with all the snow."

"*I know*. Well, not about the staying fit, but I just can't wait for summer so we can hang out outside. I hate wearing all these clothes."

I held my tongue wanting to say something sexual, but I knew I couldn't. We were still officially friends, even though I felt we both knew we were growing past that.

"Well look, I'ma let you go. I'ma try to get some sleep." I looked at the alarm clock on the dresser next to my bed. It was 3:39am.

"Okay. Let's meet up at the library tomorrow to finish that paper."

"Okay. Good night… or morning." She giggled.

"Good night morning."

"Bye silly."

THE NEXT DAY WAS A SATURDAY and I woke up close to noon. After a shower, I threw on some jeans with a nice thick hoody. "Where you going, chump?" Damian asked as I settled on the couch waiting for Moms to grab her keys and put on her coat.

"To the library. Got a paper due on Monday."

"You coming to my game right?" I loved watching him play basketball. There was something that I recognized in him on the court. Maybe it was his similar deep squat run or his extremely quick first step. Maybe it was how smooth he moved as he glided effortlessly through the opposing defense. Whatever it was, it felt like I was watching myself out there, only better, but I would never tell him that.

"What time is the game again?"

"4:30."

I looked at the large clock on the wall. "I'll make it there for the second half dude. Cool?"

"Alright." He put his hand on my shoulder. "You know how I do. I might already have like fifty by the second half." I flipped his hand off my shoulder.

"Nigga please, you might be down by fifty by the time I get there." I laughed at my own joke as I kept my attention on the TV. Suddenly, Moms was in the way. I looked up to meet her angry eyes.

"What did you say, boy?"

"What?"

"Just now. What did you say to Damian?" Fear held my mouth shut. SMACK!!! My head whipped to my right. I felt Moms hooked index finger aggressively push my chin up so that I looked her directly in the eyes.

"Don't you ever let me hear you using that word in this house again. You hear me?"

"Yes, ma'am."

"Hmmph," she released my chin. I glimpsed Damian snickering quietly in the corner as Moms went back into her room.

"Now come let me take you on your date."

"It's not a date, Moms. We' just helping each other with our papers."

"Ummm hmmmm."

While at the library, Kim and I perused through Encyclopedias and other books while writing our reports. As we worked, we made jokes back and forth while talking about music and the latest gossip. Before I knew it, it was 4:50 and Moms was coming to get me at five. I invited Kim to come to Damian's game, but she said that she had to go grocery with her mom.

"She never knows what to get if I'm not there."

We both packed up our book bags and began exiting the library. Kim stopped at the payphones and I leaned against the wall waiting for her. I watched her as she dug through her pockets for a quarter to make the call.

"Mah. We done. You coming to get me?" She looked up at me and smiled to break the look of concern that was on her face. "Well, I told you I was gonna call when I was done." Kim continued.

She listened then responded. "It don't matter, mah. I told you I was gonna call. You said you didn't have nothing to do but go to the grocery store today."

She rubbed her forehead and faced the payphone squarely. "Well, what you want me to do? You coming or not?"

Another pause. "Hold on. Japeth." I snapped my head up.

"Do you think your mom can give me a ride?"

"I'm sure she can."

"Mah, Japeth's mom gonna give me a ride." She didn't even wait for her mom to answer. She hung up the phone immediately after. "I hate when she act like that." She leaned against the wall next to me.

"What's the deal?"

"She said she tired from work, but I know it's because her bum ass boyfriend over there and now she don't want to go nowhere." She stayed silent for two seconds then continued. "That's why I can't wait to get my license."

Moms rolled up in front of the library and stopped. I asked if we could give Kim a ride and Moms said it was fine. We dropped Kim off then drove over to the community center, which was only a few minutes away.

I looked at Moms and although I knew she was excited, there was a tired look in her eyes. We entered the gym then Moms and I weaved our way through the small crowd in the entry way. Moms peeked her head around to see if there were any seats available.

The smell of popcorn permeated the warm gymnasium. I looked across the light hardwood floor as the teams huddled together on their separate sides around the coaches. I caught Damian's eye as his team dispersed slowly onto the court. He gave me a head nod. I pointed to the scoreboard that showed they were six points down. He nodded his head confidently as the timeout buzzer rang.

Moms was able to squeeze into a spot next to Pops at the end of the four-tiered bleacher. I stood next to Moms. Within a few seconds, Damian stole the ball off the dribble from the opposing team and scored a lay up on the fast break.

By the next time out, three minutes later, Damian's team was four points up. All points scored by Damian. On his way back to the huddle, he looked over at me and smiled that arrogant smile of his. His long arms hanging down at his side as he walked, taking in the cheers of his name and hi fives by his teammates with a calm, composed ease. I knew that feeling and I wanted it back for myself, but I would have to wait some time before I got there.

Chapter Thirty

THE EARLY EMERGING SPRING in March created an energetic buzz that seemed to be running through everyone's veins. It had been about a month that Kim and I were teetering on the fence of being together. Finally, I made up my mind that I was going to tell Kim how I felt while we were walking home from school one day.

During the final class of the day, my palms moistened with sweat. I started to prepare for my conversation with Kim, searching for words to express my feelings. The final bell rang and everybody was scurrying to leave the building. It looked like a racial divide as the white kids went out the side exit towards the buses, while those in my neighborhood went out the front and walked our way north.

My book bag hung off my shoulders as I walked amongst the crowd, heading to the nearby convenience store where everyone usually congregated after school. I felt a light tug on my book bag from behind.

"What's up, dark boy?" Her barely husky voice caught my ear.

"What up, pink toe?" She hit me on my arm. She hated

when I called her out for being so light skin.

"You said you had something that you wanted to talk to me about?" she asked.

"Yea, but first how'd you do on that Health test?" I responded as we walked together and split from the rest of the group. I kept my eyes fixed on all the cracks and differences in the concrete slabs that lay before us. You had to pay attention to the sidewalk on that street or one of those sudden raised surfaces would send you stumbling or laying flat out on your face.

"I think I did alright."

"Good." I could feel my heart beating rapidly and I felt a little dizzy.

We neared a set of railroad tracks that separated one part of the block from the other. I stopped right on the tracks to gather myself. My abrupt pause caused her to stop as well. There we stood in between rail one and two. Between one part of the block and the next. The shade from the large nearby trees provided a sort of reverse spotlight effect, as the sun shone brightly on either side of us.

"What's wrong?"

"Kim, I…" Somehow the arrangement of words I had in my head sounded awkward to me so I paused.

"I like you. Like really like you. More than just a friend. Umm..I wish I could say that better but I just had to let you know how I feel."

I took a breath then continued. "I mean, we talk all the time and I just like hanging with you, ya know? I can't even think of a…"

I was hushed by her lips as they pressed against mine. My eyes squeezed tightly, wanting to hold onto that feeling forever. She released my lips and her body settled back onto her heels from her tiptoed stance. She remained close to me and looked up to me with her sweet eyes. I smiled nervously.

"So you my man now?"

"Yeah!" I said confidently.

"Not yet you not." I looked at her confused.

"You gotta ask me properly, dark boy?" I obliged only to make her happy.

"Will you go with me, pink toe?"

"I'll think about it." I gently shoved her and sucked my teeth. She rocked back, moving her left foot back to catch her balance.

"Of course, dark boy." We walked across the railroad tracks.

I was settling back into the Kokomo life and certainly having Kim as my girlfriend was a big help. She was a constant source of support for me at that time. I really needed that, not just for the life issues I was dealing with, but she became the voice of reason a lot times when I was starting to slip back into my old ways. Unfortunately, she couldn't prevent everything.

Chapter Thirty-One

POPS REACHED OUT to the Fort Wayne Citadel Director of coaching and we were told that it was too late to join a team. Pops tried to explain that I had played on the team before, stating that I was ten times better than I was when I left.

"I'm not sure your son can even get back on the team in his own age group. The players have really grown with a few selected for the regional team and Billy even made it to the national team camp. I've got to be honest with you, Sonny. I don't really see a future here for your son."

My fist clenched as I listened to call after call go in the same direction. Not one premier club would take me on my terms. A few were willing to allow me to try out within my own age group of U-15, but I knew I was better than that so I declined.

Moms walked through the bedroom door where Pops and I sat, clinching her teeth as Damian helped her into the bed. She crashed on the bed, complaining that her hip and back were hurting again. She'd had those same complaints for a few weeks, but it was never that debilitating.

"Damian, go run a bath for me with some Epsom salt and fix up some of that bush tea for me, please. Japeth, can you help your brother and warm up some of that ointment for me for when I come out the bath?"

"Yes, Moms."

The soak in the tub seemed to help as she was able to walk the short distance from the bathroom to her room, although it was still slow. Damian grabbed the warm bottle of liquefied ointment from the boiling pot of water and brought it in the room for Pops. Moms lay in bed, and Pops excused us from the room before he began rubbing the oil onto her. Damian and I stood by the closed door for a few minutes listening, our ears pressed against the hollow wooden door.

"I really think you need to go to the doctor, Elaine."

"I'm fine…just had a tough day today lifting all them bags."

"I think it's much more than that. You haven't been lifting bags the past few weeks.

We decided that we had enough and slowly eased away from the door, retreating back to Damian's room. I sat on his bed and he laid out behind me. His voice was shaky and unsure when he asked, "What you think is wrong with Moms?"

"Man…I don't know. Pops sounds concerned, huh? You know it's got to be bad if Pops is telling her to go to the doctor." As soon as the words left my mouth, I wondered if it was the right thing to say to Damian.

"I know…" Damian responded before fading into his own thoughts.

I gazed at a picture of Michael Jordan dunking over an opposing Detroit Pistons player. His face was full of fury and determination; ready to overcome anything that came in his way. I wished I had the strength and words to help us both feel like that, but I had nothing. We were both helpless and I couldn't even begin to think of losing Moms, although it was a possibility.

THE EARLY SPRING WEATHER continued through April, with a few days feeling more like summer. I saw DBrown in the hallways of school towards the end of the semester, mostly around a new comer to the city, named Jason. That fat fuck. Jason was from the suburbs of Houston but he always talked about the Fifth Ward, an area known for being rough and dangerous. He talked about the area so much that most people thought he was from there.

He didn't bother to correct those who made the mistake. He considered himself a comedian and always found his material to be me. I held back from cracking his head because he and DBrown were good friends, having connected over their Texas roots.

Even without his condescending jokes about my culture or sport of choice, I just didn't like him. His cocky attitude was only based on the fact that he was from a big city.

He was always saying, "Oh yall think that's dope, back in Houston…" and the blank would be filled in with anything that was spoken about as being fun or superior.

I could see how everyone would go into a daydream state as he'd tell stories of life in Houston, Bloods and Crips, and the candy painted cars and such. People around Kokomo bought right into that fat fuck's stories, just because he was from Houston. That fat fuck got girls just because he was from Houston. DBrown thought he was the coolest guy, just because he was from Houston. Everyone assumed that he could fight, just because he was from Houston. That fat fuck.

I hated the way he'd separate DBrown from us, well really me. He'd pull DBrown aside in a way that said, "Hey *we* are cool. Leave him alone. He's going to mess up whatever we're trying to do." Even more disappointing was that DBrown listened. Whether anything like that was said verbally to DBrown or not, I don't know, but I felt like he bought into that fat fuck's theory. It really scared me that Jack would begin thinking this way as well, since he was beginning to hang around them more.

As DBrown and Jack went further and further into the life, I was still hedging my bets. The gaps of time where I was away from my friends, practicing football, were what scared me most but the gravitational pull of my dream to be the best footballer in the world was too strong. I felt I owed it to the memories of Mike and Landon and refused to give up, even if it meant losing my two closest friends to that fat fuck.

Chapter Thirty-Two

THE WORLD CUP was in the USA during that summer. It was 1994 and incredible to think that the world's greatest players were only hours away from me in Chicago. These were figures that I had only read about in a magazine at the library. I'd ride my bike up there every third week of the month until I found it on the shelves of the reference periodicals. I spent hours immersed in the world of recent football news, the commentary of the writers and other editorials.

I recorded all of the games that I could, quadrupling my football video study. With no venue to really showcase my talent, I projected myself in those games and imagined playing with the best players in the world.

That World Cup also showed me the pressure and heartbreak of football. The eyes and hearts that rest on every bit of work that you put into your game. The pride of fans and a nation that depend on your God given ability for their own well-being.

The weight of the air after failure forces your head down,

regardless of the fact you gave it your all. I'd witnessed several disappointments during that tournament, but I hid them in the recesses of my mind. I only wanted to hold onto positive thoughts, as I got closer to being able to play football again.

I was anxious for the upcoming high school season. It would be my first opportunity to show everyone I was the best player in the state. Kokomo High School was not known for soccer, but I had no doubt about the sensation I was going to be.

I had summer school for the rest of July and early August. Outside of that, my days were filled with hanging out at Kim and Trish's house although we spent less time as a foursome than before. Kim and I were limited to going to the movies and the arcade for our dates, restricted not only by our age but also the small city.

Jack made up for his handicap by either borrowing DBrown's car or taking a car from one of the local crackhead factory workers. DBrown got arrested twice that summer, once for fighting and another time for breaking and entering. The police were keeping a very close eye on him and that fat fuck.

IT WAS AROUND MID-JULY when Moms finally went to the doctor. I remember because the World Cup final had just happened. Through all of that pain, she was still going to work everyday. It wasn't until the pain became too much for her to work through that she decided to go to the doctor. Upon review, the doctor admitted her to the hospital immediately for testing. They thought there was a strong chance she had cervical cancer.

Damian and I were at home at the time of the visit. Pops called to check in on us and told us they were going to be at the doctor's longer than they expected. At that time, he didn't tell us anything about the possibility of cancer.

I know he was trying to help protect us, but that actually

made things worse for Damian and I. We knew that a longer visit at the doctor was not a good thing, so our minds started to wonder.

We talked about all kinds of scenarios but they all ended with Moms dying. We were both crying. I wish I could have been stronger for him. I just didn't have the strength to deal with Moms leaving us and being the bigger brother I felt I needed to be.

The best I could do was to fix us peanut butter and jelly sandwiches for dinner. Pops called again and mentioned that he was going to stay in the hospital with Moms overnight since the test results were expected to come in the next morning. I asked what the doctors thought it was, but he didn't give me a clear answer. Damian broke down in tears again after the call with Pops. I don't know where I found the strength, but suddenly I felt I could be the rock he needed. As I held him, I thought about all that Moms did for us. She made the money, cleaned the house, and kept us in church. I fought hard to hold back the tears.

The next day during summer school, my mind remained on what was happening with my mother. After school, I rushed home and called the number that Pops left for any emergencies.

"Hello." His voice sounded shaky.

"Pops?"

"Yes. Japeth? Something wrong?"

"No. I was just calling to see what was up with Moms. You get the test results?"

"Hold on Japeth." I could hear a doctor's voice in the background. "Japeth, I'll call you back." When he called back the conversation was brief but promising. He said they were coming home and asked if I could prepare a pot of tea.

When they arrived, Pops assisted Moms to the couch and helped her lay down. Damian and I started to run towards Moms to hug her, but Pops stopped us and asked that we give her some space. Instead we both sat on the couch across from her and waited until Pops finished pouring a cup of tea for Moms and himself.

"So what did the doctor's say?" I asked.

Pops took a sip of tea and remained quiet for a moment before answering, "Moms has cancer in her cervix."

"Cancer? Is she going to die?" Damian asked.

"Calm down Damian. She's not going to die. The doctors will have to do a surgery to remove the cancerous cells, but first they ran some tests to make sure that the cancer didn't spread to any other areas." Pops was trying to remain positive but I could tell that the news left him feeling as uncertain as Damian and I. Perhaps he felt that his hurt was becoming to0 visible because he cut the conversation short by suggesting that Moms lay down in bed.

Moms slowly rose from the couch. "Yeah. I guess you're right. Well, you guys have a good evening. You boys make sure you come in here and give me a kiss before you go to bed, okay?"

"Of course, Moms," Damian said.

During class the next day my jaw remained clenched. Damian, Kim, and I were the only ones in the house after school. There was a quietness that hung in the air, the voices from the TVs sounded ghostly and distant.

Moms and Pops returned around six that evening. The expression on their faces hung on the ledge of relief and sadness. Damian came out from his room and joined us all in the living room. After greeting my parents, Kim got up and started gathering her things. "I'll see you tomorrow, Japeth."

"You don't have to leave, Kim," Moms said as she sat next to Pops on the couch.

"It's okay. I better get going. My mom will be looking for me any time now."

"Oh, she doesn't know you're over here?"

"I left her note to tell her where I was but she probably didn't read it so...." she playfully rolled her eyes.

"Alright. Well, have a good evening." Moms responded.

I hugged her at the door, let her out, then closed the door behind her.

"You're not going to walk her home?" Moms questioned.

"No. She'll be alright. She walks from here to there all the time."

"Are you sure Japeth?"

"Moms, she's fine. How are you? What did the doctor say?" I settled into the seat next to Damian.

"Well. It's good news. I tested negative for cancer in all other areas. So it's not spreading."

We all rushed over to Moms and wrapped our arms around her. In our loving, interlocking circle of embrace it was as if the worries and fears peeled away from all of us. Moms and Damian let their worries fall through tears. Trying to be like my Pops, I held mine back. The scare of losing Moms made me feel like Malcolm X in his last days – everything was urgent.

Chapter Thirty-Three

MOMS HAD ONLY BEEN HOME for a few days from her surgery when we got the news. The factory was doing a round of layoffs and Moms was one of the workers that would be let go. Budget cuts and a new direction for the company were the reasons they gave. The layoffs were determined by seniority; those with the longest tenure were able to keep their jobs. I watched Moms cry out of fear for what would happen to our family. Pops tried to comfort her, but even in his eyes I could see concern.

Football and being high or drunk were what kept me sane. As long as I was under some intoxication, I felt shielded from reality. The burden of the situation weighed heavily on my heart and mind. The small bit of sunshine was that high school football tryouts would be held in about two weeks. I was happy to start playing again after several months of not playing a game. I had continued to practice because I knew the only thing I seemed to be able to control in my life was how that ball rolled or bounced.

Pops was only making the minimum wage of $5.75 per hour at a slaughterhouse and that would not be enough to support all of us.

When Moms was at the factory, we were barley scraping by, living on necessities only.

We got the most basic shoes and clothes, but always had food on the table. We may have had store brand cereal and such, but I was never starved a day in my life and I never knew our electricity to go out or water to be turned off as DBrown had experienced several times.

I sat at the dining table and bounced my knee up and down nervously. My hands were intertwining with each other. Pops placed a glass of juice in front of me with three ice cubes. He held a bottle of beer as he lowered himself into the chair at the head of the table.

"How are you doing, son?"

"I'm fine. You're scaring me though."

His eyebrows turned downwards, asking why without him having to say a word. Then he went ahead and asked anyway just in case I couldn't read his expression.

"You called for me like this is a mafia sit down or something. I feel like I'm going to get wacked." We both laughed, but underneath the merriment lingered something much more serious.

His laugh slowed. "Well, son. You know we're in a bit of a predicament here with Moms being laid off." I nodded my head.

"Times are going to be really, really tough, but I think we can do it. You know we had this discussion before about how we all have to make our sacrifices to make this work."

He paused for a second, looking down at the table as if that was where the words were scripted.

"Son, we're trying our best to give you a chance at your dream. I know you want to be a footballer. The best in the world, right?"

"Yep."

"It's just so hard to do every damn thing here in this country. It's *supposed* to be the place where you can be anything you want to be. Provide your kids with all they want. The streets paved with gold. The American Dream, you know? That damn dream is a nightmare. They dangle that shit in front of your face, but the truth is without the money that dream doesn't work. And di damn place does everything in it's power to make sure you don't have the key to that dream – the money. I'm starting to wonder if this was a—" He caught himself, then got his thoughts back on track.

"Son, me and your mom been talking and trying to find everyway around having this conversation but… we're going to… I hate having to ask you this… we're going to need you to find a job as quick as you can. And working that job means not playing football this season. We need every dollar we can get." His voice was soft and apologetic. My leg still jumped up and down under the table with increased fervor.

I was fifteen years old. I thought I was a man and men were expected to give up things for the betterment of their family. It was strange. I felt honored that Pops asked me for my help.

At the same time, I wanted to whine and cry about how unfair everything was at that moment. It wasn't fair that Moms had cancer. It wasn't fair that they laid her off and it wasn't fair that I didn't get to pursue my dream of playing football, but as a man I knew I had to understand that life wasn't fair.

"Okay, Pops. Can you take me to fill out some applications at the mall today?" I tried my best to sound strong and unaffected, but the droop of his face showed me that he knew different. It only took three weeks to find a job at a local fast food restaurant in town, Ricky's Burger. My first day at work coincided with the first football game of the high school season. Kokomo was playing our local rival Northwestern.

I had dreamed of playing in that game from the time I returned back to the Kokomo school system. I was really looking forward to putting a hurting on them. Instead on that day, I learned the great arts of taking out trash, mopping floors, and making fries the Ricky's way. A few weeks went by and I quickly got used to the rhythm of working at Ricky's.

"Man, this two hundred dollars a week ain doing shit."

"What are you going to do, Japeth? Two hundred dollars a week for a fifteen year old is good money," said the assistant manager at Ricky's. His name was Tom.

"I don't know. There's got to be something better than this shit." I lifted a bag of trash that I just tied up.

"I'm telling you, dude, hang in there. You're just starting. You can't expect to get it all now. You keep grinding and soon you'll be making double that."

"How much you making?"

"I make $7.25 an hour, but you have to remember I've been working here since I was your age and I'm an assistant manager. It takes time. Trust me, you keep working hard you'll get there."

"How old are you again?"

"Eighteen."

"Tom! The register's stuck again!" another employee shouted from the front. Tom disappeared to the front of the restaurant while I remained in the back with my co-worker, Andy.

"Duty calls."

There was always about an hour's time between the closing of Ricky's and when we were able to leave. As Tom was counting the money, Andy and I tidied up the restaurant. When we were finished, we closed up the store and locked the door. Tom left me with a lot to think about and forced a decision that I was trying to avoid for weeks.

That night in bed, I did the math in my head. At $7.25 an hour I would be making around $500 every two weeks after taxes. It would take me about two years to get to that point. I decided that was too long. I didn't have two years to wait for those crumbs. I knew I could make at least twice as much selling crack.

Even though I was betting with my life, I couldn't turn my back on what was actually going to make money and help the family. I justified it at the time because I felt that if the factory could lay off my sick mother, knowing that she takes care of this family, then I felt we all had no choice but to survive by any means necessary.

Chapter Thirty-Four

THE NEXT DAY THE CLOUDS in the sky won the battle over the sun. I called Jack and DBrown that morning, but neither of them answered.

"Mrs. Johnson, do you know where Jack went?"

"He said he was going down to the gym to play basketball."

"Okay. Thanks, Mrs. Johnson."

"How are you, baby? I haven't seen you in awhile. You still playing that soccer?"

"Yes, ma'am. Well, kind of. I didn't play this Fall because I got a job, but hopefully I can play again in the Spring."

"How's your grades?"

"Good. I have all A's right now, hopefully I can keep it up." All the extra work I did in St. Vincent to save my family from embarrassment in the classroom paid off tremendously. When I returned to the States, I was pretty much on cruise control because they were repeating things that I'd already learned in St. Vincent.

"Good to hear. Keep it up. You always been smart like

that. You have a good head on your shoulders. Jack needs to learn a thing or two from you."

"Thanks. I think he'll be okay. You do a good job of keeping him in line."

She chuckled to herself. "I try my best with him. Well look, I'll tell Jack to call you when he gets home."

I hung up the phone, got dressed, and walked down to the local community center. When I walked inside the gym, there was a full five a side game going on with a number of people waiting to play, Damian being one of them. I spotted Jack on the court playing, so I walked over to where Damian was waiting with a few guys that went to school with me.

"I should have known that you'd be here. How long you been down here?"

"Not too long. You see I ain't on the court yet. Once I get on, I don't plan on coming off." I smiled at his arrogance.

"You on next?"

"Yup. You want to run? We got numbers, but I'd kick one of these bums off for you if you want to run."

"Naw, I'm good, bro."

"Cool. That's probably better anyway. You don't want to get shown up by your little brother out there."

"Little dude. Please. You ain showing me up." A common friend who was dribbling nearby added his two cents.

"I don't know about that, Jay. You might want to stick with that soccer shit. Leave the basketball to Damian."

"Anybody ask you? Were we even talking to you?" He threw his hands up surrendering the conversation.

"Damn, man!" I heard someone shout from the court. The game was over. "Who's next?" Jack yelled out as he walked over to the water fountain where I met him.

"What you doing here, Jay? Thought you had to work today."

"Naw. Tomorrow."

"Oh, okay. You trying to run?"

"Naw, man. I wanted to holler at you on some business."
Jack looked at me with a strange curiosity.

"A yo! Hold up before yall start!" Jack shouted to his teammates.

"Aight. We got you, but hurry yo ass up, nigga!" One of his teammates shouted back.

"Hurry this, my nig." Jack grabbed his crotch in response. We walked off the court area and up a set of stairs. Jack tried to open the weight room door but it was locked, so we talked on the landing.

"What's up, Jay, you trying to get back on?"

"Yeah, man."

"You know things changed out here. With Choco in jail we getting our work straight from Dave now."

"I don't know that dude that well. You can make the connect for me?"

"Yeah. When you trying to start?"

"Shit. I'm ready to get some work today."

"You got the dough?" We heard footsteps and both of us looked down below the stairs. "Jack! We gonna start! You can jump in when you ready!" a voice shouted up to us from the doorway below.

"Aight, you impatient mutha fuckas!"

"Look. Come by my crib at four, then we'll swing over and get you something. Wait. What you trying to get?"

"An eightball."

"Yeah, you should be good. So come by at four, cool?" Jack reiterated as he began walking down the stairs with me behind him.

"Aight, I'll be there."

I STAYED AND WATCHED the guys play until open gym was

over, which was an hour and half later, then Damian and I walked home together.

"I told you I wasn't coming off the court once I got on."

"Whatever dude."

"You know how I get down. That's why you didn't want to get out there and get yo head bust."

"Little dude. You don't want me out there cause you'll get fucked up. That will be the end of your career."

He laughed. "That's probably true. That's how people get when I break their ankles. Get to fouling and shit. That's what me and MJ have to deal with. Piston ass dudes like you."

At home I watched TV and looked at the clock often. It seemed to be moving in minute fractions. When it finally reached 3:30, I left the house and began walking to Jack's house on Taylor Street.

I walked up the stairs towards the porch where Jack, DBrown, and that fat fuck Jason were sitting.

"What up, Jay?"

"What up." I shook the hands of each guy, rhythmically moving through a series of Vice Lords signs.

"Jack said you trying to get back to being a man out in this piece," that fat fuck Jason chided at me. I looked over at Jack.

"He ain't gonna say shit," Jack responded.

"How the fuck I'm going to snitch on you when I'm out here doing the same shit? That would be fucking stupid."

"Yeah. Exactly." I snapped.

"What you tryna say, I'm stupid nigga?"

"I'm not trying to say anything. That's exactly what I'm saying." Jason rose up from his seat and my stance remained still.

"You's a disrespectful little nigga. You lucky you they friend or this would be a problem, corny ass nigga."

"I'm lucky. Yeah. Aight. Jack, let me holler at you for a quick minute." I motioned for us to go inside. We went to Jack's room and I shut the door behind us.

"My dude. What the fuck? What are you doing telling DBrown and that fat fuck Jason about my business?"

"Man, they cool. They ain't gonna say shit."

"That ain't the fucking point. What I discuss with you is between me and you. I don't want mutha fuckas to know what I'm out here doing. Especially when I don't know all the shit yall out here doing."

"You don't be knowing shit because you be out playing soccer. That's yo bad. We choose the fam over everything. You don't."

"What kind of fucked up thing is that say? What, cause I'm trying make something of myself with football?"

"Soccer."

"It's football and that's beside the point. Yall mad cause I got shit to do?" Jack stood with a scowl on his face.

"My dude, you don't *have* to do it. That's your choice. You ain't even on a team."

"I will be though and when that time come, I gotta be sharp. I don't know why you don't understand that?"

"Dude. When it was me, you, and Mike we were always kicking it together. We grown now and I don't expect us to sit around and play video games all the time but damn. You ain never around." Jack took his beeper from the waist of his pants and looked at the number on it.

"Yo, what the hell are you talking about? I been at all the meetings."

"Once a week nigga?! That's about it." We both remained silent for a few seconds.

"Look man. My bad for telling them niggas, but I was happy to see you coming back. We good?" He held out his hand.

"Yeah. We good. Who hit you on the beeper?" We showed each other some love.

"Trish. I'll hit her up later. Let's go get you some work."

"They coming too?"

"Yeah. They gotta re-up on their supply."

"Aight. Let's roll."

We left the porch and walked to a small house that was ten minutes away from Jack's. There were two guys I didn't recognize sitting on the porch with Rottweilers on thick chain leashes.

"What up, Poo and Pork?" DBrown said greeting the two young men.

"What up, DBrown? Who's this little nigga?" The darker of the two said as he nodded his head in my direction. The dogs barked and we all stood back at a safe distance.

"Come on man. Yall know this dude. This is Jay. My nigga from way back."

"He good. He's with us," Jack added.

"This the dude Choco be talking bout?" Pork asked.

"Yeah." Jack looked up and down the block.

"Aye little nigga, shouldn't you be out playing kick ball?"

"Naw man. I'm just hanging."

"You just hanging. What kind of answer is that? You know where you at?" Pork looked at Poo and laughed.

"Yeah, I know where I'm at."

"Pork, leave this dude alone, man. Can we get in or what?" Jack jumped in again.

"Naw, fuck that. DBrown and Jason can go in but not yall. You mutha fuckas gotta wait." Poo drew a gun and put it on his lap while it pointed in the direction of Jack and I. Poo and Pork tightened the leashes on the dogs, allowing Jason and DBrown to pass through the front door. Once they passed the leashes loosened again and Poo put the gun back in his pants.

"This is some bullshit, Poo and Pork."

"Naw, Jack. You on some bullshit. Bringing new square mutha fuckas around here. You know Dave don't like that shit."

"He's fam though."

"I ain never met him," Pork responded. "Me neither," Poo added.

"Aight, man. We'll just wait for Dave."

"Yall better walk yall ass around this block or something and come back."

"Damn. Aight. Let's roll, Jay." Jack and I walked around the block and he explained that even though Dave worked at one of the factories as a cover, he was still very paranoid about getting busted.

By the time we got back to the house DBrown and that fat fuck Jason were outside talking to Poo and Pork. This time they allowed us in the house. Upon entering we were patted down and the gun that Jack had was removed from his hip before we were escorted to the kitchen in the back of the house. Jack showed some love to Dave.

"What up, Jack? You good?"

"Yea, I'm good Dave. This is my boy Jay. He trying to get on."

"So I hear. Aye yo partner. You mind stepping back out into that living room while I deal with Jack?"

"Cool." I exited the kitchen area, took a few steps into the living room, and sat on the couch. The sports announcers on the TV were talking about the basketball game that night. Through the window I could see the greyness of the evening giving away to the blackness of the night.

I tried not to look into the kitchen where Jack and Dave sat together. I didn't want to appear suspicious, so instead I took quick glances between the kitchen and the TV. I was in between glances when I felt a nudge against my shoulder.

"Move over nigga." I looked to my right and there was empty space. I noticed Dave looking at me from the kitchen.

"Naw man. You don't see all this over here." The larger man grabbed my shoulders and shoved me into the open space. I sprung up and punched him in his chest. He pulled a gun from his belt and rested the edge of the barrel on my forehead. Sweat immediately beaded and ran down my face.

"You not so tough now are you, little bitch. Huh?" I didn't speak for a split second while I thought of how to handle the situation. In that time, I weighed the option of showing respect and apologizing or gaining respect and standing my ground. The wrong choice could mean my brain sprayed on the wall behind me.

"Fuck you. You ain shit cause you pulled out a gun. What you think I'm scared to die? Pull the trigger!" His eyes softened and he stood there with the gun at my head.

"Aye put the gun down, Antoine." Dave said from the kitchen. The gun was lowered from my head. Once it was back in his belt, I punched him right in his jaw.

"Don't you ever pull no fucking gun on me. We supposed to be Peoples and you playing some bull shit." The next thing, I knew I was being thrown against the wall by Dave. His large hands almost encircled my skinny neck and his face was only inches away from mine.

I thought to myself that this was the man who once burned a crackhead to death for fun. The man who beat a woman so bad that she has permanent mental damage. The man who was the leader in the Kokomo Massacre only few years before and this same man now held my neck in his hand.

"That's my little brother you talking to. Who the fuck are you?" I didn't know what to say and I knew no matter what the answer was, I was going to be wrong. All I could think about was how disappointed my parents would be at my funeral.

"Japeth." He released my neck then walked back into the kitchen.

"Come on in here uh…what's you name again, little dude?"

"Jay and Peth. Japeth."

"Sit down, Jay. And Antoine, I told you about fucking with people. You gonna get yourself fucked up messing around." His attention turned back to me as only he and I sat in the kitchen. Jack waited in the living room.

"So what you doing trying to get some work? You look

a little too clean to be out here working."

"I gotta get some money. This is the only way I know how."

"You ever did this before?"

"Yeah. I was selling for Choco." He nodded his head.

"So why you coming back now?"

"My Moms. She got laid off and we need money. I'm not in this for play shit. I gotta help out my family."

"What about your father? He around?"

"He's there but he's not making much."

"Who's your peoples again?"

"The Walkers."

"Walkers? Hmmm… I don't know any Walkers. Wait. That little basketball dude. Damian. That's your kin?"

"Yeah. That's my little brother."

"I be seeing him up there at the park playing. Little nigga can hoop. He might make it to the league if he keep his head straight." He looked towards the living room with a thoughtful stare, then took a deep breath before looking back at me.

"Usually I wouldn't fuck with someone like you. You got a nice family and two parents that are around. But I think you're in a fucked up situation and I want to help you out. But don't fuck this up. Don't make me regret this decision."

"I won't." He reached in his pocket and pulled out a tied off sandwich bag with an eighth of a gram worth of cocaine.

"Three hundred and fifty." I pulled the money from my pocket and placed it on the table in front of him. I waited while he counted a month's pay for cleaning up trash at Ricky's. When he was satisfied he nodded his head towards the living room.

Jack and I left the house and went straight to DBrown's to cook up. During the five-minute walk, Jack kept on talking about what happened at Dave's house. He kept asking me what I was thinking and telling me that he's seen people get the shit stomped out of them for even talking to Antoine wrong.

He continued as we entered DBrown's house, recounting the entire story to both DBrown and that fat fuck Jason. The story made DBrown smile and that fuck Jason sat straight faced and only said, "You a stupid mutha fucka."

I kept my job at Ricky's as my cover. I needed to have a means of explaining why I had money. Although I hated that job, it ended up being where my journey in football picked up again but not before I found myself in more trouble.

Chapter Thirty-Five

I OFTEN FOUND MYSELF under the cloak of the early morning darkness, serving little white rocks to the first shift crew heading into their factory jobs. Kim didn't like that I sold drugs. I always reassured her that I had Lucille and no one was going to harm or rob me, but the reassurances fell on deaf ears. I kept the gun in the small of my back like Malcolm X did in his time carrying a gun.

I snuck out of my bedroom window every morning at 3:30 and stayed out until about five. I was the only one willing to get up that early, so I developed a sizeable, loyal customer base. I enjoyed the quietness of the world in those early morning hours.

My mind often drifted to dreams of glory and fame in football when I wasn't busy exchanging crack for cash. The mental visions were short because I needed to stay on the look out for cops and possibly anyone that wanted to rob me. Football at that point remained a distant dream.

I still practiced when I could, but I started to question if I would ever make it. I carried the guilt of not delivering on my promise to the spirits of Mike and Landon but my family's well-being came first. I had to be responsible.

I found ways to sneak in an extra five hundred dollars every two weeks to my parents, under the guise of random hustles; but that was only a quarter of my profit. They would have been so disappointed if they knew what I was doing, but the extra money helped keep us afloat. I don't think my paycheck from Ricky's alone would have been enough for our stability.

I tried to find a way to legitimize the other fifteen hundred every two weeks, but until then I kept my extra cash in a shoe box deep under my bed. Eventually, I started spending some of the money on Kim.

I bought her shoes and whatever clothes she wanted. I also treated myself to the latest sneakers, polo shirts, and jeans. We kept all of the adults in our circle thinking that someone else, anyone else, was buying all of these new things for us. Each item was assigned a different person and reason.

The weeks flew by and December arrived quickly. During early mornings, I would stop by a local convenience store, stand by a local church, or even just walk briskly in some direction. I wanted to make sure I always had a good reason for being out, in case the police ever bothered me. I tried to be as buttoned up as I could about selling.

I operated at odd hours. I kept a low profile. I made sure that I was safe in all that I did, but the thing about that life is that no matter how prepared you are trouble just finds you.

For me that was the morning of December 4th. I remember it was cold and there was a light snow that felt more like a drizzle. I was out walking around and selling as usual. A person whom I'd never seen before walked past me and said "you holding?" without stopping.

I didn't recognize the face so I kept walking. It was only he and I on the street, so I heard when his feet stopped about five feet behind me. I heard the rustle of a jacket.

I turned around and the skinny man who was only a few inches taller than I had a knife in his hand. He lunged at me but I dodged the sharp end of the knife. I lifted my bubble coat past my waist and pulled out Lucille as the man regained his balance.

He started to lunge at me again as I took a step back, cocked the gun, and fired all in one smooth motion. I let two shots spray from the barrel into his stomach. He doubled over in pain and rolled to the ground. Then I ran.

I cut through yards and alleys all the way home, snuck in my window, removed my clothes, flushed my work down the toilet, and put my clothes over the heater vent in my room. I let them warm up until the chill from outside was gone then hung them back in the closet before climbing into bed.

The time on the clock was 4:43am. I needed to be down at the bus stop for school by six-thirty. I went back and forth in my mind about playing sick for the day so that I didn't have to go to school.

Then I decided it would be better for me to be at school in case the cops came to my house. If they came, they would quickly find out that I wasn't really sick and it would be down hill from there.

That day at school, I wondered whether the guy I shot died. On one hand, I didn't want him to die, but on the other, if he didn't he could seek revenge. He didn't appear to be a gangster. He looked more like a crackhead, but sometimes you couldn't tell. I didn't even know why I pulled my gun and shot him. It was just a reaction.

I cursed myself for having the gun; then again, if I didn't have it, it might have been me on the ground. Just then, I realized that I had the murder weapon in my room. I eyed the clock all day.

I called home during lunch, but no one answered. Kim had her lunch period with me as well and she asked if I was okay. She mentioned that DBrown was acting funny earlier too. I kept praying that either the cops didn't go to my house or if they did, that no one was home.

The last bell rang and I hustled out the doors. I got home fast through a combination of sprinting and walking. When I arrived there was no sign of the cops or concern on the face of Moms or Pops. I went to my room, changed my clothes, picked up the gun and stuffed it in my bag.

"Moms, Pops, I'll be back."

"Where are you going?"

"Just going to take a run, Pops."

"Okay."

I ran to a local convenience store and bought a hammer and ammonia. I took those items to a wooded area on the north end of the city. I wiped the gun down with a cloth, broke it into pieces, and buried the pieces in different places within the wooded area.

I returned home sweating after the run in the cold winter air. Pops was at work, but Moms was resting in bed.

"That was a long run. How was your day today?"

"It was fine, Moms. How about you? Are you feeling okay?"

"Yes. I'm fine. Just tired."

The next day at school, I ran into Jack after second period. He asked me if I talked to DBrown. He told me that DBrown's uncle got shot the day before and that he was in the hospital. He told me about how DBrown was trying to be unaffected, but that his eyes were mindless.

It was dangerous to be around DBrown when he was hurt, so Jack was trying to dodge him. I still couldn't believe that I almost killed that guy, then to find out it was DBrown's uncle made me feel worse. It was another scene that played on my mind in replay along with the death of Landon and Mike. During lunch, I snuck out along with a few other Vice Lords and smoked a blunt.

I needed to put myself into a haze. It was the only way that I could function.

Later in the day Jack and I were at the park hanging out by the swing set. We talked as cars drove up and down the street through the park. Some of the cars stopped and whistled at us.

Only Jack was available to answer their call. He either took a ride around the block with the person in the car or went to their window before returning to the swing set, twenty or thirty dollars richer. Then, a black long body Cadillac with gold rims pulled up and stopped by the curb. Dave rolled down the window and motioned for me to come over.

I ran over to the car and he told me to get in. Antoine and Poo were in the backseat, so I was forced to sit in the front next to Dave. We drove off from the curb and I looked through the back side window at Jack alone on the swings.

"What's up, little man?" Dave asked.

"Nothing. Just hanging."

"Yall out there working, huh?"

"Just Jack. I'm out. Need to re-up."

"When you run out?"

"Few days ago. Just been busy. Need to come through tomorrow." Dave was driving outside of the neighborhood and towards the north end of the city. I didn't want to ask where we were going. My hands poured sweat. The winter hat on my head became damp from the perspiration that was forming on my forehead.

"You weren't out yesterday morning?" I thought through the few customers that I saw and weighed the chances that Dave had already talked to them or that he would be talking to them.

"I was out for a quick minute, but shit wasn't hitting so I went back in quick." He was silent in his response and remained silent for the rest of the ride. We pulled into an apartment complex that was nestled across from the wooded area where I buried the gun.

He pulled into a parking spot and excused Antoine and Poo from the car. They said no words in their exit.

"You know Ole Taurus got shot yesterday, right?"

"Yeah, I heard about that from Jack today."

"Jack, huh?" I twisted my hands together and tried to pretend as though I was warming them.

"Yeah. Told me today in school."

"You know that I know you were out there yesterday morning, right?"

"What you mean? Yeah. I was out there for a quick minute."

"Not a quick minute, Jay. You shot Ole Taurus. Don't lie to me." I said a silent prayer in my head, asking for forgiveness of all my sins and that my family be blessed in my absence. "If only I would have stayed in St. Vincent…" I thought to myself, but it was too late now.

"See that right there. You told on yourself."

"Huh?"

"Don't lie to me mutha fucka. I know you shot Ole Taurus. Now tell me what happened." I explained the events of the morning before. Then he told me how I had fucked up business because the cops were all over asking questions and such.

He lit a blunt, took a puff, and asked how football was going. I filled him in on how I was being rejected by teams and because of my mom's cancer, I couldn't even play for the high school team.

"You need to keep yo head on that soccer shit, little man. I look back and I wish somebody would've made me stick with baseball. I was good as shit, but then I started in this Vice Lord shit. This ain for you, Jay. This is for niggas who ain' got shit like me."

"So why don't you move on and leave it alone?"

"I'm in too deep now. I'm committed to this shit, ya

dig? Ain't no turning back for me. You still got a chance." He turned on the car and reversed out of the parking space.

"Yeah, but yall are like my family. You know? I don't have nobody else here outside of my parents and my brother."

"Yeah." He took another pull from the blunt before passing it over to me. I gripped the burning blunt between two fingers.

"I hear you, but you got somewhere to go. Nigga still got dreams and shit." The smoked tickled my throat and caused me to cough.

"I'm for real, nigga. Tell me what them other niggas you run around with dreaming about."

I took another pull from the blunt answering the rhetorical question. Dave's deep voice murmured, "I'm just saying dude… you gotta follow that dream. Like I said, I'm stuck. I ain going nowhere. That dreaming shit is for you young niggas. Yall got time. I'm twenty-six dude. I made my decision young and I don't want to see you stuck like me."

I extended my arm, passing him the disappearing blunt. "I hear you, dude." If it wasn't for that nudge, the story of Japeth Walker would have been different.

Chapter Thirty-Six

THE CONVERSATION I HAD WITH DAVE stuck with me for a few days. I told Kim about the conversation. "I don't know nothing bout no soccer but I know that's your shit and I think you gotta try babe. I don't understand why you don't just play at your age level?" She asked the same question every time the topic came up.

She didn't get it. I couldn't deal with the frustration of stooping to that level. I was better than kids in my age group and I would not accept, what I interpreted as disrespect, to my talent. US youth football had to accept me on my terms or not at all.

After I promised Dave that I would continue to try at football, he took me off the streets. He gave me $1500 every two weeks in cash so that I could continue to help my family and have a little spending money for myself. I still worked at Ricky's too. I was at Ricky's when Walter's dad, Mr. Hernandez, walked into the restaurant.

He recognized me and asked how my parents were

doing. I told him that Moms and Pops were okay. He went on to tell me that Walter made varsity as a freshman, the first to do so in our high school's history. I shared my struggles with football while I continued removing the trash from a table nearby where he was sitting.

He sat quiet for a minute then mentioned that if I wanted to play indoor, there was a Mexican league in Indianapolis. It was a men's open league. Most of the guys were between nineteen and thirty and games were every Sunday night. I told him that I was interested, but that I would need to make sure that Pops could give me a ride.

When Pops came to pick me up, I told him about the talk I had with Mr. Hernandez. The next day he and Mr. Hernandez spoke. The team was open to having me play since they were usually short on players. The first half of the indoor season was almost finished, so they told me that I could join the team when the new season started in January of 1995.

When we arrived for the first game I remember not being able to feel my legs. Soon after entering the building we spotted the team. We walked to the other end of the facility near the arcade games and Pops introduced himself as Mr. Hernandez's friend and soon we were all shaking hands and exchanging names.

The buzzer sounded, marking the end of the game for the other teams. We entered the field through the hockey style door and began warming up. My touches on the ball were feeling good, but my legs were still feeling wobbly.

With me, we had just enough players to play the game. Five field players and one keeper. I'm not sure how Mr. Hernandez convinced them to allow me to play, but I noticed a disappointing look or two as some of my teammates looked down at me. For all I know, he could have told them I was big and athletic and only half that statement would be true.

The buzzer rang and I was directed to play up front. I

stood over the ball and began to feel dizzy. My mind was rattled with doubt that I tried my best to fight, but felt like I was on the losing end, then the whistle blew.

The other team rushed us trying to gain possession of the ball. The first half moved quickly and the rust on my game was apparent. I didn't play well, but at least I was fit and could run around.

The game was tied with four goals each midway through the second period and something just clicked when I received the ball near the halfway line. My legs felt steady underneath me. My touch made me feel as though I was back in St. Vincent with the Wicked 7. My vision seemed clearer.

I turned with the ball and easily beat the onrushing defender with a change of direction exploding into the space behind him before slipping past the last defender and then rocketing the ball into the lower corner of the small goal.

Offensively, I dominated the remaining ten minutes of the game, scoring two more goals and adding an assist to help my team win seven to four. The smiles on the faces of my new teammates said more of their acceptance than any of their broken English comments. It felt good to be back playing the game.

The competition was decent. It didn't completely bore me and if anything else, those players understood the passion behind the game and that was important. I played indoor football like futsal before I even knew that futsal existed. I displayed all the flair and trickery that I'd kept sharp in the basement, on the porch, and in the backyard over the last several months.

A couple weeks passed and the crowds grew bigger every week to see the league's newest star. Most people called it the Mexican league, but there was a mix of Hondurans and El Salvadorians amongst other cultures in the brown skinned league, though Mexicans did make up the majority.

It was about mid-season and we had just won another game,

keeping our undefeated streak alive. I was sitting on the bleachers next to Moms. She was saying something about Mr. Barney when a defender from another team approached us.

"You play very well. Where are you from?" He looked Hispanic but had no accent.

"Kokomo."

"No, where are you from originally? You can't play like that being from Kokomo."

"Really?" I snapped back.

"Hi, I'm his mother, Elaine. Nice to meet you." Moms extended her hand to meet his.

"Nice to meet you. Jose Del Toro. Mother huh? I thought this was your sister, Japeth."

"Whoa whoa whoa. Ease up on that, dog."

Jose pushed the palms of his hand towards us, feigning that he was putting on the brakes. "Aye. Easy. I'm not trying to hit on your mother, Japeth. I'm married. But what I am more interested in is your age. See, I coach a youth team here in town and I hear you might be interested in playing."

"What team do you coach?"

"The Dynamo FC U-18 premier boys team. So, is it true that you're only fifteen?"

"I'll be sixteen this Friday." He smiled and the pace of his words increased.

"I'd love to have you come out and train with us as soon as possible. We're getting ready for The Dallas Cup. You heard of it?"

"Yup." I knew that it was one of the tournaments where the best youth teams in the world played.

"We won the national championship for our age group last year so they invited us to be a part of the super group. It's going to be incredible and I think you have the talent to help us out. What do ya say?" His hand was outstretched, hanging in the air in front of me. I couldn't believe my luck. After all the shitty situations and bull shit that I had gone through over the past couple years, I finally got a break.

When we told Pops about the chance meeting, he was very skeptical about the story. The next day, while I was at school, Pops and Coach Jose had a discussion. Pops was convinced and his excitement was oozing by the time I returned home from school. Pops and I shared a childlike exhilaration going back and forth with "What if" scenarios. Then the question hung between us like a ghost. I gave our ghost a voice.

"How are we going to pay for this?"

"We'll figure it out, son."

After talking to the team coordinator, Pops found out that it would cost four thousand dollars to make the trip to Dallas. It was a weeklong tournament, which meant hotel costs alone could be one thousand dollars. Then there was money for plane tickets, food, a rental car and gas.

Pops got rid of cable TV and he sold the TVs that Damian and I had in our rooms. He was able to scrounge up one thousand dollars over the next few months through his efforts. Dave gave me an additional one thousand dollars; beyond the money he gave me to help cover the family's bills that I sprinkled in over the months in small increments. As the time got nearer, Pops broke down and asked Mrs. Johnson and Mr. Barney, our neighbor, to loan him the money. They both were able to provide two thousand dollars each.

When I saw Mr. Barney, I thanked him. "Ain nothing to it, young blood. You just go out there and show them boys how to play, alright?" He stuck his hand out for a low hanging five, when I swung to hit his hand he quickly moved it and ran it through the side of his head. "Too slow my man." He continued scraping the early morning frost off of his windshield. I smiled, then turned around to defrost the car for Pops.

The early March winter air finally began to thaw enough for the Dynamo team to play outside. The day of that first practice I could not concentrate on anything in school. After the final bell rang, I got home as fast as I could, grabbed a quick snack then Pops and I drove to Indianapolis.

We turned on a road that seemed to be heading deep into the woods, but soon it opened up and a large open area with six football fields were before us. Walking out to the field area felt like my first game with the Kicks team in PAL. That memory bleeding into the remainder of that day when I found out that Mike was on his deathbed. I forced myself to focus on positive things but I held onto the motivation from that moment. Soon the team gathered into a circle and began stretching. There were two black guys on the team. One of them sat next me.

"What's your name, man?"

"Japeth."

"Malcolm." He held out his hand.

"Named after Malcolm X?"

"My dad loves Malcolm X. Surprised you know of him. Not too many people seem to."

"My dad is a huge fan too. Made me read the autobiography when I was in the seventh grade."

"Damn. That's serious. My dad just made me read it last year."

After a few minutes of small talk with Malcolm, Coach Jose called out to me, cutting off our conversation. I rose up from my butterfly groin stretch to meet him.

Coach Jose shook my hand and welcomed me to practice. I could feel the eyes of the players burning holes of curiosity into the side of my face. The team finished stretching and gathered before Coach Jose's tall frame. The sun beamed off of his tanned brown skin as he began, "Alright boys, today we're going to get started with some three hundreds, move into a game of knockout, then get into a full sided game."

"You sure bout those three hundreds?" the other black guy on the team asked.

"You scared of messing up your hair, Shane?" Coach Jose responded, clearly making a reference to Shane's growing afro.

"I'm sure you guys noticed there's a new player here with us today. This is Japeth Walker. He's sixteen, but remember - skill has no age." I cringed inside when he mentioned my age. I wanted my new teammates to first judge me based on my skills and not focus on me being two years younger than them.

He looked down at me and winked, then sent us to the touchline. We ran across the width of the field trying to meet certain time standards on each run. Markee, from the Wicked 7, made me see the importance of being fit. His voice was in the back of my head. "It's when you tired that you make mistakes."

Malcolm was fast and had a beautiful stride that made it look like he wasn't even trying to run with speed. His tall, slender frame glided over the blades of grass, but I was still the fastest player on the team.

We moved onto knockout, a king of the hill kind of game. If you lost your ball or had it knocked outside of the confined area, you were out. The game went on until there was one person left.

My change of speed, creative dribbles, and ability to hold onto the ball created whispers from those that were out of the game. When the game was done, I stood in the squared off area by myself like a king watching over his newly conquered land.

"That, gents, is skill." Coach Jose announced.

I was placed as the lone striker on the B team for the practice game. I scored all three goals in a 3-1 win over the A team. I'd proven to everyone that I deserved to be on the first team, outscoring Malcolm who was a US youth national team forward.

Pops and I were leaving the grounds when I saw an animated older lady next to Coach Jose, her index finger was pointed at Coach's face. Her bleach blond ponytail that hung through the hole in the back of her baseball hat flung and bounced around as she talked. I wondered if her anger had anything to do with me.

That Thursday, we had a practice game against a team from Elkhart. I started in place of Justin, who was the usual attacking midfielder. Jalani Thomas, who was from South Bend, joined Malcolm in the starting forward positions. Jalani was also black, which made for an unusual situation of having four black players on one team.

The football pitches in the States looked more like the segregated south. Whites and a few "acceptable so called negroes", as Malcolm X would say, played football. The blacks played American football and basketball. The first team we scrimmaged against was a classic example of the type of football teams that existed at that time.

Elkart didn't have a guy under six feet and for the most part they were what we called "big, country fed" boys. They were all white. We were clearly the more skilled team, but Elkhart relied on a very physical game.

Malcolm and Jalani were struggling to get looks at goal, as the Elkhart Blaze constantly interrupted the flow of the game. I was adjusting to the new position of attacking midfielder and the addition of Jalani while attempting to model my style of play after Cam from Bagga.

In the end, Malcolm and Jalani each scored one goal to give us the 2-1 win. I was on a high from the victory and anticipation of going to the Dallas Cup. The next day that fat fuck Jason would nearly ruin everything.

Chapter Thirty-Seven

"JAY BOUT TO DO HIS THANG with that soccer shit down in Dallas," Jack said as we walked home from the convenience store after school that day.

"It ain shit. That's a sport for pussys anyway. Real niggas in Dallas play football." That fat fuck Jason always had something smart to say and I lost my patience with him.

"Fuck you say?"

"Haha. You hear this nigga's voice crack like a bitch." I hit that fat fuck square in his nose. It felt good to watch him hold his bloody face in his hands. Jack and DBrown pulled me back away from him.

"What the fuck is wrong with you, Jay?!" They both made sure that I was calm before tending to Jason, who was now on his knees with his face in his hands. I left the group and continued walking home. As I walked away I could hear Jack say, "I told yo dumb ass to stop fuckin' with him…"

I stopped by Kim's house and Miss Beverly let me in. I

greeted her and then noticed a small bowl of chips on the dinner table, a sign that Kim had just gotten home.

"Hey, Japeth. Kim told me you going down to Dallas to play soccer soon."

"Yeah. It's a big tournament, so it should be fun."

She nodded her head approvingly as she exhaled her cigarette smoke. She sat in the couch in short shorts and a tank top. The revealing clothes showed that Trish more inherited her mother's body type than Kim. I figured that Kim must have taken on her dad's body type. I'd never seen him. She burned all her pictures of him after he left, which was three years prior to when I met her.

"That's good. You keep it up. Don't' be like half these bums around here ripping and running the streets."

"I'ma do all I can."

Kim walked out of the bathroom and I followed her into her room. I told her about the Jason incident and she peppered me with questions about how everything unfolded.

"What if the police saw you? You know how they be around every corner. Yo ass would've been locked up and behind bars instead of going to Dallas next weekend."

I knew that she would react that way. It comforted me to see her concern. A few minutes after Kim calmed down, Trish walked through the front door.

"Whoooo... I heard your son-in-law done went and busted Jason's nose today!" Kim jumped up from the bed and swung open her door.

"Yea... AND?!?!?"

"Oh hey Kim! I didn't even know you was here. What's your issue?"

"You out here talking smack like we can't hear you and you probably don't even know the story."

"Bitch! I do know the story..."

Miss Beverly stepped in. "Aye! Aye! Aye! Watch your language little lady before I come over there and smack the piss out of you."

Trish continued, "Sorry mah. I *do* know the story cause Jack was right there when it happened."

Kim slammed the bedroom door. "Aye!!! Don't be slamming no GOT damn doors up in my house!!! You don't pay a damn bill around this mutha fucka." Miss Beverly's voice boomed through the shut door. Kim threw her body down on the bed next to me where we laid not saying anything to each other.

I wondered how much longer I could exist living between the two worlds of youth football and my neighborhood. It felt like no matter how well I did on the field, the streets would always have a grip on me.

I wasn't confident that I could ever escape the life. I broke my train of thought and noticed that Kim had fallen asleep next to me. I looked back to the ceiling and daydreamed about winning the Dallas Cup the following weekend. I never thought it would be more than a dream.

Chapter Thirty-Eight

ACCORDING TO GRANNY, Cam had some tryouts in England, but nothing materialized so he was heading to Trinidad to play football professionally. Blue was also a professional footballer in Trinidad. Hulk, Front Seat, and Markee were all still playing in St. Vincent, but with no real competition their talent was beginning to wane.

"Them boys does only really play when they on the national team now. I talked to Hulk and Blue the other day up di road. They looking to get some scholarships like Dready. I guess he been talking to his coach about them."

It was ironic that she mentioned the superstar striker from Layou because we were scheduled to have a practice game against his team, the last practice game before we left for the Dallas Cup. Dready was a junior by this time and was voted the best player in college that year, leading his team to a national college championship.

I read about him in the magazines when they covered the collegiate scene. The name William Cole, or Dready as he was known in St. Vincent, was always mentioned in the discussions and articles of the best players in the nation. He was a second team All-American his freshman year and a first team selection his sophomore and junior years.

Their stadium had a decent crowd that muggy, Wednesday afternoon. The band played loud, adding to the energy of the feverish IU supporters in Bloomington, Indiana. On my way out to the field I spotted Kim, Trish, DBrown, Jack, Dave, and Z in the bleachers, then I saw Dready.

He stood near the halfway line and I took my opportunity to meet the Layou legend.

"William?"

"What up yout man?" He lifted his head in my direction. He was much taller than I thought at six feet four inches. I jogged over in his direction and put my fist up to give him a pound.

"I'm a Vincy. Heard a lot about you when I was back in Layou." He hit a pass in the direction of another player then threw his hand up to signal that he didn't want a return pass.

"Where you from?"

"I was up by First River. Played for the Black Stars when I was there."

"What!? Wait, you the man they call Bird?" His voice shrilled.

"Yeah."

"Alright dred. Heard good things about you. Let's meet up after di match."

"No doubt."

The game finished and it was true what they said about Dready. He was simply a goal scorer. I saw nothing especially skillful about him but if that ball was within twenty-five yards of the goal he was going to find a way to get it into the back of the net or damn close.

Our keeper halted most of Dready's attempts, keeping us in the game before I scored two goals and had two assists. The game ended 4 – 2. Dready scored the two goals for Indiana University.

After each goal I scored, I'd look up in the stands to where my crew sat. They'd throw their signs up and I could hear them say, "That's my nigga!" or "Yall can fuck with him!" above the rest of the college crowd. They were out of place amongst the drunk college kids, but they were my people and I was happy to have them there.

After the game Dready and I were talking with Moms, Pops, and Damian in the parking lot when the IU head coach approached us. I assumed that he was coming to talk to Dready, so I was surprised when he reached out to shake my hand. He removed his shades and gushed about how good of a performance I had and handed Pops his business card.

"We'd love to have you right here, wearing the IU uniform next year," Coach Smith said.

Everyone in my family looked around at each other. "I'm finishing up my sophomore year of high school this year."

"You shitting me?!!? You're only a sophomore? Forgive me ma'am," his Tennessee origins shining through in his response. "Sir, lets talk on Monday morning. I am very interested in having your son join our program."

Coach Smith moved on, walking towards a grey Lincoln. We all continued talking and decided to have Dready up for a home cooked meal in the coming weeks before he left campus for summer break. Two days later, Pops and I were leaving with the team to go to Dallas.

I noticed that Justin was not amongst the group at the airport. "Shane, where's Justin and Andy?"

"Lets go get some cinnamon rolls." Shane responded. I told Pops that I would be back.

We were only a few feet away from the rest of the team when Shane started to explain. "You causing some serious stuff to go down."

"Me? What I do?"

"Man. Justin and Andy's parents are mad cause you on the team."

"Why? We're winning and they were still playing. I don't get it."

"Dude. They were playing on the wings. They were both *star* central midfielders before you came. You shouldn't technically even be on the team." He paused to order his cinnamon roll with extra icing.

"I hear you. That kind of sucks. Now we're down two people."

"Yeah... but not really. I didn't like them too much and I don't think very many people did either, including Coach Jose. Speaking of, his job is now on the line. Justin's mom is on the board of directors for the club and she apparently has this whole report in on him. She's trying really hard to get him fired."

He took a bite of his cinnamon roll as we walked back toward the group. His mouth full as he said, "It doesn't surprise me. She's a bitch. I heard they quit when they found out that Coach Smith was interested in offering you a full ride scholarship. Justin has been trying to get a scholarship there for like ever, but they keep pulling dudes from St. Louis and Michigan over him. His mom was always saying Coach Smith doesn't recruit in state. Everybody knows that ain't true. He hollered at me but I just didn't want to go there. I wanted to get out of Indiana. Same with Malcolm."

"Ahhh. I guess that makes sense."

"Yep. Coach Jose was supposed to get a couple of my boys from North Central High School to fill in on the wings. These dudes are dope. They play for Inferno."

"Yeah?"

"Yep. Last time I talked to them they were thinking about it, but hadn't made up their minds yet." We turned the corner, where the waiting area of our gate became visible again.

Shane took the last bite of his cinnamon roll and threw the cardboard box in a trash can. "Ahhhh shit..." I turned my attention to where Shane was looking. Two young black men stood next Coach Jose, large soccer bags were slung over their shoulders.

One of them was tall, dark, and bald, similar to Malcolm. The other was short and light skin wearing a bright smile. All seemed right in his world as he kept his eyes focused on Coach Jose while Coach Jose spoke.

"Aye," the tall one said to Shane. They embraced with a manly hug.

"So is this the infamous Japeth," the short one said to me as he reached over to give me a fist bump.

"Well, I don't know about infamous, but I'm soon to be famous."

"Bryan Jones. Coach Jose was just telling us how you been getting down out here. Can't wait to play with you man."

"Likewise, heard good things about you, too."

"Larry Marvin," the taller one said then gave a simple head nod. I nodded back.

We boarded the plane and after a few hours we landed in Dallas. Our first game was the following day against the B team from Madrid. We quickly dismissed the notion that we were the usual team of American athletes who were dumb and clumsy footballers when we won 5-0.

Malcolm scored one, Jalani had two, and I put the other two on the board. Only a few critics took notice, but it was more respect than we had before the game. I was impressed with the wing play of Bryan and Larry.

It was exciting to watch them run past defenders. They fit beautifully into the fluid style of play and there was a chemistry that was automatically building within our team.

The next match we tied a very talented Dutch team 3-3. I had one goal and one assist. Larry scored the other goal. Several players on that Dutch team were called into their first team a few months following our game. They all played pivotal roles in that team winning the Champions League that year.

We went out to dinner that night as a team to celebrate. The common ground between the white and the black guys on the team was larger than I'd seen before in other mixed environments. I was particularly struck by our center back, Derek Shea. Derek told Larry and I how he spent the early part of his childhood in the trailer parks of Detroit until his mom moved back to Indianapolis to live with his Grandma.

"I didn't start playing soccer until I was ten, when we moved to Indy. I didn't want to play at first; I thought the game was for girls but Grandma forced me to play. She said I needed something to keep me busy. Plus even if I wanted to play in Detroit, we didn't have money for that shit. We didn't even have money for food. That's why I'm so skinny now."

He reminded me of Harry, the gap-toothed kid from middle school who left me to die at that detassling job, but I somehow felt a kinship to him. There was something genuine about his spirit, something relatable and familiar.

Much like Malcolm X's experience when he made his pilgrimage, I realized that the diversity issue in US soccer wasn't strictly along black and white lines. Derek was white, yet he used to view the game similarly to how my friends viewed it.

I learned to not see the issue with US soccer as a race issue only but one that was affected by its public perception and economics. I believe that it was the diversity of culture and thoughts that made that Dynamo team stand out in the US and to the world.

The football media said our style of play was like watching jazz in motion. "The Americans Finally Got It!" one of the German newspapers exclaimed. The article went on to talk of how there was finally an American team that broke the mold of fast, strong but haphazard, unknowing players. The article called us the "Bebop Boys."

The audience at the tournament started to refer to us as "The Bebop Boys" as well. We were all from the hip-hop generation, but we understood the reference to the free, improvisational style of playing jazz, with unpredictable punctuations and rhythms. Each artist on our team was able to take over under the spotlight.

As the Duke Ellington of the team, I had adopted Cam's style, but made it my own. Along with my pace I frequently attacked players one on one then created opportunities off of that penetration, while Malcolm and Jalani built off of the team's imbalance with their speed and imaginative play in the final third. After two more wins, I began to wonder if we could actually win the tournament.

The buzz around our team was building, as evidenced by the growing crowds. Top Division I college coaches as well as professional scouts were scattered amongst the casual fans.

During our game against a top French club, we encountered a pair of brilliant forwards. The smaller of the two, Patrick Apolline, was like a combination of Malcolm and Jalani. I really admired his game. He was strong, quick, unpredictable, and had an incredible competitive spirit.

It was because of his hat trick performance that the game was pushed into overtime and then penalty kicks. I also had a hat trick that game. Although we didn't speak the same language, there was an understood competitive respect between us when we shook hands and acknowledged each other after the game. It was similar to the type of respect that hip-hop artists carry for each other - loving, but with a competitive edge.

The day of the final game was cloudy and rainy. Luckily the pitch was slightly elevated so excess water was able to run off down the slope surrounding the field. The slick pitch played to both of our advantage with both teams being very skillful and fast. The Brazilian team we played was overall more skilled, but we had more pace.

I had their toughest defender on me like he was a second layer of my dark skin. I struggled to get an effective touch on the ball. Towards the end of the first half he tried to intercept a pass coming in my direction and slipped. I collected the ball and pushed it diagonally through their defense to Bryan. He chipped the ball over the on rushing keeper. It was the goal of the tournament for my vote. Not only for its beauty but also because it won us the game.

When that final whistle blew, the crowd burst into celebration. I ran and jumped on Malcolm, wrapping my legs around him and throwing my fist in the air declaring victory. Soon I was at the bottom of a mountain composed of all of my teammates.

The mount of players eroded and I was embraced by Pops. He squeezed me tight and whispered in my ear, "I'm proud of you, son." I thought about Moms and Damian and wished they were there with us. I collapsed in Pops' arms overcome with emotion. It was finally happening. I could feel it. I was back on the road to being the best footballer in the world.

I could feel Mike and Landon smiling down on me and it felt good to finally give some honor to their memories. A young reporter tapped me on my shoulder. She congratulated me on the win and asked me a few questions. I only remember the last question that she asked me, "You play with such passion, where does that drive come from?"

"I love the game, so it's nothing for me to give it my all but my family has definitely been a source of inspiration and my friends Mike and Landon. I can't let those people down so I always do my best, even when it gets tough."

Chapter Thirty-Nine

IT WAS THE FIRST TIME an American soccer club won the Super Group at Dallas Cup, so we became the darlings of US soccer. Malcolm and Shane had already accepted full ride scholarships to UCLA and would be joining that team in the fall.

Bryan was going to Southern Methodist University and Larry was on his way to the University of Virginia. Jalani was committed to UCLA as well, but had to complete his senior year of high school.

I was also getting tons of scholarship offers and it was exciting to read about myself in the monthly football magazine. The enthusiasm even trickled over into national sports media with a short article in the May issue of *Sports Elite*, the leading national sport magazine.

US Soccer's Future?

Sitting in a Motel 6 on US 31 in Kokomo, IN, I await what I suspect to be a massive 16 year-old based on what he's done on the soccer field. He's a key piece in what is being called the greatest youth soccer team in United

States history. He's arguably the best player on the best youth team in the world
– he's also it's youngest. His performances at the Dallas Cup in March, have
earned him an invitation to train with the U-18 national team. Walker has
already played at the youth national team level for St. Vincent and The
Grenadines, so the US is currently expediting his paperwork so that he can
play in the upcoming match against Norway.

I open my room door after hearing a knock and see an average size
kid at 5'9 who would be 140lbs soaking wet along with someone I rightfully
guessed was his father. I invited them in and I couldn't help but be impressed
with his confident stride. The kid walks like he's good. He takes a seat on the
bed and Japeth Walker and I begin our talk.

Professional and college scouts have their eyes on Japeth, who goes by
Jay. "I've got a lot of offers and I'm talking to coaches at every tournament we
go to, but I haven't made up my mind yet." Jay has some very talented players
around him as well. A team comprised of six national team players across
different age groups – all entering or planning to enter top DI programs- but Jay
is a true rarity.

"He's a very special player. One who could single-handedly turn a
game around with a piece of magic. His impact is irreplaceable," says a top DI
college coach. It's this kind of talk that has the US Mens national team
excited for his arrival in hopes that he can take US soccer to the next level.

It's to be seen if this young kid has the shoulders and strength to
make the United States a winner on the world stage. One thing is for sure, in
his mind there's no question of what he can do. "We're going to change the game
in the US forever."

I was skeptical about my growth as a player if I chose to go
to college. I was already playing against the best the country had to
offer every weekend.

Most of the players were lifeless and had no passion, their
skills more suited for the schoolyard kick ball tournament. I could
only be considered to be the best footballer in the world if I
competed with the best and showed to be better than them.

Coach Jose and I had several discussions about my next

move. "In the meantime, your focus should be 100% on playing well for the U-18 national team. That is priority number one," he said. I knew he was right and Kim echoed the same thought process.

She was so proud of my success. I loved that about her. She made it feel like we were a team against the world. I tried to keep my mind focused on the U-18 national team game in Norway, but it was difficult. In my neighborhood, life was moving as usual and I wasn't exempt from getting touched.

I came close to getting into a fight with someone at school, when DBrown stepped in and took on the fight for me. At the time I was upset because I knew I could handle my own, but Kim made me realize that I was lucky that DBrown came to my defense.

"You don't know what could have happened in that fight. You could have gotten stabbed, shot, or arrested and then what dummy?" Over the next few days, I stayed home as much as I could trying to limit my interaction with the world before I left for Norway.

THE AIR IN OSLO was bone chilling cold when the wind blew. Coach Jerry Adler decided to try a 4-3-3 formation with Malcolm at center forward, Jalani on the left and me on the right up front.

Our middle consisted of Larry on the right behind me, a short guy from California in the middle, and Bryan on the left. In the back Derek Shea and Shane were on the wings. Our combination of speed and skill dominated the Norwegian defense. I had a tremendous game in particular, showing skill and a nose for goal. I scored all three goals in the 3-0 win.

The day after I arrived home, I was on the porch with Jack and DBrown catching up on all things Kokomo. Who did what, new female conquests, new crackhead stories and drama. Jack was mid-story about some fight that happened when Moms told me there was a call for me.

"Is it one of those college coaches?"

"No, he says he's from Catalonia."

"A college in Catalonia?"

"I don't know Japeth, you want to talk to him or not?"

"Let me see what this Catalonia business is all about. It's just weird someone calling from a college in Catalonia." I picked up the receiver.

"Hello?"

"Japeth?"

"Yes. Who is this?"

"This is Antonio Wex, Head Assistant at FC Catalonia." I never heard or saw his name in my football magazine, but he did have an accent that I assumed was Spanish.

"Hi. How are you, sir?"

"Fine. Look, we want you to come over for a tryout. We've been seeing you since the Dallas Cup and saw you in Norway with the national team." I stood in the hallway staring out at Jack and DBrown on the porch.

"Hola. You no understand?"

"No, no, I heard you. To be honest with you I just don't know whether to believe you." He laughed a hearty laugh.

"Fair enough. Should I speak with your madre?"

"No, my dad would be the better person to speak to. He deals with all the football stuff."

"Very well then. Very important I speak with your padre when he home." He gave me his number. "Hope to see you soon. Adios."

"So who was it?" Moms asked.

"Some guy who said he was from FC Catalonia." She gave me a questioning look.

I went back out to the porch. DBrown was saying something, but I found it hard to listen. Then the phone rang again and Moms shouted out, "Japeth! Coach Jose!" I went inside and picked up the phone.

"Hey, Coach Jose."

"Did Antonio Wex call you yet?"

"Yeah, I just got done talking to him."

"You don't seem that excited?"

"Why should I be, Coach? The guy claims to be from FC Catalonia. Sounds like hoax to me. Some of these college coaches are really—"

"He's real."

"What? He's real? What do you mean he's real?"

"I mean he's real. He's really who he says he is."

"Are you serious? This is not a good time for a joke, coach. Are you for real?"

"Si Mijo!!!"

"So let me get this straight. Catalonia, the famous football club, wants me to tryout for them?"

"What, you don't understand my Spanish? Yes!!!" Moms was jumping up and down in front of me. My heart pumped like a rapid-fire sub machine gun, but I couldn't move. I ended my conversation with Coach Jose and Moms squeezed me in her arms.

"I'm so proud of you, boy. This is it. You're on your way to being the best in the world!"

DBrown and Jack let themselves in the house to see what was going on. When I glanced up, I looked past them. I could see Pops' car pulling up in front of the house.

"Sonny's here. We have to go tell him now." Moms and I both rushed past DBrown and Jack. By the time Pops stepped out of the car Moms was draped on him.

"Elaine, what's wrong? What happened? Everything okay?"

"Catalonia, Pops. They called."

"What? What are you talking about?"

"Did you hear him? Catalonia called for our son. They want our son!" Damian stood on the passenger side of the car with his basketball shoes in one hand and duffle bag draped over the other shoulder.

"Wait…wait…calm down, Elaine. What are you talking about they want Japeth?"

"Some guy named Antonio Wex called and said he was with Catalonia and they want me to come over for a tryout," I said.

"Wait…Antonio Wex? That name sounds familiar. I think he was a stand in coach for them a few years ago."

"I don't know, but Coach Jose says he's the real deal. He left a number for you to call him back."

"Excuse me, Mr. and Mrs. Walker," Jack chimed in, "but what are you talking about?"

"Catalonia is one of the biggest football clubs in the world and they want Japeth to come tryout for their team," Moms answered as she wiped the tears of happiness from her face.

Pops added on, "If this is true, it's like if the Lakers were to ask Damian to come tryout for their team. But this is probably for their academy team so something like trying out for the Lakers practice squad."

"Oh, dang. Aight. Jay you got skills like that?" Jack said with a big smile.

"Yeah, I do what I do out there, you know?"

Damian came over and gave me a hug. "It's about time you started getting as good as me. Feels good, huh?" I slapped him in the back of the head then DBrown and Jack jumped on him and wrestled him to the ground.

"You ain never too old to get your butt kicked," DBrown snarled.

"Aye don't go hurting my baby now."

"Oh Elaine. Let the boys rough him up a bit. It's good for him. I need to get inside to call this man back."

Chapter Forty

THE OFFER ON THE TABLE after two tryouts and a month of negotiation was that my parents would have paid travel to come see me once a month, Moms medical needs would be taken care of by the club, as well as the remainder of our mortgage. The Walkers snuggled ourselves in a blanket of security.

We sat at a local seafood restaurant for a celebratory dinner with my family, Kim, Uncle Jimmy and his wife. I was still amazed that I was going to be a part of the famed Catalonia club. I'd met one of my heroes and got to talk to him for a few minutes before his training session. I felt as though I was floating on air when Coach Antonio escorted me around the grounds.

The final person I met was a man I'd watched on video since I was young, whose name I'd heard Uncle Jimmy and Pops talk about since I could remember – the head coach, who was simply called The Coach.

If I accomplished nothing else, everything we'd been through was worth that moment. A moment where Pops could shake hands with one of the greats he admired since boyhood.

I clawed through my shrimp and lobster, not really engaged in the discussion around the table. I was daydreaming about playing against players from around the world when Kim elbowed me in my ribs.

I looked at her, smiled and felt sad because neither of us wanted to talk about the decision that was before us. It was rare for her not to speak her mind, so I knew the situation was difficult for her. My own confusion brought back thoughts of having to leave Renell, who I still missed, even though I loved Kim.

I was set to leave for Catalonia on November 5th. A few days before my flight, I was sitting in Jack's living room as we watched a movie. DBrown wasn't around much for my last week in Kokomo and I asked Jack about it.

"He had a half a kilo on consignment and his dumbass spent too much money on drinking and shit. Now he's out there trying to get his money back up." I knew that meant DBrown was out robbing people, stores, and possibly out selling fake drugs. Jack looked down at his beeper.

"Man... this nigga Jason stay hitting me up, man."

"I don't know how you fuck with that dude."

"He's alright. It's just sometimes he want to be around too much."

"So yall moving half a key now?"

"Yeah, man. Where you been? We been moving half a key each. We out here getting money, dude. Streets is hot right now though, so we gotta stay low and be careful. Po Pos is all up in this bitch. You know they put cameras in them street lights at the park."

"Word? Damn. Make sure you be careful out there."

"Don't worry about me. They ain gonna catch the kid."

"Where's Mrs. Johnson?" I asked.

"Work."

"Damn, she aint never retiring. How she doing?"

"She good. Getting on my nerves though."

"What she doing now?"

"You know how she do, always talking bout how I need to be trying to go to school and shit. I swear I can't be around her for two minutes before she start up with me." He mocked her voice as he continued, "What you need to do is be studying your school books instead of tryna be mista cool out here in these streets. You little soms a bitches don't know how good ya got it."

"Well dog…she ain lying, though. My Uncle Jimmy was saying the same type of shit, before I got signed with Catalonia."

"I know, right. Like why do I need to go to school? You go there to get a job right?" He paused. "Shit, I already make more than all them professors. Plus, this is home, man. Fuck I want to go someplace else for?"

"Well, that's your choice, bro." There was a moment where neither of us talked. In the quiet of our conversation I thought about where we both were in life at that point. It always felt as though no matter how hard I tried with football, I was being pulled back to the hood lifestyle.

Finally, I was going to be able to escape it. I knew I was lucky, but I also worked my butt off to get to that point where I could take advantage of the luck that came my way. DBrown loved the life, so there was little hope for him to leave but I wondered about Jack.

Jack was different. He actually had hopes of doing better in life. I remember in some of our conversations as kids, he said that he wanted to be an engineer. He was really good at math too, so I definitely think he could have made it. Instead, the allure of fast money and the life was more attractive to him.

My heart ached at the thought that it might have been the last time that I saw Jack alive. I wanted to get on my soapbox and preach to him about doing something better with his life, but I would have felt like a hypocrite. If it wasn't for the chance meeting with Mr. Henandez at Ricky's or my discussion with Dave, I would have probably been moving a half a key with tunnel vision on the drug game as well.

"Anyway. You going over by Trish and Kim?"

"Naw, man. I'm going to be hanging out with Malcolm tonight down in Indianapolis."

"Cool."

A few days passed and it was time for me to go to Catalonia. Pops and I sat quietly in our first class seats peering out of the window of the airplane. I was not yet tired of the beautiful descent into EL Prat, the Catalonia airport. I loved how varied the terrain and scenery was on our way in, flying over the deep blue water.

Looking out, the series of close houses looked like a pan of Rice Krispy treats, the mountains providing a curtain for the city. We flew over what looked to be some manufacturing plants then a few factory buildings, one of them with the letters ZAL written on top.

I reflected back on my first PAL game and how the heartbreak of not playing was trumped by the soul altering news of Mike's death. I thought of that fight that Jack and I had with the Capones only for those guys to become our friends. I thought of Choco and wondered how he was doing in jail. A guy like Choco doesn't live for very long, that was something that even he knew.

I thought of that Labor Day weekend only a few years back, when that drive by shooting caused Landon to die, bleeding out his life in front of me. A scene I still saw in my nightmares frequently. I thought of Damian and his success as a basketball player and I hoped I'd get the chance to see him play in college.

A feeling of relief and pride came over me as I thought of Moms and Pops. I was proud that I was able to do something that had eased their lives. Our hospital bills and mortgage were able to be paid off due to my talent and my hard work.

All because Catalonia finally saw in me what I realized

years before. I was the first American player to join La Joventut, the football academy of Catalonia FC.

Today it's seen worldwide as the best youth academy in the world, but back then, it was just a regular youth academy. At that time the Netherlands youth system was hailed as the best in the world.

The philosophy between the two schools of thought was very similar since we shared the connection to The Coach, who was a Dutchman.

The philosophy of Total Football, or what we called Passa Passa in Catalonia, was a key shared vision. In this system, no player was ever out of place, creating a sort of fluidity in the way the game was played.

It didn't take long to get our luggage. Hernando, our driver, was waiting for us as usual. It was in our talks with Hernando that I first understood the Catalan spirit. I don't remember the details of our discussion, but I do remember hearing "more than a club" numerous times. The words held little meaning to me at that point.

The city was amazing with it's combination of wide and tight winding roads. There were moments when no buildings stood grandly over us and in those moments we were in awe of the mountains and beauty they provided to the landscape.

Our right turn onto a two-lane street gave us a clear view of The Stadium. There it stood grandiose and seeming to lean into its rounded end. "Dis is heaven here. Heart of a country," Hernando said. He said that every trip at that same point. It was a sight I was sure he had seen many times being a local citizen, but he still had the same glazed over look in his eyes.

The gate was the line that separated the world of Catalonia the country and the pride and joy of its youth. The future football superstars of Catalonia were housed in the estate: La Joventut.

Chapter Forty-One

IN THE QUIET SERENITY OF LA JOVENTUT, sixty some heartbeats pounded vigorously red and blue. Sixty some minds with the same goal – to make the first team. I was probably the only one there who had a different goal. Mine was to be the best footballer in the world.

Pops stayed two days before returning back to the States and I was alone for the first time in my life. There were only a few kids there that weren't from Catalonia, most being from Brazil or Argentina. I was intimidated by where they were from more than the actual people. Those countries had given the world some of it's greatest players. I laid in bed that night by myself, my roommate was supposed to arrive the next morning, and I barely slept. I was certain that all of the kids there were footballing gods in the making.

I glanced at the clock and saw that it was 6:45am. Breakfast was served at seven, so I didn't bother taking a shower. I quickly brushed my teeth, threw on my school uniform, and walked down the hall to the cafeteria. Other people were leaving their rooms as well.

They were in groups of familiar beings, while I walked with no friends. The feeling reminded me of my years as a kid before I met Mike and Jack. Curious stares fell upon me.

I continued my journey alone through the breakfast line, selecting a banana and a bowl of cereal before walking to an empty table. I took one bite of my cereal when a guy with dark, shiny skin took a seat across from me.

"Where are you from?" he said in an up and down sing songy rhythm that pegged him as native to somewhere on the continent of Africa.

"The States." I could tell in his hint of a reaction that he found my accent just as funny as I found his. His name was Ibrahim and we continued talking throughout breakfast.

"Well, the practices are not hard like the practices back in Senegal. In Senegal, you have to watch your legs. A man, and a *BIG* man, will try to break them so he can brag about it later when he is getting drunk with his friends. This is not good where I am from. But here. Here it is much harder because it is a mental game."

He leaned over the table and lowered his voice to a whisper. "Everything must be perfect. Everything. Every push of the ball. Every run. Every stretch...... Perfect."

The hard pronunciation of "perfect" vibrated in our little conversation bubble. He leaned back up and laughed to himself as he took a large bite of his buttered toast. "But we will see how you do, American." Ibrahim said with a grin on his face.

"I tell you this because I don't want you to get your hopes up, but they bring you here to make money off of you, not to put you on the first team."

"Why not? I thought that was the whole purpose of the academy."

"Pfff." He began rising from his seat. "Oh boy. You Americans are truly a special group of people. You believe everything you see on TV. Come on. We need to get over to the bus."

The classes were challenging and I felt lost on that first day, primarily due to the language barrier. Everything was in Catalan, the national language. I had a translator to help me but she seemed to always be a step or two behind the teacher, which made her more of a distraction.

The coaching staff told me that education was very important to the academy, which was very appealing to Moms and Pops, but for me education had little to do with my life goal. Soon the monotony of the day went away and I was finally on the green training pitch. The soft thumps of balls being knocked back and forth echoed on the field. Ibrahim and I warmed up together. The whistle blew and the session began.

There were drills designed to quicken your foot speed and build stamina, but the ball was always there in some way. After a demanding practice I stayed out on the pitch to run some extra drills by myself while everyone else hit the showers in preparation for dinner.

The stink of my performance that night weighed heavily on my mind as I ran through drills that I had been doing by myself back home in the States. I had just finished my pendulum drills full of quick touches, before a few other kids emerged from the locker room and a game of two on two was started.

Before I knew he was my roommate, I was impressed with Oier Perez's ability on the ball. His movements were deceptive and quick and he seemed to read the game very well. He was short and small. In a way he kind of reminded me of my cousin, Smally, in St. Vincent, both because of the way he was built and the way he turned into a bothersome presence when he lost the ball.

"You play well. What is your name?" he said as he sat on the grass stretching his legs.

"Japeth. You?"

"Oier Perez" his chest puffed out when he said it.

"Are you from Spain?"

A flame seemed to burn in his eye. "No. I am from Catalonia. Sant Pol Del Mar."

Over dinner I learned that Sant Pol Del Mar was a beachside village where life was similar to Venice, California. Aside from surfing and the walkways where people would roller blade near the beach, I had no idea what that meant. When I thought of California images of Compton, South Central and Dr. Dre videos came to mind.

I started training with the Line B team and spent weeks learning the principles and tactics of playing for Catalonia. The Line B team was the lower performing bunch of players ages fourteen and fifteen. The guys looked at me with shame as if I were a charity case. There I was struggling with kids a year or two younger than I and these were the worst of the group. My steely confidence had taken a hit and for weeks I floundered while Oier shined with the Line A team in our proper age group.

Ibrahim's words played on repeat in my mind, "They bring you here to make money off of you, not to put you on the first team." I started to believe it and my dream began to dilute. I was free falling into an average mind state. I would find ways to sneak alcohol or cold medicine into my room. I would drink either or both to force myself to sleep. I had a building feeling that I was going to be cut from the program and that would mean losing all of the security that we had as a family.

Everything rested on me and I felt like I was letting everyone down, including Mike and Landon. During this time, the nightmares were more frequent and so I increasingly drank more at night in hopes that I could sleep more deeply and not see those graphic images.

My conversations with Pops and Moms helped, but more so acted as a band-aid than the true mechanical fix. Oier believed in my ability and tried to help build my confidence, pointing out areas where I had been successful and telling me things that the coaching staff said to him about me, like: "Japeth has such great control of the ball, his decisions just need to be better."

Everyday passed the same. Breakfast in the morning, school until three o'clock, a short break or study time, then practice from six to eight in the evening. What changed was the dynamic or the feelings that went along with those days. Most days I was sad and frustrated, but there was the occasional glimpse of joy when I was just hanging with Oier and Ibrahim.

A couple of months passed and Coach Artiga pulled me aside before practice started that evening. He told me to come to his office after the training session. During practice, my mind was consumed and I couldn't focus on playing. As a result, I played horribly.

In the shower I was so distracted by my thoughts that I didn't even bother to cup my balls and male member as I usually did in the open prison style shower. I tried to have positive thoughts about the meeting, but I knew they were going to let me go. By the time I was done dressing, I decided I would go to college when I got back to the States. I planned on joining Malcolm and Jalani at UCLA.

My steps were slow and tense, leading me to the office where my dream would end. I knocked on the office door, even though everything inside of me wanted to turn around and run. A voice responded so quietly that it seemed to slide under the door. I turned the knob and there stood Coach Artiga and The Coach. Coach Artiga pointed for me to sit in a chair that rested just a few short feet inside of the door.

"Hey guys, before you say anything. Let me start. I want to say I'm sorry. I let you guys down. I know you have to send me home. It's hard for me to accept that. This is my only dream in life and it sucks that I can't really pull it off, but I understand."

"Japeth." The Coach chimed in, "We're not sending you

home." His Dutch accent gave lots of "shhh" sounds to his sentence. "You have nothing to worry about. We know it can be hard to adjust to life here. You are away from home, in another country with many things to get used to. The football will come. I have seen you myself and have no doubt that you will go very far here." His hand massaged my shoulder as he stood over me.

Coach Artiga added, "Yes, Japeth. Your talent is undeniable. It will take time to learn the system and how we play here at Catalonia. That is why we have you with a younger team."

"I know, but I'm struggling to play with those guys. I just don't know if I can make it with players my own age. I thought that both of you might be feeling the same."

"No. Nothing of the sort. Listen, we're flying in your parents for an additional weekend this month. You need family support very much at times like this. Our system is easy once it's in your blood, but the injection of it can be tough. We realize this and try to help the process along as best we can. Some make it. Some do not, but I have been watching you and I think you have what it takes to be a great star in this game."

The Coach's words, accompanied by Coach Artiga's approving look, were the sunshine bursting through the dark clouds. When Moms and Pops came the following weekend, I was already in better spirits.

Seeing and talking to him heightened my energy and suddenly the engine of that dream was chugging again. Not roaring quite yet, but the pistons were beginning to fire.

Chapter Forty-Two

MY FIRST COUPLE MONTHS at the academy gave me insight as to why Ibrahim struggled with the demand for perfection. In simply being part of La Joventut it was guaranteed that you could play anywhere in Una Legua, Spain's top football division. Ibrahim was in Catalonia long enough to develop a "good enough" attitude.

His family fought so hard to get out of Senegal that they felt the world owed them a favor. Nearly every word they spoke dripped of it. They'd say things like, "Why should I break my back doing this? I get paid whether I do it or not." I've had to do things that I didn't care about to advance in life, but this was football. I just couldn't understand how someone could treat the game in that fashion.

I reapplied myself, burning away the pity and self-doubt that nearly swallowed me whole. I didn't drink as much alcohol and cold medicine at night.

I had the thought that if I could flood my mind with positive images of success for thirty minutes before I went to sleep that I could drown out the images of death. The nightmares we're still there, but there were less of them.

Armed with my change in attitude, I begun to skyrocket through the youth ranks at Catalonia and eventually earned a starting spot on the reserve team. I even got the occasional call to sit on the bench of the first team.

It was an honor to be within the same twenty-two names as players I could only read about a couple years before. It turned out I wasn't the only one beginning to find success as a footballer.

Cam was picked up by the Los Angeles Chivas and they were spending their pre-season in Spain. Mama was able to put us in touch with each other. We talked briefly on the phone and planned to meet in his hotel lobby a few days after he arrived.

He was easy to spot when I arrived in their hotel lobby that Saturday evening. He had grown an inch or two and was now about five feet eleven inches, just an inch shorter than myself. He shuffled his way towards me with that same deceptive pigeon toed walk.

We reminisced about old times as we sat at the oak bar that night. The bar nearly invisible if it weren't for the random neon lights that hung on the wall spelling out the names of Catalonian beers. The lobby transitioned into a party spot during the late night hours, but we stayed and talked amongst the crazy party attendees.

A few beers and we were chatterboxes like we were back hanging out by the post office in Bagga. His mother was doing well, but he still had heavy resentment towards his father who lived in London. Blue was still playing in Trinidad and playing well. "He had an offer to go to the States too, but he said they ain have enough money." I shook my head. Blue hadn't changed one bit.

"Markee and Hulk gone to England to try out for a first division team."

I nodded. "Didn't you try out for some teams there too?"

"Yeah, but it ain work out. Them man say I ain tackle enough. I's a boss on di pitch, me ain no tackla!"

I touched on a nerve and quickly tried to soothe it. "Well, you already know how they do. It's nothing but long ball and hard tackles over there. It fits a player more like Hulk."

"True. That's why I ain sweatin it."

"What about Cat Eye? What's he up to?" I asked.

He sucked his teeth creating a disapproving squeal. "He gave up ball you know? He said a man from SVG can't make it in the game, so it's a waste a time. I try to push him, but he naw listen to me. I just hope he keeps his head straight. You know he's a man who could mix up in thing easy."

Cat Eye and Jack were similar in that way – easily mixed up in things. I heard that Jack got caught driving with three kilos in Lafayette on his way back from Chicago. I was sad when I heard the news, but rationalized that it was better jail then hearing he was dead.

I still carried that fear around that I was going to hear that DBrown or Jack were killed, but so far they'd beaten the odds so I was becoming less worried. When I met with Cam, Jack was still on trial but it was pretty much a given that he was going to do some time. It was only a matter of how long. I explained that situation to Cam and shared my fear for my little brother Damian.

I asked Dave one favor before I left and that was to make sure that he had all Vice Lords looking out for Damian. I didn't want him to be able to join the gang and I didn't want him getting harmed by anyone else. He was a good kid, with no real demons that I knew of, and I wanted to keep it that way.

"What about that guy... What's he name? Choco?"

"Man...Choco. Choco got into some shit with some GD's in jail. Shit didn't go right. They stabbed his ass up in his cell while he was sleep. Over one hundred holes."

"You alright dred?"

"Yeah, I'm good. Just funny how somebody is here one day then just like that, they're gone. Well, on to brighter things. So how you end up with the Chivas anyway?"

"That was crazy breda. So I'm down in Trinidad playing for my team. Just a regular league game. I doing me thing you know. Running di field, controlling di ball. Well after the game, a man come up and say him want me to come for a tryout in the States. I was thinking this man is bullshittin me, right?" He paused and took a swig of his beer.

"Well long story short, he was for real...he organized di plane ticket and thing for me to go LA. I went, did my thing and them man make a good offer. Team jamming good right now too."

"Oh yeah. I have a few buddies of mine who are playing for UCLA over there in LA."

"Yeah man! I think I met them. Malcolm, Jalani, and Shane? Them man can play."

"When you meet them?"

"Chivas play them in a scrimmage game. Good team, man. They win the national championship last year." Talking to him brought back great memories, as well as a few bad ones. The conversation forced me to verbalize issues that I didn't with Oier or Ibrahim.

I spoke about how the word around Kokomo was that, that fat fuck Jason set Jack up. The story of Kim tearing my heart to pieces when she cheated on me with that fat fuck Jason. An expression of my fear that I may lose my mother way before I felt I should.

Our booze filled conversation, full of passion, failures and ambitions, continued long into the night. We exchanged email addresses and messenger names. We promised to stay in touch. A manly hug between us and we both went back to our worlds and mine was about to change forever.

Chapter Forty-Three

WE LANDED IN KIEV on a Sunday afternoon, greeted by a mob of press. The majority of the aggressive crowd attacked The Coach and I. They had many questions about my selection into the team for such a crucial UEFA Champions League match. This was before social media, so hardly any of this so called informed press saw me play. All they knew was that I was an American and Americans could not play football.

The rumbles had grown to a roar. The displeasure that I was selected to the first team at all was always an issue. It was worse now that I was selected over my roommate, Oier Perez. The Catalonians, especially, were not happy that an American was taking a spot on the team over another Catalonian.

That night as I watched the news and other shows I saw how they poked fun at my baggy jeans and hat tilted to the left. Some of it was outright racist. I had my team's support, but I felt very alone.

Over the next couple days, I began to form a closer

friendship with the star Brazilian attacking midfielder, Breo. We talked before, but it was always professional. Witnessing the emotional stress that I was under, he kept me under his wing and helped me deflect the ill feelings I felt.

THE TEMPERATURE MUST HAVE BEEN around fifteen degrees on that April day. The Coach told me to be ready because he may need to use me. "Been ready," was my reply to which he just laughed.

The match didn't start well for us. After seven minutes we were down 1-0 after a Kiev United forward capitalized on a blundered save. The match was competitive for the remainder of the first half with a lot of back and forth action.

Breo showed a few moments of brilliance with some penetrating runs deep into the heart of Kiev's defense. We went into the halftime break with high spirits, hoping to take it up a level for the second half.

Again, at the start of the second half, Kiev scored early. It was almost as if you could see the life drain out of the team. A few minutes into the second half, Coach pulled me from the bench and told me to warm up. My body vibrated from nerves and the frigid temperature. The UEFA Champions League quarterfinal was being televised in the USA and would be my first time playing as a professional.

I warmed up for fifteen minutes. Coach motioned for me with a wave of his hand. I stood in front of him and he looked me in the eye with his hands on my shoulders and said, "In for Cardona. Take us home."

Running onto the pitch at the sixty-two minute mark, I immediately heard racists taunts of "nigger boy," "monkey," and animal noises in the roar of the home crowd. It was scary but suddenly the words of Pops' speech to me on that beach in Layou came to mind and I knew I had to make it my fuel.

It felt like there was a slow motion movie playing in my head that was showing all the moments and lessons I learned in St. Vincent, playing for Dynamo, and the last two years at La Joventut.

At the seventieth minute mark, Breo intercepted a ball in our defensive third and sprung it to me out on the left wing a little past the half field line. I had already taken a quick glance at the defense's positioning.

I received the ball and turned quickly. The defender trailing behind me paused in anticipation of my next move. I took a touch to my left then cut inside and ran past him. The ball approached a second defender. He tried to beat me to it.

I got there first and pushed it left around him and into open space as I ran to his right. The path of the ball and I created a wishbone shape. I caught up to it about twenty yards out. The keeper had begun to rush out of the goal. Boop!! I chipped the ball over him and into the goal.

Our small number of supporters and team bench exploded. I lost my mind. I was so excited that I ran over to the TV cameraman screaming and throwing up a Vice Lord sign, then pounding my chest in triumph. I kissed the crest on my jersey.

Then I lifted my jersey, exposing a t-shirt with the flag of my heritage - Gold, Green, and Blue, three diamonds sitting perfectly in the middle. I screamed into the camera "Mike and Landon! That was for yall!"

The excitement caused my heart to beat fast, releasing tiny burst of joy that would not allow me to stop smiling. I wanted those few short minutes to last forever. At the eighty-sixth minute I tucked in a curling shot to the corner, cementing our position in the semi-final.

That game lit a fire inside of me. Most of the press finally accepted me and suddenly in a matter of two hours I had gone from lonely and sad to elated and famous worldwide.

On the plane I remembered a quote Pops always said, "When you start making money, don't stop to count it." My goal was closer, but I still was not there. All the doubts about my talent and what I could do were erased for a night. For that night and the morning after I was the most talked about footballer on the planet. "The American Delivers!!!!" one of the headlines read the next day.

I played in my first league game that weekend. We won the game convincingly 7-1. I scored five. There were fifteen games left in the season and we were in a heated race against our archrival for the number one spot.

When I started playing we were in second place, six points behind our rival. In those fifteen games I managed to average an unprecedented three goals a game. I dazzled crowds with my wit, dribbling, and creativity. Every game was harder to score than the one prior. I still managed to get shots off and I paid the price many times receiving tough tackles and cheating punches to the face.

In those last few months of the season, I solidified a supreme confidence in my game. The Coach spoon-fed me extra doses of praise to help keep my confidence high and growing. The Coach knew the more confident and arrogant I felt about myself the better I would play.

He encouraged me to take advantage of all the extra attention from women. He even sent me few big name models, which I had fun with, but they weren't really my type - too skinny. He didn't have to tell me not to settle down, my first priority was football. I was just having fun and enjoying the spoils of being a football superstar.

For the final game of the Champions League that year, I was sore from the beatings I had taken in league play and I was nursing a bruised right ankle, but somehow I still managed to play in the game against FC Milan.

On that chilled evening against Milan the whole team seemed to be a step off. Our passes weren't quite connecting and we weren't reading each other properly. I was able to break through the tough Italian defense a couple of times but I was missing that next gear I usually had due to the ankle injury. With all that said, I was able to volley home a goal from a left wing cross with my injured right foot. I could have sworn that I'd broken my ankle as bursts of pain exploded through it.

Unfortunately, Milan hit the back of the net three times winning the game 3-1. Our spirits were dampened from the loss, but after the game in the locker room The Coach told us if we stayed together, we would win it the following year. He was so confident in this notion that he told the press the same thing.

The press was hard on me in particular for our loss, saying that I lacked the big game mentality. I thought that finishing the season as Una Legua champions by one point over our rivals proved that I was a winner, but I was wrong. It wasn't enough. It was the beginning of me learning that no matter how big the accomplishment, it was never enough.

Chapter Forty-Four

DURING THE SUMMER BREAK, I went back to Kokomo for a few weeks in May and Damian and I visited the Pendleton jail where Jack was serving his time. The jangle of chains and heavy steps against the concrete floor caught my attention. Behind the protective glass a thicker bodied Jack appeared and squatted down onto the circular stool. He sat down and we both picked up the phone that rested on each side.

"What took you so long?" He started the conversation.

"You know where I been, dude."

"Of course I know. Happy for you, my dude. I hear shits going good for you out there. That soccer shit is really paying off, huh? I should have stayed my ass in the game. I would have been right out there with you, my dude."

"How you holding up in here?" I asked.

He replied that it was shitty, giving the security officer a look of disgust. We continued for about five minutes, with him doing most of the talking. He was struggling with the loss of

Mrs. Johnson, who had passed a few months prior from cancer. I had spoken with her before she moved onto the next life and knew that her heart was heavy with disappointment over Jack.

"Some people just going to be who they gonna be. My lord knows I did my best with 'im," she expressed to me. "Japeth, I'm so proud of you. Out there showing 'em black folk can play soccer too," she laughed lightly. "I can't wait to see you on TV, boy." She never got to see that goal against Kiev United.

A few minutes into Jack's conversation with Damian, the security guard let us know that we had two more minutes. A light that had briefly come to his eyes, the old Jack, blew out at the sound of the security guard's voice like a candle in the wind.

Damian and I didn't talk much on the way home. I was lost in my thoughts of Jack, and how prison had changed him. It was eerie to think of how close I was to ending up with the same fate, the only difference was I never got caught. Damian jolted me out of my sobering thoughts.

"That place is depressing. I never want to go there again Jay." I glanced over at Damian. He was staring at the road ahead, his face void of expression.

"Yeah, it is. And we didn't even see the inside, you know?"

"Yeah, I know. That's what's scary. I was looking around that place when we were waiting. Place feels like death, man. Worst part is Jack. He's so cool. So cool. I don't know what it is about him, Jay, but he looks cold."

"Yeah, I know," I said.

That night we had dinner at a family style mega buffet restaurant. While chowing down on an overflowing plate, Moms and Pops took the opportunity to drill their parental speeches into me yet another time. The topics ranged from money management to girls to home maintenance. Uncle Jimmy was with us too and of course he added his two cents.

The sight of an ailing family patriarch made the speeches

bearable and somewhat understandable. His body was feebler than I'd ever seen it. His voice was also shakier. A few kids ran up to the table, excitement and nervousness filling their bodies. In Spain, I couldn't go out without receiving attention so I recognized the look in those kid's eyes.

I prepared myself, wiping my mouth with a napkin when they opened their mouths and asked for an autograph from my little brother - Damian the high school basketball star. That old twinge of jealousy panged within me.

"Japeth, you was thinking them boys were coming for you?" Uncle Jimmy laughed out loud until tears fell from his eyes. Pops and Moms joined in with a few of their own jokes.

I laughed about the situation as well but underneath, it burned me up that even though I had become a world footballing superstar, I still didn't matter as much as the local high school basketball star in my own home town. In this case it was my brother, which made it both easier and harder to swallow.

Before we left the restaurant, I ran into an old acquaintance from high school, Erika Julane. "Hi Japeth!" she exclaimed as she jogged toward me, her bubbly smile bringing a high energy to the environment.

"Hey, what's up?"

"It's been so long! How are you?" Her voice hitting a higher pitch and hanging onto the last syllable at the end of every sentence.

"I'm good. Are you working here now?"

She rolled her blue eyes. "Yes. I have to make some money during the summer before I go back to school."

"What school do you go to?"

"IU."

"How is everything down there at IU?"

"So awesome. I love it down there. It's so fun. School's a bit of a bore, but once I get into the Kelley School of Business, hopefully it will get better. And you… Mister big soccer star!"

"Yeah well…I'm not bored for sure. I love my football so I'm having a blast."

"I'm friends with a few guys on the IU team and they just can't believe that I went to school with you. They didn't even believe me at first until I showed them your picture in the yearbook. Come to think of it, there's a guy on there who says he knew you too."

"Who?" I knew Dready had already graduated and was playing professionally in the States.

"Billy Mouser."

"Oh yeah! I used to play ball with him up in Fort Wayne a few years ago. Tell him I said what up?"

"Okay. Oh! And you remember Walter Henandez? Little Mexican kid who was real good at soccer too? He's down there as a walk on. He was starting during the spring season, so I think he might get to play during the fall. Who knows though. When those recruits come in…."

Her voice faded away. She glanced over at a manager. "Well, hey, I better get back to work. Call me later. Do you have my number?" I shook my head no, so she wrote her number down on a white napkin and handed it to me. I called her later that night and I told her that I would come pick her up so that we could hangout. When I picked her up we talked briefly, then we ended up having sex.

"I've always wanted to do that with you," she said finally.

"Why didn't you?"

She looked at me as if I was stupid and said, "You were with Kim! I didn't want to deal with her."

My mood dampened for a quick minute at the thought of my ex-girlfriend. I still had strong feelings for her that I couldn't shake but I buried the thought and regained my senses.

On the drive back to her house she laughed a lot and even

when she wasn't laughing, she was smiling. I hoped that she didn't ask that question I heard so many times in different languages over the past few months. I hated answering that question, but my answer was always the same.

I pulled up in front of her two-story house and she leaned over and kissed me on my neck. "So where does this leave us?" I was on automatic pilot when I responded, "You're a great person. I had a great time with you tonight, but I can't get into anything serious right now. I'm just at a place in my life where I can only commit to one thing and that's my career."

I always gave a little break to let the words sink in then continued with, "I hope you understand where I'm coming from." It was my standard I just wanted to fuck line, but it was also the truth.

Chapter Forty-Five

IT BROUGHT A SMILE TO MY FACE to watch Moms pull up in her new cream Maserati. The positive effects of her treatments radiated through her smooth, clear skin. It was quite a magical thing to think that through realizing my dreams I was able to fulfill the dreams of others. That was worth more than the money.

I would occasionally ride around the old neighborhood in Moms car, seeing a lot of faces that I didn't recognize. I would drive past the park and it would be empty. On one of my rides around the neighborhood, I saw a few acquaintances heading into the community center. I stopped and talked to them for a few minutes.

"Man, these young folks ain't the same as us. They don't hang like that. Little mutha fuckas be inside playing video games and shit."

I found myself lost in my memories as this old acquaintance spoke, but shook free in time to catch his invitation to a party later at The Place to Play. The *Kokomo Perspective* came by my house to interview me later that afternoon.

The reporter was an older gentleman that I remembered seeing at Damian's games a few years prior. We talked about my life in Spain and my recent selection to the men's US national team. When he asked if I felt that the US could make it to a final, or even win a World Cup in the near future seeing that they made it to the quarter final in 1994 I answered, "Not without me."

"That's not off the record is it, Mr. Walker?"

"Why would that need to be off the record? It's the plain truth and everyone knows it. This is not a secret." My supreme confidence had deep roots in the fact that I worked so hard and endured so much to get to that point.

I thought I was destined to be the best footballer in the world. When you can literally see something bigger than you at work in your life, as evidenced in my life by close calls with death and danger, it's impossible not to sound arrogant or cocky to those who do not understand that aura.

When the interview was over we had dinner as a family, a dinner filled with stories and updates that made us laugh and some that made us reflect on how fortunate we were to be healthy and alive. From time to time I'd glace over at Moms and be reminded of her sickness. Her body had filled out a little bit, but still wasn't back to its regular size. All reports from the doctor continued to be good, but I was still uncomfortable with the thought of Moms having cancer.

Later that night I went up to the Place to Play with Z, who just arrived from one of his trips up to Chicago. The spot was an old game room that was converted into a party space. We stepped into the heavy smoke filled room and I saw faces that I knew. Finally, that piece of home came back to me. I showed love to all my people then glimpsed Trish across the room. I walked over to her.

"Shout out to Jay in house." the DJ shouted into the mic. I raised my beer in acknowledgement to the crowd.

"What's up, Trish?"

"Hey."

"How you doing?"

"I'm fine." She wouldn't look at me and seemed bothered that I was even talking to her.

"Well, I thought we could talk but I guess not. See you another time." I started to walk off.

"Japeth." I turned back to her. The party light flashed across her face and revealed some swelling on the right side of her forehead.

"I'm sorry. I do want to talk."

"What happened to your head?" I asked.

"Oh nothing. Bumped it on the sink this morning."

She asked me how I was and congratulated me. "You was always talking about how you were going to be a soccer star." She said that she and Kim spoke about me all the time and I took the opportunity to ask about Kim.

"She lives in Indianapolis now. She was going to come down tonight, but she ended up not making it."

"Aww that sucks. It would have been nice to see her. How's she doing though? She live by herself?"

"No, she got a boyfriend she living with down there."

"How long she been with him?"

"About a year now." I wanted to ask more but held back.

I noticed a guy approaching us from the corner of my eye as the dance floor became full when Noreaga's "I Love My Life" came blasting through the speakers.

We made eye contact as he walked across me to get to Trish. She quickly introduced me but didn't reveal his name. He immediately excused himself and Trish. I eyed them through the cloud of smoke. I asked Z if he knew anything about Trish's boyfriend. He told me that he was new to town and came from St. Louis. He was a cousin of a few of our friends.

I was at the bar waiting for another beer when I saw a group of people heading toward the door. I followed the crowd outside where I saw Trish and her boyfriend fighting in the middle of the street. The fight was not one sided so the crowd just stood around and watched. I was uneasy, but there looked to be a chance that she would handle him so I let it go.

Seconds passed then suddenly he seemed to get an extra burst of strength that she couldn't match. He swung a wild desperate punch that hit her flush in the face. The cracking sound was explosive and jarring like the sound of a Blackcat firecracker. She hit the ground and fell into an unconscious state.

The crowd stood still. I started pushing through from the rear of the audience. When I reached the front, I was getting ready to swing on the guy. Then Trish's little cousin emerged and beat me to it. He began slicing into her boyfriend.

The fury-blinded boy, who couldn't have been more than fourteen years old, was turning Trish's boyfriend into a human sprinkler. A group of guys jumped in to defend Trish's boyfriend and then the whole scene turned to a melee of violence. I backed away, confused about what side was which in the violent bunch.

The sound of gunshots cracked through the air and everyone bolted off in different directions. The sound of sirens could be heard off in the distance. I took off and ran through familiar alleys and yards and made it home quickly without ever being tracked by the police.

The next day the front page of the *Kokomo Perspective* read, "Two dead, seven injured, two arrests in late night brawl." I thought to myself that if it wasn't for Trish's cousin being a step quicker, I could have been among the dead, injured, or arrested. Again good fate intervened and I was thankful, but I also knew that I couldn't continue to put myself in compromising positions. I couldn't risk my destiny.

Chapter Forty-Six

WHEN I ARRIVED IN LOS ANGELES for national team training camp the skinny kid who set the world on fire a few months before had transformed. I was stronger, leaner, with more powerful legs. In the locker room, I changed into my training kit for the day while the guys cracked jokes about me eating, saying that I had finally gotten over my eating disorder.

Every time I stepped on that practice pitch, the echo of voices from La Joventut played in the surround sound theater of my mind. I heard them talk about the USA as if we were the kid who never got picked for gym class.

I felt Americans deserved more than to be the joke of the football community. It pissed me off to see American players and coaches be complacent with the attitude that Americans weren't as good as other countries in football.

I knew that from playing on a few US youth national teams that there would be a few of these kinds of players on the team. When it came to the US national teams, I did have a reputation for being very demanding. I transferred the attitude of striving to achieve perfection that was ingrained in me at the academy and the desperation to overcome adversity from my background, to my US teammates.

I was trying to raise the bar on our level of play as a nation and selfishly I didn't want their bad habits to rub off on me and lower my play. My former Dynamo FC teammates, Malcolm, Jalani, Larry, and Bryan, appeared to have a similar mindset and practiced like their life depended on it, but as I predicted that fire was missing in some of the other members on the team.

This one player in particular kept giving the ball away during a keep away, possession oriented game. He was laughing and talking about basketball with another player. When he lost possession again, I jumped in his face and cussed him out.

"Hey dude, kiss my ass okay? Fucking asshole."

I crashed my fist against his mouth. His head whipped around and his body followed. I balanced myself over him. "Boy you really don't know who you fucking with. I ain one of your bitch ass talk and do nothing friends. I will fuck you up."

The team captain shoved me from over the guy on the ground. "Get away from him, dude! Fucking prick."

"Shut up. This ain even got nothing to do with you." Malcolm held me back from attacking the captain.

The captain stared at me blankly then said, "Dude you're an asshole." By this point the head coach, Sampson Ludvig, stepped in and cancelled practice for the day. He shouted for me to meet him in his office immediately.

My anger continued to simmer as I walked slowly through the locker room and to his office. He stared me into his presence then he gave me a slight shove across the threshold.

"What the hell you push me for?"

"Sit down!"

"Man, you ain bout to just be yelling at me like you crazy."

"Sit down." I felt as though I had won that fight. Series tied at 1-1. He got me with the shove into the office.

"Just what the hell is your problem, Japeth? You run around out there like you're some kind of raging drill sergeant, shouting at the guys every minute. That's my job, not yours."

"Well coach—" He cut my sentence off immediately.

"I'm not finished." I felt another pang of disrespect as he reclaimed a leadership position between the two of us.

"Now, no one will ever say that you are not talented. Probably the most talented player the US has ever produced."

"Probably?" The shock in my voice made obvious by the way it cracked. He narrowed his eyes in at me again telling me to shut up.

"Yeah *probably,* because you're a piece of shit teammate. You really think these guys are going to go to war with you when you're smacking'em and cussing at'em like that? I want to kill you and I'm not even on the field with you. Sure you can play, but you can't do it alone. You *need* those other ten guys out there with you. You better get your shit straight, son."

"Son? I only have one father, Sampson."

"God Damn it!" The base of his clinched fist pounded against the desk. He rose from his chair and stared down on me.

"I'm trying to help you out here. Can you just shut up for five seconds! God Damn it! In all my years I've never had someone so talented be so fucking stupid! And I've had some pretty stupid son of a bitches."

"Listen. You can call me a piece of shit teammate all day, but the fact is that I don't have these problems with my club team. You ever think about that? You ever hear anything in the press about me having problems with my Catalonia team? No, you haven't. That's because I don't have to force them to see how important it is to take the game seriously. Here, that's the shit that annoys the hell out of me. The players don't care whether they win or lose and as a matter of fact they pretty much expect to lose. You can see it in the way the practice and play. You don't do shit, so I have to step in take on that role. I'm helping you keep your job, so you should be thanking me."

He shoved his body back into his office chair. "Get the fuck out of here and don't bother coming to practice tomorrow or to the game this weekend."

I never saw the battle for supremacy ending like that. I never would have imagined he would pull me from the team since his job was on the line after several losses and I was his star player. Baffled at first, I stayed in my seat and glared at him across his messy desk.

"You're a fucking cunt, you know that? I can't wait til they fire your ass and bring a real coach in here." I stormed out, threw on some shorts and t-shirt and darted out of the locker room.

The closer I got to my car in the parking lot the more the hurt began to surface. I shoved my way through a small group of media who were already asking questions about what happened at practice that day.

One cameraman in particular lodged himself in front of my car door, the rapid clicks of his shutter catching my naked hurt that I thought was visible to all. "Move!" He took a few extra clicks.

For the second time that day, my hand made contact harshly with a face. There were screams of pain from the ground where the man lay, his face in his hands. I snatched the camera from around his neck, jerking him around on the ground in the process before raising the camera behind my head then slamming it down against the concrete. SMASH!!!! The pieces of the camera seemed to be running away from each other. I kicked one of the larger pieces.

The picture of me kicking the smashed camera was the visual seen around the world with the story of my dismissal from the national team and assault on the cameraman. The more the cameras were around me, the more they saw my flaws and I hated it. I wanted to create a new, clean version of myself but these situations kept following me.

Chapter Forty-Seven

I LEFT LOS ANGELES and went straight to Catalonia. I had a drink and went to sleep as soon as I arrived at my condo. The next day The Coach was knocking on my door. I let him in.

"Hey Coach. What's up?"

"How have you been Japeth?"

"To be honest coach, I've been better."

"I'm sure you have."

"Would you like something to drink?" I asked.

"Yes. Water please." I grabbed The Coach a bottle of water from the nearby kitchen.

"Thank you."

I lead The Coach through the short hall and down the three small steps into my living room and we took our seats on the plush couches.

"Well son, you've got quite a mess here."

"Yeah."

"What happened?" I explained the situation to him.

"Your feelings are certainly understandable, but your

reactions are immature and lack any kind of thought. Your thinking is flawed, Japeth, although your intentions are good." He paused for a moment and took a sip of his water.

"Look, son. I'm not here to judge you. As far as I'm concerned, you do your job for the club so there's no consequence here. As for me, I personally care about you as a person. I don't want to see you get hurt or worse, get yourself killed. It seems spanish to me for you to act this way, but it's your life."

The Coach nibbled on his bottom lip for a few seconds then exhaled hard through his nose. He then rose from his seat on the couch. "I'll see you at practice tomorrow," he said as he walked out my front door.

I dropped down on my king sized bed and turned on my five-disc CD changer. As I laid in bed, the thing that made me feel the worst was that Damian undoubtedly heard about the situation. I always felt a responsibility to set a good example for him and although we joked a lot on each other I knew he looked up to me. He copied nearly everything that I did. He saw the dedication that I gave to the game of football and he applied that to basketball.

He later told me that when he was younger, he didn't even know most people didn't take their craft that seriously. The way I went about things was the only way he knew how to do it so it was normal for him, which is why I feared the influence this incident might have on him even though he was already in high school. I called him later that day and explained everything to him and he understood. With a clear conscience, I was able to return to training camp.

I found refuge on our practice fields. The large rectangle of perfectly manicured grass releasing that fresh natural smell. The grounds slightly softened from the daily watering. In that space there was only football. The Coach pulled me to the side one day during practice. "You know, if you keep playing at this level this year, you could be voted as the best player in the world." He looked me in my eyes to make sure I got his message. When he seemed satisfied, he sent me back to train with a "Keep it up son".

Two years passed and I still had not received that award. I lead the Catalonia team in scoring every year. I won the golden boot for Una Legua every year. I lead Catalonia to two UEFA Champions League titles back to back. I embarrassed our rival with multiple goal performances and maintained an undefeated record against them in the last two seasons.

I did not react negatively when crowds across Europe threw bananas at me, made ape noises and called me a nigger although I was very close to jumping into the stands and whopping some ass on several occasions. Despite all of this, I still was not recognized.

I was a revered figure within the communities of Catalonia. I was given the nickname Déu, which is "God" in Catalan. If you knew anything about how spiritual and how seriously the Catalan people revere the church, you'd understand how high of an honor that is.

It was summer again and after spending a summer in Brazil with Breo and another in Kokomo, I was ready to try something different. I decided to spend the next summer in New York City.

Greg and I stayed in touch over the years and he was known as one of the best lyricists in hip-hop. That summer he was getting ready to release his third studio album called *I Am Me*. I knew Greg as a boy on the stoop, but he got involved in the streets of Brooklyn in his teen years. He didn't get too deep into the drug game but it was deep enough to threaten his life.

After a botched robbery left Greg with two bullets in his back, he refocused himself back on the music. While we ate at a high-end restaurant in New York, he mentioned that he was thinking about starting his own music company.

He said he was tired of the executives trying to push his music in a pop direction. "If my music ain't about truth then it ain't about shit. They want me to sound like MC Hammer but that's his truth. It's not mine. You see what happened when he tried to be gangsta. They don't care though, they just want to sell."

I was gently cutting through my steak when our waiter came over and told me that Mr. Faraldo would like to see me at his table. The waiter nodded his head to the right toward a large circular table with several older men sitting around it. Their tailored suits had a little glimmer under the muted restaurant lighting.

I put my napkin on the table and walked over to them. Mr. Faraldo motioned his hand for me to sit in the empty seat next to him.

"Hello fellas, how can I help you?"

The table of six guys looked at me. No expression. No response. Finally, a short fat man spoke.

"You's Jahpeth Walker, right?"

"Japeth. Yes"

"I told you fucks that was him! This fucking guy cost me thirty grand against Milan! The fuckin guy isn't from this planet!"

I began looking for the different exits. There were two cups of hot coffee and a jagged steak knife within reach. But my mind began to ease at the sound of laughter.

They were very free in showering praise on me for my talent. After a few minutes of talking I thanked them for the glass of wine then took a picture with them as a group before going back to the table with Greg.

We finished our dinner, had a few drinks, then stepped into Greg's chauffeured black SUV. I got the impression that he felt insulted that they recognized me and not him.

One of the Saturday nights I was in New York, Cam happened to be playing against the New York/New Jersey Metrostars. I took a couple of my younger cousins to Cam's game and he played extremely well. I can't even remember a time he gave away possession. The ending score was 0-0 and it was an entertaining game but not nearly as interesting as the rest of the night.

Chapter Forty-Eight

AFTER THE GAME Cam signed a few autographs and I did the same. The reporters that were there asked me about my thoughts on the game and I told them that I was impressed with the level of competition in US league.

Cam and I met up later that night at a spot I was renting for the summer. We drank a few shots then left to join the New York nightlife. The first spot we hit was supposed to be the hottest club in NYC at the time, Bungalow 8. The women in the club eyed shoes, watch, and your choice of drink before they even looked at your face. My six hundred dollar black leather shoes and tailor made button up shirt signaled money to them, so a few women asked me with their eyes to engage in conversation.

That night I was not in the mood to deal with a random hook up, especially with that type of woman. She would want to hear about the best hotels in the world, food, clothes, and any thing about a rich lifestyle that she could add to her own collection of wealthy things to try or talk about. I had a nice lunch and threesome earlier with two beautiful women from Puerto Rico.

My needs were met for the day.

We left Bungalow 8 around 3am and decided to hit up a Vincy basement party in Brooklyn. The music at Bungalow 8 was pretty good, but the high-energy blend of hip-hop and R&B vibes fizzled to a slow death in the standing crowd.

I called a car service to come pick us up from the club. We arrived in the Crown Heights section of Brooklyn at a quarter to four in the morning. The soca music was thumping all the way out in the street. We walked past a few people smoking or having private conversations in the dark driveway on the way to the basement entrance.

The basement had a cellar entrance with steep steps leading down to a near pitch black area. We were about to disappear down into that darkness when someone shouted out, "Cam!?" Both Cam and I turned around. Cam recognized the guy as a classmate from Barrouille Secondary School. They shared a quick embrace then Cam introduced me to the guy nicknamed Shut, because he used to always block domino games.

"You ain have to tell me who this is. Ya forget me is a footballer? How me ain goin know the best player in the world." He shook my hand.

"Come lets go get something to drink." He escorted us down through the open cellar door and into the darkness of the basement, the ceiling only about four or five inches higher than my head. The only light in the basement was a string of Christmas lights that ran along one side.

There were some spots in the basement that were pitch black and others where the figures were silhouettes. The sweat on their skin glistened under the faint light as they whined and jumped to the tunes the DJ was playing. Shut grabbed us a few beers from behind a table at the back of the crowded room.

The party was full of thick, beautiful mostly Vincy women. In between jumping around, I danced with a couple of them.

The energy stayed high for the next hour with the drinks flowing, the music pumping, and everyone dancing.

In the midst of partying, I noticed that one of the shadowy silhouettes looked vaguely familiar. I glanced over a few times then realized that I did know who it was. I walked towards Joanne, Renell's friend from St. Vincent. My eyes strained in the darkness but I admired her tall, strong body.

The closer I got I could see that she had beautiful dark skin that seemed to glow under the Christmas lights. A flat stomach, toned arms and supple C cup size breasts. Her lower body was thick and curvy flowing outward from her small waist. Her legs were toned but full to compliment her round behind. She spotted and ran towards me, then wrapped her arms around my neck.

"Boy you ain change a bit, except for all this height" You look good man! Ya turn big star on me, huh? What you doing here in Brooklyn?"

"Taking some time to relax and live it up a bit."

We chit chatted for a few minutes then my favorite soca song at the time came on. The unmistakable beginning, with only the guitar strumming smoothly came through the speakers.

I grabbed Joanne's hand and positioned myself behind her as the song came in. That was the first song we danced to but we continued to dance together for the rest of the night.

At the end of the party I could not find Cam, so I went outside with Joanne figuring that I'd run into him eventually. The darkness outside was replaced with the morning light. The soft morning rays revealed Joanne's high cheekbones, perfect teeth and radiant dark skin. Her dark brown eyes held a sexiness that pulled me into her orb.

"You are absolutely beautiful," I said to her.

"Thank you but," she got closer to me, "you think that's going to get me to give you this?"

I laughed. I saw Cam walking down the street, back towards

the party house, with a girl he was dancing with earlier. One of my cousins was hanging out on the sidewalk with his wife and saying his goodbyes to a few other guys. He asked us if we wanted to go to breakfast with them.

I looked over at Joanne. She said she would only go if we made sure her friend that she came with got home safe. I called for car service, which arrived in fifteen minutes. I paid the driver then went to a local diner for breakfast where Joanne and I laughed and flirted with each other amongst the crowd.

The morning sun was at its full intensity when we arrived back at Joanne's apartment. I walked with her into the building where we hugged good bye in the common entrance and exchanged numbers. It was the beginning of one of the most important relationships in my life.

Chapter Forty-Nine

I SLEPT MOST OF THE NEXT DAY, which was a Sunday, occasionally waking up and checking my phone. There were several text messages, but none from Joanne. I went out that night with Charles. Every buzz in my pocket I quickly reviewed, but still nothing from Joanne.

There were a lot of women in the party that approached me that night, but for some reason I had no attraction to them. The next day, I finally received a text from Joanne that simply said, "Tomorrow?"

I responded "My flight leaves tomorrow night at 11:30. Can we do breakfast?"

"No. I work on Tuesday's. I can try to get off early and we can do an early dinner."

"What time?" I responded.

"Lets aim for 5."

"Any requests?"

"TOBU. Near where I work and I've heard good things."

The next day went by quickly. I spent most of the day

saying my goodbyes to family members around Brooklyn. That evening, I pulled up in front of TOBU's a little before five. Joanne arrived wearing a colorful flowing dress that seemed to playfully cling to her curves.

"I guess you look alright." I joked as I smiled.

"I know I look good but thank you, Mr. Walker. You could have done better, but this will work." She said as she straightened my collar.

We hugged each other then I alerted the host that we were ready to be seated. As we followed the host, Joanne reached out and placed her hand in mine. I looked back at her and she smiled in return.

During dinner she told me about how she moved to the States when she was fifteen. We talked about the types of jobs she had to do to pay for school, but she noted that the nursing degree was worth it. She also spoke about how her and Renell were not friends anymore.

The two stopped talking because Renell married Joanne's uncle who was in his sixties. "It would be different if it were for love, but I know all she looking for is the money."

When I checked the time and saw it was 7:43, I knew that I should have been leaving to get to the airport but I didn't want to. Reluctantly, I called for a car to pick us up. When I dropped her off, I escorted her to the main door of her building. We kissed and said our goodbyes. I promised to be in touch from Catalonia.

On the flight to Catalonia, I thought about Joanne. She managed to be everything I wanted in a woman without me saying a word.

There were even qualities about her that I did not know I wanted until I met her. I landed in Catalonia with a yearning to be back at the TOBU dinner table.

———————————

BLOOD PUMPED. THE BODY'S HEART beat nakedly without its usual skin to cover it. Eyes were staring at me. I screamed then realized it was yet another nightmare. When I finally fell back to sleep, I saw Mike, Jack and I laughing on the playground in elementary school. Then I saw him on the ground of his living room, lying lifeless. I awoke and called Joanne.

"Nightmares again, babe?"

"Yeah. I keep seeing both of them. I can't get rid of the images."

"You sure you don't want to tell the team doctors about it?"

"They'll think I'm crazy and that it will affect my play on the field."

"You ever think that might be true, babe?"

"Naw. If anything, its fuel."

"I don't know. You barely sleep. That can't be good for your body."

"Well that just means I have more time to talk to you."

"You're so stupid. I love your crazy butt, though."

"I love you too, babe."

"Okay. I gotta go. Patient needs me."

"Okay. Can't wait to see you next week."

"Me neither. Love you."

The first half of the season was almost finished and we were nearing the holiday break. The year was very bumpy thus far. The Coach decided that he wanted to use me as an attacking midfielder at the beginning of the season and moved Breo up front to the forward position.

I struggled in my new role. The press and fans were cruel to The Coach while I learned my teammates movements and particular likes. The Coach was called everything from a idiota, cony, cara de cul, to a canell del sexe. In English that's everything from an idiot, pussy, and ass face to a sex doll.

The fans couldn't understand why Coach would change a system that was working so well, had won us championships, and had us rivaling some of the best attacking teams in history. My name was synonymous with "merda" (shit).

During our last game before the break, I was knocked off the ball about thirty yards out from our goal. I thought I was fouled. The player who dispossessed me had one dribble then blasted a shot into the back of our net. My mistake cost us the game as we lost 2-1.

The next morning my phone rang at about 10:30, waking me out of a short sleep. I thought it was going to be Joanne, but instead it was The Coach on the other end.

"Did I wake you, son?"

"Yeah, it's alright though. What's up, Coach?"

"You want to meet me for a cup of coffee?"

"Uhhhhh. Yeah. Where you wanna meet?"

"Bar Queardi" he replied.

"Okay. Meet you there at twelve?"

"Sure."

I pressed the button on the phone and felt a pit in my stomach. Becoming more awake, I realized that I had to go out in public but I wanted to remain within the walls of my condo. I did not want to hear the anger of those fans on the street or even worse, see the look of disappointment in a child's eyes.

Being a Catalonia player was a special circumstance in which you not only played for a major club, but really for an entire country. A rebellious coastal city seeking independence and with every loss the community felt as though they were less entitled to that right. It was much more than football. This was not only their lives I was out there playing for every game, it was their legacy.

The drive to the Nou Barris wasn't as bad as it was in my head. The shouts did come my way and there were one or two glares, but nothing too bad. I intentionally ignored eye contact while walking in the streets. I wore sunglasses with a red Indiana University cap drawn low to shade my face as I walked toward the sign that read "The Supermarket" in Catalan.

I walked to the back of the store then up a stairwell to the terrace. My eyes searched the area for Coach, but I only saw a couple giggling with each other over a plate with a half eaten prosciutto sandwich.

I sat at the table furthest from them. Seeing me walk to the table drew their attention and by the time my butt hit the steel chair, the woman was waving in my direction. Her date, who must have been around my age, walked over to me and extended his hand. "Want to tell you how great player you are. I big fan. You. Best player in the world. Hang in."

"Thank you, much appreciated."

The young man also stopped Coach. The two talked for three seconds before Coach came over and took a seat at the circular table where I sat.

"Nice gentleman, that guy."

"I know. He is, isn't he? What did he tell you?"

"Oh you know, hang in there. I have you on the field and you are the best. Don't be worried. And I'm one of the most brilliant footballing brains." He paused looking around for a waiter to place his order. When he saw no one, he turned back to face me. He pulled a handkerchief from his pocket and wiped the sweat on his forehead. "The kid's right, you know."

"About you having me?"

"No. About me being one of the best footballing brains. That's what made me so good on the pitch in my day. I'm not going to say the best because I don't believe in all that best ever stuff, but I was certainly of quality."

I smiled. "Yeah, whatever Coach. What's up? You didn't look too happy walking over here." His scowl returned.

"Fucking cocksuckers in the office. This new management doesn't give a piss about football, Japeth. They only care about the fucking money. Fucking pricks."

"Wow Coach. They really pissed you off. What happened?"

The waiter finally arrived and took our orders, breaking the conversation. Coach asked for a black coffee and I got a vanilla cappuccino. I looked over Coach's shoulder and waived bye to the couple that was beginning to walk down the stairs.

"These guys have no respect for the game. It's all about power. Can you believe they're trying to tell me what to do with *my* team?"

"Well, what do they want you to do, Coach?"

"They want me to get rid of Breo. They want us to play a more direct style. They feel we'll score more goals, which means more time on sports show highlights, more fans, more jersey sales, more money."

"What happened to Passa Passa?"

"I know, I told you. Fucking pricks. We play the most beautiful football in the world. That's what the fans come to see, but they don't get that. They're not footballers, Japeth. I don't understand how you can have non-footballers running a football organization. This is what happens." The waiter arrived and placed our drinks on the table.

"So what are you going to do, Coach? I mean these guys sound like some stubborn assholes. Doesn't sound like you can get anywhere talking to them."

"You're absolutely right. We just have to win. Winning will do all the talking we need. That's the life of a manager. You win, you keep the job. You lose, you're searching for the next opening."

He took a sip of his coffee then exhaled loudly. "We just

have to win."

"Have you told Breo?"

"No. You know how he is. He's playing well right now and I want to keep his head there. You don't tell him either. This is between me and you."

"I won't say a word Coach."

"Anyway, I also wanted to tell you that you're playing better and better son. I know the match yesterday was a tough one, but keep your head up."

"Thanks, Coach. I feel like I'm getting better too, but it's like every time I start feeling really good, some shit like last night happens. It's frustrating."

"I understand, Japeth. When I was on the Dutch national team the coach did a similar move with me and it took me a while to grow into that role. You have to have patience son. Trust me."

"Easier said than done. I just hate letting our fans down, especially the young ones."

"And you think I don't? It's part of the process, Japeth. We owe it to ourselves as professionals to push our limits. If we do that, there will be uncomfortable periods but the outcome will be so much greater." He swallowed the last gulp of his coffee before continuing.

"Enough about football, son. How's life? How are things with Joanne?"

"Really good, Coach. It's scary how much I love this woman."

"But you still…you know?"

I rubbed my forehead with the tips of my fingers. "I still fool around a bit, but I really do love her."

"I see. That is the life of a young man. Skipping and diving from woman to woman." The volume of his laugher was hearty with a timber that hinted at memories he didn't voice.

"What about Jack? How's he doing?"

"Oh boy. Jack?" I shook my head and took another sip.

"Jack. Well, he's doing alright, but he got in some trouble in there recently."

"For what?"

"I guess he got in a fight and ended up beating a guy with a bar of soap that was tied up in a sock. Real jail shit."

"Oh. I've never had anyone close to me in jail, so I can only imagine what that's like."

"Not easy Coach. I mean, I have other friends that are in jail too, but Jack is the only one I really stay in contact with like that. There's the other guy I was telling you about, DBrown?"

"Oh yes. The crazy one right?"

"Right. Of course he's in there too, but I haven't spoken to him in a long time. It's been years."

"Maybe you should write him?" Coach suggested.

"I might. Maybe after this trip to St. Vincent I'll send him a letter."

Chapter Fifty

WHEN WE ARRIVED AT GRANNY'S, we joined the twenty some people hanging around on her porch and in the front yard. Moms pulled me aside at one point and told me that she really liked Joanne. "I know. Me too Moms. I really love that woman." She smiled at me then placed her hand on my arm and gently guided me towards Granny's room.

"Where yall going?" Pops shouted out at us.

"None of your business," Moms said with a smile. "I want to talk to my son. Is that okay with you?"

The door lock clicked behind us. "What's up, Moms? How are you?"

"I'm good, Japeth. I would love to see you more often, but I understand. My son is a big international footballing star. It's been a few days since we've talked so I wanted to know how you are doing. Are you okay?"

Her eyes carried a hypnotizing effect. I told her about my struggles of being in a new position and how the city hated me at the moment. I tried my best to explain how I loved the appreciation from the fans but found myself struggling with being such a public figure. I told her again about the perfection of Joanne.

"Is she going to be my daughter-in-law?"

"Maybe Moms. I don't know, but maybe."

"Alright, so this is serious, huh?"

"Yeah."

"Okay. That's good. It would be nice to see you settled down. Just be careful she's not after your money."

"Naw, she ain't like that Moms. Granny already gave me the speech on that." I said as I laughed.

"Good. Well Japeth, I have something I want to share with you." She clasped my hand inside her palm.

"Japeth, the cancer came back. It started in my ovaries apparently, but has now spread to my lungs." I had a million words in my head, but none would come together to form a coherent sentence.

"Doc said that I have some time, but that it's definitely terminal. He guessed it could be about three years, maybe four if the treatment really kicks in."

"Why?" That was the only word I could get out.

"I don't know, Japeth." She wiped tears from her face. "Doc said it was undetectable in my ovaries and you know…from there it just…"

"They couldn't detect it? Isn't that what all those crazy machines and doctors are for?"

"Shhhh. Keep your voice down. I haven't told everyone yet and I'm not ready to. I don't want everybody feeling bad for me. I want to enjoy this time. This might be the last time I get come home and I want to have fun, you hear?"

"So who all knows?"

"Pops, Damian, and you. I want it to stay that way. Okay?" The sound of laughter, voices arguing with each other, and music all meshed together as background noise. If it weren't for that noise, the silent room with old pictures of Granny and Grandpa would have been haunting.

"I'm okay, Japeth. Don't worry about me. I've lived plenty life and to see you and Damian living out your dreams is the most important blessing of all."

I sat still for a moment and stared at the rug on the floor. I took a deep breath, then looked at Moms.

"How was your flight? First class?"

"Duh. Nah me?" She smiled. We wrapped our arms around each other tightly.

"It's going to be okay, Moms, we gonna make sure you get the best treatment and you gonna beat this damn thing. Okay?"

I heard a sniffle that accompanied the warm tears that soaked through my t-shirt. "Okay, son." There was a light knock on the door.

"Japeth?" Grandpa's voice penetrated the wooden door.

"Yes, Grandpa." I could hear the low voice of Granny behind him muttering something.

Grandpa unable to keep his voice low responded, "But ah my room. How can you tell me, I can't go in *my* room?" Granny's response was low and short, probably not more than a word. Then we heard Grandpa walking away.

"Coming out now, Old Man," Moms shouted as she wiped her face. She rose to her feet then looked at herself in the mirror. When she was satisfied with her appearance, she turned and patted me on the shoulder and I opened the white, wooden door that separated us from the rest of the world.

"How you gonna hold me damn room hostage?"

"Oh whatever, old man, you could have your room back." We continued to hang out for that night, having conversations with visitors, eating, and listening to the radio.

The next day was Christmas. We exchanged gifts and had a big breakfast that forced most of us to take a nap afterwards.

When we awoke, we got dressed and visited many family members, eating a little bit from every place we visited. Our last visit was Mama's. "Boy, how you stretch so long? Oh jeez you. This boy tall like coconut tree," Smally said to Damian. It was the first time that I saw the six foot four Damian feel slightly uncomfortable about his height.

"Dem Walkers always been tall people, you know?" Mama replied as she set a plate of tri tri cakes down on the table. Jessy grabbed one of the fried fish patties from the plate and asked me how life was as a big, rich footballer and about Joanne.

"Joanne went to visit her auntie but she'll come by later. Football is fun, but it also has its challenges."

"Yo, you could organize a tryout for the team? You remember how me used to clean up man back with the Wicked 7?" Hulk slurred as he poured himself a glass of St. Vincent Strong Rum.

"Hulk. Dem days long gone dread. You can't play no more." Smally said.

"Wha ya mean, Smally? I was part of the Wicked 7. We used to run things all through the islands. National team. Di Wicked 7 dey. Championship team. Di Wicked 7 dey." He sucked his teeth. "Di Wicked 7 used to run things in St. Vincent man. Nah true, Japeth?"

"That's true." Hulk staggered to a seat. Out the corner of my eye I saw Jessy and Mama hiding the liquor bottles outside.

"Yeah, that was then, but we talking now. Watch the state of you? You think you can get out there and play with fellas like Japeth, Cam, and Markee now?"

"Man, look. Me ain't never claim to be no big skills man, but I done break plenty foot for them man. If not for me, them man might not be playing now. With me on the pitch, man afraid to touch man like Cam, Markee, and Japeth." He took another drink.

"And what anybody ever do for me? Only Markee does ever come and say here take a little four or five hundred. Them man Cam and Japeth making millions! Them naw even give me anything to go buy bread."

"But Hulk you never asked me, so I never knew you needed anything."

"Wha ya mean, Japeth? I live in St. Vincent. You live in Spain. A how me naw goin need anything? You never even bother to send me a jersey. You naw send nothin! And you a send Mama money. What for? She have money!" Jessy walked over to Hulk and gently grabbed his arm. He ripped his arm away from her. She hunched over, locked eyes with him and whispered something to him. He got up and they went outside.

"Don't bother with him Japeth. That's just di Strong Rum talking," Smally said.

"How long he been like this?"

"Been awhile now." Seeing the state of Hulk was a downer and there was more bad news to come.

Chapter Fifty-One

I WAS GETTING PAID about 2.5 million Euros every year so under my parents advice I had a weekly meeting with my agent, Jeremy to review my finances. We reviewed what investments should be made, what should be saved, and any new interesting investments that I should consider. It was the same meeting over and over so I developed a trust with Jeremy.

Occasionally, I would let periods pass where I would have him manage my money for me. It was never longer than a month or two, usually when I got really busy and needed to prioritize other things.

I only asked that there weren't any new investments, outside of stocks, without consulting me. That season I remember leaning on him to take care of my portfolio. I needed to be laser focused on improving my play or there would not be any money to manage.

I grew accustomed to playing in the attacking midfielder position and we had a much better second half of the season. We repeated as Una Legua champions for the third time in a row and we won the UEFA Champions League title as well.

I was the top scorer and named player of the tournament. Even with those accomplishments, I did not receive the USA player of the year award due to bad blood with the USA Federation. Instead it went to Jalani for his incredible play in Holland. It did not bother me that the USA did not recognize me as the best player in the country, but I was pissed that the World Committee withheld their acknowledgement of my play.

I wanted the title of best player in the world badly. It was a lifelong want dangling in front of me, rightfully mine but unfairly given to someone else because of their bias against Americans in football. Even though I was proving that an American can play football, the World Committee always found a reason to award someone else, usually another European. It was a slap in the face to me and what I was trying to accomplish in memory of my dead friends, Mike and Landon.

The World Cup was that summer and the USA barely qualified as one of the final teams to make the tournament. I was out of favor with the team since the incident with Sampson. First, there was an official suspension by the USA Federation, then it became a personal thing between Sampson and I. He didn't want me on the team because he thought I was an undermining influence and I wouldn't play underneath him because I knew he was a fucking idiot.

The world cried out for my presence on that team. At the same time, there were also those that felt that Sampson was right to exclude me. They said things like, "maintain integrity of the game," "get rid of the brats," "gangsters don't belong in football," and for the very blunt, "keep the black in his place."

With the support of my fans, I felt validated in my feelings towards Sampson, his fans, and the system. When the Federation stood behind him and made no attempt to see my side of the story, they picked his side in my eyes.

Around this time, I realized that this was nothing new for me. I was always at odds with the US football system. As a kid, I was faced with their indirect opposition in the way of finances and opportunities to play. I almost gave up playing several times because of their indirect pressure or lack of concern. Now as an adult I faced the system head on and they fundamentally disagreed with me as a human being. It was hurtful, but I knew I had to continue being me. I, personally, was bigger than them and knew it would only be a matter of time before they gave in. I just hoped it wouldn't be too late for me to make a difference.

The main attraction of that 2002 World Cup USA team was the partnership of Malcolm and Jalani. Jalani was the top scorer in the Dutch league. He was an unstoppable goal-scoring machine and other top clubs were beginning to bid heavily for his services.

Malcolm was still a silky goal scorer. His biggest improvement was his aerial game. If the ball was in the air, he was going to win it. That added another dimension to his partnership with Jalani, which was needed for that team's more direct style of play. Bryan and Larry fell victim to politics. Sampson had his special group of players that he liked and would always pick over anyone else.

I watched the games from home much to the dislike of most of my family and friends. They thought that people would perceive me as a selfish punk for not being there in person to support my country, but I didn't care. I felt "the country", meaning The Federation, wasn't supporting me.

I was the one that was suffering the most. I had to sit and watch as my friends played and cemented their names in World Cup history. I was feeling down at that point and things still continued to get worse.

I was watching the French team play Brazil when I heard Moms' quick footsteps. I looked up and saw her running into the bathroom. I followed. When I got there, I saw her throwing up a neon orange liquid.

"Are you okay?"

"I'm fine." Her body hurled another time. I rubbed her back.

"It's okay, Japeth. It's just part of the treatment"

"Well this sucks, Moms. They can't get you anything better with more money?"

"I don't think so, hun." My mobile phone rang from my pocket. I glanced at it.

"Jeremy. I'll call him back." I said more to myself, but did say it audibly.

"Answer it hun. It might be important." I hit the green button on my phone.

"Make it quick, Jeremy."

"Jay, I'm begging you. Please get your butt over to that tournament and show the people you care."

"No. Is this what you called for? I don't have time for this mess right now." Moms threw up again and was breathing heavily over the toilet.

"Fine. I just think you're making a big mistake. Is somebody throwing up?"

"My Moms. Is that it?"

"I was really calling to talk about the money, but we can do that another time."

"Look Jeremy. Just handle it okay? Isn't that what I pay you for? Anything new and worthy, then talk to me but don't bring me no BS Jeremy. I don't have time to waste. Understood?"

"Understood. Send your mother my love." I hit the red button.

"Japeth, I don't think that's smart son."

"What's not smart, Moms?" I continued rubbing her back. She wiped her mouth then rose to a standing position.

"Letting Jeremy handle the money like that. You need to keep a close eye on your money."

"Moms. It's fine. He deals with billionaires okay? Trust fund babies. If they can trust him with their money, why can't I?" She took slow steps to the sink, turned on the faucet and washed her mouth out with water then mouthwash.

"Son, that may be so, but that's the way your father and I had the contract drafted up and we did that to protect you."

"It's fine, Moms. Trust me."

"I don't like it, Japeth."

LATER THAT AFTERNOON, I WATCHED Patrick Apolline score the first goal of his World Cup career. Throughout the tournament, he played a key role on the French team that summer. He was the second highest scorer behind their great midfield maestro, Bezane.

Patrick's play from the right wing was as exciting and menacing as it was years prior at the Dallas Cup. Since Dallas we became good friends. We played against each other during youth national and professional games and had a Bird and Magic type of relationship. Watching him play gave me both the most joy and envy during the 2002 World Cup.

The only advantage about me not playing in the tournament was that I was able to rest the entire summer. When I arrived in Catalonia the press were waiting for me with questions about The Coach.

The mob of questions hurled my way just sounded like the usual noise until one of the reporters held up a popular Spanish newspaper. "Sacs de Catalunya a l'entrenador de tall" (Catalonia Sacks On The Edge Coach) was the headline that stared me down. I refused to be intimidated by the news and snatched the paper from the hands of the reporter.

The article insinuated that it was a contract dispute over money, but I learned that afternoon, from Coach, that was not the case. It was about power. It was about who's philosophy was the right way forward for the club.

The new coach, Coach Luis De Coster, invited Breo and I to dinner a few weeks later. We had not even ordered the bottle of wine when De Coster announced to Breo that he was moving him to the left wing position.

There was a brief back and forth between the two of them. Breo telling De Coster that he was not playing left wing as forcefully as Coach De Coster was demanding that he would.

"You are too selfish and I have watched you squander too many opportunities," De Coster explained to Breo. There was some truth to what he was saying, but I did not admit that to De Coster. By the end of dinner, Breo had begrudgingly accepted his role. The first few days of practice De Coster was asking me to play more balls over the heads of defenders instead of quick small passes. It was the beginning of the end for the great Catalonia era.

Chapter Fifty-Two

ONLY AFTER A MONTH OR TWO of De Coster's leadership, I started to find it hard to wake up for early practices. I found joy in the final whistle of the training sessions. In the locker room, there was a stillness where there was once foul language, exploits of the night before, and laughter about times past.

I walked into that drab locker room one day and there was a curious silence. Everything in the room felt slow, except Breo. Breo's arm was pumping in and out of his locker grabbing items and tossing them into a gym bag.

"Breo, what's going on man?" Oier stretched out his hand to stop me. I pushed through it.

"These mother bitches are sending me to Italy."

"What? That's some bullshit. For real?"

"The good thing is that I don't have to play for that stupid runt. He knows nothing of football and I feel sorry for all of you." He moved his hand around pointing to the entire team.

A week later De Coster brought in Gerrit Bakker. He was a Dutch striker who finished second in scoring to Jalani the past two years in the Dutch league. His strengths as a striker were his physical presence at six feet three inches and his goal scoring instincts.

Frustrations within the team were growing day by day. De Coster was a coach who wouldn't think twice of berating you in front of the team or press. When mid season arrived, we were showing the affects of the harsh coaching method as well as the fatigue from the World Cup summer. We were in second place, eight points behind our rival in the league.

Joanne visited me in Catalonia for a few days before we went to Indiana for the holidays. She arrived on a Tuesday. On Wednesday night we went out with Oier and his wife for dinner. We had a great time and agreed that we would all go out to a club the following night.

Knowing that Oier's wife, Victoria, came from a wealthy oil family in Venezuela, Joanne expected her to be snotty. She was surprised that Victoria was actually a sweet person, even though I tried to tell her that before.

The following night after dinner at La Peix, we went downstairs where the club section was in full swing. The music varied from salsa, merengue, hip-hop, and electronica. The club was closing at 4am, so we all decided to get a jump on the exiting crowd and left a few minutes before. Outside of the club there was a small crowd.

We were waiting for our cars from valet when I overheard aggressive voices. "Look at that black whore bitch." Another voice chimed in. "I've seen gorillas lighter than that."

There was laughter from a group of individuals. I turned and saw four bald white men. Joanne turned around as well. "Don't look over here niggers. Especially you, you, black bitch."

I sprinted towards the group of men and punched one of them in the face. His body fell backwards and laid limp on the ground. The fight was one versus three and soon I was the one being slammed on the ground by the police. The cuffs they placed on my wrists pinched into my skin. I had a black eye and a bloody lip, but my three opponents had several broken bones.

After a few hours of explaining the situation at the police station, I was released. A trial date was set for three weeks later. The next day, different versions of the story were all over the media. De Coster had his assistant coach call and tell me that I was suspended for four games without pay.

The assistant coach explained I was very irresponsible and my behavior was ignorant. He said I was unprofessional and that I behaved like an animal not a gentleman. He paused for a moment then continued saying that De Coster expected more out of me. My response was, "Fuck off" before I hung up the phone and continued watching TV in my condo.

A couple minutes passed and the phone rang again. I picked up. "Yo, I said fuck off. Don't call me with no more bullshit. If De Coster got something to say, he can call me himself."

"Japeth?"

"Moms?"

"What's all that about? That's how you talk to your coaches? You know I raised you better than that. You better act like you have some brought-upsy."

"Sorry, Moms. They just suspended me for four games. I'm just really upset about it."

"Did you get to explain what happened to them?"

"No. They don't care. De Coster didn't even call me. He had his assistant call me."

"It's okay, Japeth. Keep your head up. Pressure makes diamonds."

"Yeah."

"Remember God don't give you nothing you can't handle." She said.

"I know, Moms."

"Hey, so I have a little more bad news. Your grandpa is sick. We're not sure what it is but we're bringing him up here for treatment."

I didn't say anything. I reminisced on our times talking about cricket on the porch in Layou. I could hear his laugh. I thought about how I was always too busy to call as often as I wanted to over the past few years and how I never followed through on getting him tickets to one of my games.

He died in his sleep a day before the flight was scheduled to leave. The official cause of death was complications from diabetes. The night of this death, for the first time in several months, I drank some cold medicine to fall asleep.

Before falling into a deep slumber I remember that being the first time I contemplated going to another team. It felt disloyal to the team and country, but to stay felt like a betrayal to myself.

Chapter Fifty-Three

MY FIRST GAME BACK after my suspension, I was pissing away the ball nearly every time I got it. During the second half the defensive midfielder who was marking me got close and held the back of my shirt out of the referee's sight. He then whispered into my ear, "Heard your friend Mike couldn't take it in the ass." I had to watch the replays in the locker room to find out what happened next. I watched myself on the TV screen turn and punch the defensive midfielder in the face. His neck snapped back violently.

I was suspended for fifteen games by the World Committee, which was most of the remaining league season and all of the Champions League, unless we made it to the final. The guy who was on the receiving end of that punch was out for the rest of the season. His jaw was disconnected and his cheekbone was cracked. He couldn't play for about a year after that punch. He never regained form and retired after a year of trying to come back.

The incident was the headline in every newspaper and a topic of discussion on every news show. My condo became my safe haven. I had a growing library of DVDs and books that gave me a mental escape.

I usually watched the movies by myself. Different lady friends would come over every now and then and Joanne would visit occasionally from New York. I tried to get her to move in with me, but she refused until we were married. "I've worked too hard to get this job and you want me to just up and leave it without any security," she would argue.

Moms, Granny, and Mama loved Joanne. They said that she "came from good people."

"You see that Joanne, she's a classy gal. Somebody gonna take she away, if you don't do right soon," all of them warned every time I talked to any of them. I knew they were right, but I didn't want to commit to her when I still had some playing around to do.

I couldn't imagine life without her, but I also loved the feeling of being wanted by others. I loved that carnal spark in a woman's eye. It made me feel like a man and until providing for Joanne gave me the same feeling, I was hesitant to commit. Marriage was important to me and I wanted to honor it.

I was at home watching a movie one afternoon when the phone rang. I looked at the caller ID. It was Moms.

"Hello."

"Hey, Japeth. How's it going?"

"Ah. It's okay Moms. Just trying to get through this period, you know?"

"Yea. Have you been reading your Bible?"

"Yes. I've read some of proverbs here and there."

"You going to church?"

"No. I haven't been. Too many people, Moms."

"Okay. Well, listen. I went in for my check up today. They say there's some new treatment available that may help a lot."

"That's great news, Moms. Why you sound so down?"

"Well. It cost a lot, Japeth. Money we don't have in the accounts you set up for us." I had invested enough money that would allow them to live off of the interest. They both received one hundred thousand dollars each annually.

"How much is it?"

"One point four million."

"Wow. That is a lot. How do you feel about it? Do you want to try it?"

"It seems interesting and I'm willing to try. Doc said it could help add a few years."

"Okay. Let me call Jeremy and I'll call you back."

I called Jeremy at his office and on his cell phone, but there was no answer. An hour passed and he didn't return my calls. It was unusual for him to not call me back within fifteen minutes.

I called each phone three more times. I was worried, but I decided to access my own funds so that I could get Moms secured before making sure Jeremy was okay.

I logged onto my account from my laptop and saw a zero balance staring back at me. I called the bank and they told me that my agent removed all of the funds and said he was taking the money to another bank.

The next day the police found Jeremy's body on the floor of his apartment. All the money that I thought I was investing was gone. After weeks of investigating the death, the cops found that Jeremy was gambling with my money and he owed big.

From what they could piece together, he had a bad run, borrowed some money from a loan shark and the vig ran his tab well into the millions. He robbed me to pay them. They declared it a homicide, but one of the officers told me that he thought it was a suicide.

Jeremy and I were cool, or so I thought, so the news was upsetting but I also felt he got what he deserved. I was really pissed that I was now out of the money to help Moms with the new procedure, plus I knew I was going to hear it from her and Pops about trusting Jeremy.

I withdrew all of the money from Moms account to help pay for her treatment. Even with full withdrawal of her account, I was a few hundred thousand short. Pops account still had money, but I didn't want to completely deplete the money they lived on. I called a number that I hadn't dialed in some time.

"Japeth, what's up? Long time no chat."

"Dave, what's up? I know man. You know how it gets crazy busy over here."

"They still got you on suspension for that bullshit?"

"Yeah."

"Yo. I ain gonna lie. When you stole on that mutha fucka I was buggin out. They showed that shit on the National Sports Network on replay. They be talking shit about you, but they don't know where we come from, man. That's the way you handle a mutha fucka when you a Vice Lord."

"You know how it go, but hey man look. I gotta roll outta here in a minute to get to a photo shoot, but I need some help."

"What's up? What you need?"

"A couple hundred thousand. Moms is trying to get some special treatment and I'm a little short cause this punk ass lawyer stole my dough."

"Stole your dough? What?"

"A man, be cool. He's already dead. He was fucking with the mob and somehow that shit was handled, but I still don't have my loot."

"Alright man. Give me a week and I'll pull the funds together for you. Ain't no thang man. I got you."

A week passed and two hundred thousand dollars was deposited into the account that I requested. I transferred the money to Moms account for her to make the payment. I was happy at least one thing was able to get solved, but my situation with football was still a sore spot.

Chapter Fifty-Four

I FELT TOUCHES OF REGRET watching my teammates from the bench during games. Their faces that once beamed brightly with enjoyment were now tight with apprehension. The words of encouragement to each other during the games had become mean spirited. De Coster would stroll up and down the sideline and be pleased when he heard a player curse out another for a mistake. I felt like I let them down. I let the fans down. I let the ghosts of Mike and Landon down.

The black media across the world continued to support me, while my jersey sales slumped in suburban areas. My critics wrote that I was already washed up and that I would never regain form.

They labeled me a hot head who wasn't mature enough to handle the pressures of professional football, some pointing to my culture as a reason for my lack of maturity. De Coster perpetuated these sentiments by making comments to the press like, "He has all the physical attributes but he's got to get stronger mentally. I want warriors on the field."

I wrote Jack a few times letting him know what happened

and how things were going for me. His letters back to me made it clear that the past few years put us worlds apart. He now followed a new code of conduct and I was supposed to be following a new set as well. In one of his letters he told me that Jason, that fat fuck from Houston, got transferred to his facility.

Two weeks after he arrived they found him dangling from the corner of his bunk bed. The update provoked worry in me that one day I could be getting similar news about Jack. I needed that solitary time for an introspective look at myself. I think life is like that. You get on this ride and it's very easy to forget what your grounding principles are, what your north star is. The suspension actually gave me time to refocus and it crystalized during our final game of the season.

As luck would have it, we made it to the European Champions League Final. We were going to be facing a very strong Italian team, lead by Bezane. When I looked across the pitch during warm ups and saw the smiles on the players faces contrasted with the defeated look of our team, I knew that was going to be my last game as a Catalonia player.

With my name on the rumor mill, I was already receiving bids from other top teams. Even though I was considered a gamble in the football community, the offers that were coming in were record breaking and I had to hire a temporary lawyer to help manage the negotiations.

With the knowledge of this being my last game for Catalonia, I gave all that I could plus ten percent in that game for the people, not for De Coster. The game was competitive and tied at 2-2 with two minutes left in regular time and I had a free kick opportunity about twenty yards out from the goal.

I glanced at the goal and wall that was set, and then focused my attention on the ball. When the referee blew his whistle, I hit the ball with the inside of my left foot and my connection was solid.

I looked up to see the ball clear the wall. It was swooping around and down into the far side netting. I was sure it was going in the back of the net, then suddenly, Clank! It hit the cross bar and zoomed out towards our goal.

The ball flew past me, to an opposing forward who then took a long shot from half field catching our keeper off of his line. He scored and they won 3-2.

PATRICK APOLLINE HAD RECENTLY revived his career with a transfer from an Italian team to a top tier English team, The London Choppers, mid season. The recent appointment of Coach Samir LeClerc, was having an affect and they were beginning to flourish as a team.

"Coach LeClerc is a real players coach. He understands players and how to get the best out of them. I really love it here. You should come. We can do some damage together," he said to me.

"That's not a bad thought, Patrick. You and I playing together? That would be dangerous."

"Seriously. I'm talking Champions League, Premium League title, The Cup, what else? I'm serious. Let me set you up with a meeting."

"Definitely. Who should I talk to over there? I'll tell my lawyer to hook it up."

Reporters still asked whether I was planning to leave the club and I lied saying, "Things have been better but I am happy here in Catalonia. This is my home away from home."

Management also began to make a strong push for me to stay at Catalonia. I think they were reminded of my greatness from the Champions League final performance. They were willing to get rid of De Coster to make me happy. I had until the end of summer to make my decision but I wanted all offers on the table by the end of June so that I could make my decision before the Fourth of July.

The offers came in on time and the two front-runners for me were another Spanish team and The London Choppers.

I weighed all sorts of factors including the cities, team culture, coaches, and money. I also thought about where Joanne might be happiest.

I had conversations with all those closest to me. Moms had the best advice when she told me, "playing your best football makes you happiest, so go where you think that would happen. Everything else will fall into place."

I knew that London would be where I would enjoy my football most and that was the decision I made public on July third. The deal was the most money they ever paid for a player and still to this day, I have the highest salary of any player in history.

When asked about the amount of money spent and my reputation for getting in trouble, Coach LeClerc answered with his French accent, "I personally think we got a deal. There is no amount of money a club can put on being able to secure possibly the greatest player of all time. When you think of all he's done it's a real possibility that he'll go down as the greatest and I'm excited about the opportunity to manage him."

Patrick and I agreed to meet in London a few weeks before pre-season training started in late July. He wanted to show me around London and help me move in.

The house that the Choppers organization had purchased for me was much bigger than my condo in Catalonia. I needed new furniture to fill all the rooms, so I had Joanne help.

We went back to Kokomo to visit for a week. Everybody was doing well. Moms was in recovery from her recent treatment and looking better. Pops had picked up painting as a hobby. He said that he got restless doing nothing. Damian was named Division I college player of the year and was on his way to the pros.

Joanne, Damian, and I visited Jack. He was happy to see us and shocked at Damian's height. He made a few jokes about how big he was and offered him a warning about fooling around with girls too much before we settled into our conversation.

Jack's upper body was littered with tattoos and markings that I could only assume were scars of survival. He surprised me when he said that he'd been catching some of the games.

"You have TVs in there?"

"Yeah, we got TV up in here. I be catching 106 and Park and shit. For real though man, you be doing your thang out there. I'm proud of you, Jay." We talked about running around the streets of London when he got out. "We gonna do it just like how we used to back in the day," he said.

"When you supposed to get out anyway?"

"Two more years, man."

I nodded. "I want you to meet my lady"

He lit up, "You brought her?"

Damian put his fist to the window and met Jack's against the thick glass before leaving the room. Damian left and Joanne entered in his place.

"Wow Jay." He prompted me to hand her the receiver. "Good to meet you, Joanne. Heard a lot about you. So tell me, how you deal with looking at his ugly face everyday?"

"Well, I don't. That's why I stay in Brooklyn." He laughed and they had a short conversation before our time was up.

"See you in two years, pimp," Jack said.

"Alright. Hit me up when you're out." I both feared and looked forward to the time Jack was free.

Chapter Fifty-Five

I ARRIVED IN LONDON on a cloudy day with a drizzle of rain, what they would call a soft day in England. The crowds overflowed the area at the airport. I watched from the plane's window as hundreds chanted my name in hysterical bliss. When I exited the plane, I was whisked off to a nearby SUV then taken to my new residence.

Patrick and I hung out later that night and had dinner. We talked about life and how things were going for him now that he was a father. He was ecstatic especially since he had a boy and spoke at length about how he was going to go about making him into a footballer. He frequently mentioned that his father wasn't there to show him how to play.

The next day I arrived at the training grounds. I met the team and joked around with a few of the guys before heading out to the pitch for training. The grounds were full of flashes from every angle accompanied by a mishmash of voices.

We had a quick warm up then the coach called us in. He welcomed us to a new season and introduced me. We all sat down around him in a loosely formed semi-circle listening to his ambitions for the year.

"We have to take the season one game at a time. We have to enjoy our football. Most important, above the trophies, play for the joy of the game. If you have fun, the rest will take care of itself." Hearing that sentiment was like receiving a perfect full body massage that leaves you not wanting to move. I was wrapped in his comforting cocoon.

Everybody's touches were sharp and quick, the rhythm of play much faster and more aggressive than Catalonia. I struggled to keep up with the pace, but over the next two weeks of pre-season I did well enough to earn the respect of my teammates and the press in attendance. There was a buzz in London amongst Chopper fans that we were definitely going to win the title that year, something that had been eluding the team for many years.

Over the next two years, I played the best football of my career but it still was not good enough to be voted as the best player in the world by the World Committee.

I was losing faith in the mission that I'd set out on since being that boy watching Pele highlights on a VHS tape after Mike's brutal death, but life continued to move on.

Moms was hanging on and getting better. I liked to think that she was hanging on to see me crowned as the best player in the world. Perhaps she wanted to see Damian win a professional basketball championship.

He already won rookie of the year his first year in the league and was voted an All-Star for both years of his career. He led his New York team to the playoffs both years as well. It was only a matter of time before he reached the mountaintop.

Mama and Mrs. Barney passed away in 2003, Mama dying of cancer and Mrs. Barney succumbed to Alzheimer's. Mr. Barney, her husband and the neighbor with whom I had the closer relationship, didn't last much longer. He entered the other side of life six months after his wife passed.

Moms said that his existence after his wife's passing was full of material things - new car, mobile phone, expensive clothes, shoes, and a new computer. Yet there was nothing he could buy to fill the void that Mrs. Barney left in his life.

I was sitting alone on the corner of my bed in my Hempstead house when suddenly the sun poured in through my bedroom window. It felt as if God was reaching out to comfort me with those rays of sunlight. The thought of Mr. Barney suffering alone, anxiously trying to fill the hole in his life, played off of the same sheet of music in which my life rhythmically beat.

Within fifteen minutes of hearing that story and after a few paces around the house, I was on the phone with Coach LeClerc asking to be excused from practice for the next two days.

He agreed and the next morning I arrived at JFK. The smugness of the summer air was replaced with a crisp winter chill. I waited inside of the airport for five minutes before Charles texted me to let me know that he had arrived. It was a matter of hours before I was engaged to Joanne.

Throughout our celebratory dinner that night, I couldn't stop looking at the ring that I placed on her finger, which I had designed two months prior. I looked at the way her ring sparkled. The gleam from it tried it's best to exude the class and quality of Joanne, but didn't stand a sparkling chance.

Chapter Fifty-Six

JACK GOT OUT OF PRISON in January 2005, followed by DBrown in March of 2005. I received calls from both as soon as they were released. After a couple of months of talking to Jack, we fell into a new rhythm that was close and brotherly in it's own way, but the experiences we had in those years apart created some distance between us.

When I talked to DBrown, he asked when I was going to fly him and Jack over to London. His voice was like a time machine pulling me back and suddenly I could feel my body vibrate with the bass from the speakers in the trunk of his old Caprice.

I could smell the weed from the blunt that was being passed around the car. I could see girls ducking to look through the window of the stopped car. The nostalgia was intoxicating, getting me high on its fumes, and I was helpless to his question. "You know I got you, bro. I'ma hook something up so you and Jack can come through."

We were at the top of the Premium League table the last week of March 2005. My blood rushed with anticipation for the following week.

As luck would have it, Joanne would be in New York working on wedding arrangements, we didn't have any games during the week, and we were playing a team at the bottom of the table on the weekend. I had that game marked as one that I was sure Coach LeClerc would rest me for and so I bought tickets for Jack and DBrown to come out for that whole week.

When they arrived at my house, I could tell they were impressed. After the initial joy of seeing each other for the first time in years, our conversation was bumpy. "Man, you gonna have us eating all that exotic shit? You know I don't fuck with that shit." DBrown started as he and Jack laughed and shared the Vice Lord handshake.

"Shit for real dude, I just want some mac n' cheese, fried chicken and shit. I'm not fucking with no damn fish eggs or no shit like that. Well...I'll fuck with some lobster but you know what I'm saying." Jack said with excitement dancing in his voice.

"Yall mutha fuckas is crazy. Been eating too much of that damn slop and shit," I replied. It wasn't long before the difference between years in jail and football success dissipated and it was like it was 1989 again. That week we went out clubbing every night and enjoyed everything that came with it - women, weed, and alcohol.

I was making headlines that whole week and Coach LeClerc was pissed at me. Joanne was pissed too, as the media had a few pictures of me around other women. Luckily nothing was incriminating, but Joanne knew something was up.

Coach LeClerc and I sat in his office while he explained the importance of being responsible not only to myself, but to my family, team and the city. I heard him and it all made sense, but I was having too much fun. It felt so good to just be Jay and have someone pass me a blunt without some damn health hazard reminder.

It was confirmed. I was not going to play in the game on

Saturday, because Coach LeClerc was resting me. He knew I wanted to party with my friends so he gave me the day off. I went to a popular West Indian club with the guys Friday night. The night was unusually warm and the sounds of laughter, clinking glasses, and music beat the silence of the night to a non-existent pulp.

We pulled up in front of Kilimanjaro with "Where I'm From" by The Game humming out of the car speakers. The line was about two blocks long and I felt all those eyes following my red Aston Martin as I slowed to a stop for the security I hired to park and guard my car for the night. The three boys who had come from little Kokomo, Indiana stepped out of the car and into the night.

I'd been in the position of fame and popularity for years, but this time it was different. It wasn't just me. It was us. I felt like we were the guys we used to look up in the neighborhood with their 8Ball jackets and all the pretty girls at their disposal. There we were in London with the spotlight on us. Three Vice Lords who had made it, but the night wouldn't end well.

Although Jack and DBrown had never been to a West Indian party, they enjoyed the way the women moved their waist seductively with an attitude that begged your eyes to stay focused on it.

I was dancing with a popular soca artist, Marisha, from Barbados. We always had a thing for each other, but never officially dated. She was rolling her large, soft behind back on me, grinding into my mid section when I felt a nudge that knocked me off beat for a second.

I turned to see a short, dark skinned guy with dreads stumbling wildly against his own knowledge. His speech was loud and boisterous. He offered no apology. Not even a look of acknowledgment. I opened my mouth to curse at him then Marisha placed her palm on my hip, guiding me back onto her behind as she circled it around. "Don't do that. You can't see he's drunk?"

Five minutes later and about thirty feet away from Marisha and I, DBrown was face to face with the drunk dred.

I rushed over to the two guys to prevent them from getting any closer to each other. When I arrived my head was rocked back with a punch to the face. The next few seconds were blurry to me, but I can only remember throwing a flurry of punches against a never ending army then hearing gun shots.

What I remember next is slowly opening my eyes and the dark, high-energy club surrounding had been replaced with the muted cream colors of the hospital. There were tubes connected to my nose and arms. I was still half sleep when I saw that Joanne was asleep on the couch a few feet from my bed.

"Joanne," I said, surprised to hear my voice come out as a whisper. I cleared my throat and tried again, "Joanne." This time my voice carried it's way to her eardrum.

"Hey babe. How are you feeling?"

"I don't know. What happened?"

She rubbed her hand over the top of my shaved head. "You got shot, babe. Doctor says you're lucky you got hit on the right side, cause if it had been the left, you woulda been dead."

She paused and stared into my eyes. The reality of what she said was too much for me to digest and forced my eyes away from hers. The silence carried on for another minute or so.

"Where's Jack and DBrown?" She gripped my hand and tears began to well up in her eyes.

"Jack's fine."

"And DBrown?" She looked down.

"He didn't make it, babe."

I almost flung myself from the bed, but the immediate pain halted my plans. "Where's his body? I want to see the body. I don't believe you."

"He's gone, baby. I'm sorry."

————————

A COUPLE MONTHS PASSED and I hadn't touched a ball at all as I recovered from my injuries in the brawl. DBrown's death plagued my heart and mind. Another close friend gone and I had begun to wonder if it was just a matter of time before Jack and I were in the sky with DBrown, Landon, and Mike. There was always something in me that kept me feeling like that little naive kid thinking that bullets wouldn't strike me and if they did so what, I was tough.

Laying helpless for weeks let me know just how tough I was when everyday tears had their own drag racing competition on my face. It was in the eyes of Joanne, Moms, and Pops that I saw the true stupidity of risking my life.

In those moments and all moments after, I looked at Joanne with the same reverence and respect as though she floated in the crisp, blue sky on a puffy white cloud. All the other women were no more.

My near death experience spiked Moms stress levels. Her cancerous cells showed themselves again in her body. The doctor found a lump in her breast. He recommended that she have her right breast removed and she agreed.

I was doing my physical therapy in Los Angeles and Joanne and I were able to visit Indiana frequently to help Pops out with Moms during that period. Damian was continuing his success as a professional basketball player in New York and could only join on the day of her surgery.

I got great pleasure from seeing him enjoy his life, with no apparent demons to battle as I did daily. There were two unexpected big wins in my life and the fact that his life was not marred by the dramatic downfalls that I experienced was one. The other was having the privilege of being Joanne's husband.

It was through her that I finally began to really heal. She's the only person that I felt I could completely open up to. I always underestimated the value of talking about my true feelings when it came to the deaths of Mike and Landon, but she provided me with such loving comfort and support that I couldn't help but to share my feelings.

I was surprised to find that the more I talked about it with her, the less I had the nightmares. I no longer needed to take cold medicine to force myself into deep sleeps and the only haze I needed to be under was her love.

Chapter Fifty-Seven

OUR WEDDING DATE was set for July 17th, 2005 and that week came quickly. We had the bachelor party earlier in the week, which was like the scene out of the movie *The Best Man*.

"You not gonna hit that tonight?" Jack asked.

"Nah man. I'm bout to be a married man. Yall deal with that." Patrick came over to where Jack and I were talking and wrapped his arm around Jack's shoulder.

"I'll take her if you can't handle her, Jack." Those around me laughed. I looked over towards the bar where my Uncle Jimmy was taking a blunt from Jalani. He puffed it, inhaled and coughed. Then he passed the burning blunt to Derek Shea who did the same as Uncle Jimmy. The three laughed.

The other nights leading up to the wedding were more of a collective unity of the women and men. Joanne tried to remain calm, but she progressively unraveled as the week went on. The night before the wedding she called me.

"Babe, we should have just gone to the courthouse. These people are driving me crazy."

"I know, babe. We'll be married tomorrow and all will be well."

"I know. I can't wait. I love you so much, babe. Can't wait to be Mrs. Walker."

"I can't wait either. I love you."

"I love you, too."

Our wedding was the next day. Everything didn't go as planned, but the day was still perfect. While the reception party scourged on, Breo and I took a break and sat down at an empty table together. A waiter brought us two drinks.

"This is a beautiful wedding, Japeth."

"Thanks, Breo. When you gonna get yourself a wife?"

"Ha. I'm a long way away. Too many to choose from."

"True."

"What made Joanne the one for you, because you were worst than me." I took a sip from my drink.

"You know what it was, man. I got to a point where I realized life was so much better with her. I couldn't let her get away from me, so I had to do right by her. She is all the woman I need." I took another sip of my Hennessy.

"When you have that feeling, Breo, that's when you know it's time."

He nodded. "Well, I haven't had that yet." Dave walked over to the table where we sat.

"Hey Jay, when you have a minute come find me."

"Alright Dave. Give me a few minutes. You met Breo, right?"

"Yea. I met him at the bachelor party." They shook hands and Dave walked away from the table.

"He's a cool guy. He said he works at a factory in Kokomo, right?"

"Right."

"He kind of reminds me of my father." He paused for a

short moment. "He taught me everything I know about the game. He'd watch me play in the park then walk me home. During our walk home he would explain to me things I could do better. He told me the spotlight was on me when the ball was at my feet. I knew the better I dribbled the ball the more Papa would enjoy my play. I could still see the smile on his face today."

"What happened to him?"

He took a drink and continued. "The boss in the slum, Ricardo, wanted to have sex with my mother and when my father fought back they killed him. I found my father on the side of the road in a gutter with his dick in his mouth on my way to school."

Breo threw his head back and finished his drink. He placed the empty glass on the table. "That is why we are the best in the world at what we do. Without a ball at my foot I, and others like me, are just elementary school dropouts who would be left to dwell and die in the slums like my father. You know why your country is not good at the game?"

"Why?"

"You have no hunger. No need for the game. There are not enough Japeth's playing the game in your country. You know what happens to the players that don't make it in this country? They're accountants, businessmen, doctors. You know what happens in Brazil, Africa, Eastern Europe? They live poor and die poor."

Throughout the conversation his voice carried on different notes ranging from happy, sad, to anger with ease like a seasoned saxophone player. I was very familiar with how those emotions could rise to the top of your psyche so quickly and hide again in a blink.

Chapter Fifty-Eight

WHEN I RETURNED to training camp near the end of summer I was a refined assassin. The group of Choppers that I returned to were also different. There was dissatisfaction, a feeling of shame and anger that each individual carried with him.

There was a collective boulder that rested on all of our shoulders. It was a boulder that our Chopper family held up with us hand in hand. We were determined to win championships after coming in second for the league title three years in a row and failing to reach the Champions League Final every year.

Coach LeClerc picked the right pieces to fit into a sensational puzzle. Our style of play was fluid and unpredictable. Our offensive prowess was too much for most teams. The ball always flowed through me. I scored goals and fed Patrick to his best goal scoring season. I wanted to repay Coach LeClerc's faith in me.

Although he was upset about the shooting incident, he didn't once flinch under the pressure from the press or front office suggesting that I be put on the transfer market. They said that I didn't have the killer instinct needed to win another championship. Coach LeClerc never wavered from his opinion that I was the best player in the world, arguably ever.

Our team featured one of the greatest Dutch players ever in Kevin Has. He was an extremely skillful and creative forward. Patrick's fellow Frenchman, Mamadu Dior, was our clean up man in the midfield. He was about six feet two inches and two hundred pounds with excellent distribution, speed, and crunching tackles. Our back line was led by a pair of twin English center backs, Tony and Adam John, who were typical English hard men.

We had four wing players between our outside wingers and wing backs that seamlessly and frequently interchanged positions. Mario and Thomas usually started in the midfield while Martin and Robbie started in the back. Our keeper, Andreas, was a six eight brick wall from Germany.

We went undefeated in the league that season, finally winning the title. We also won the European Champions League and The Cup that year. It was a tremendous year of football that didn't end at the club level.

During that summer of 2005, the US Soccer Federation fired Sampson. The new coach, Demetril Vasile, called me as soon as he knew he was hired.

"Japeth, I know you've had your problems with the US team in the past, but this team needs you. I need you. I selfishly want my chance to coach the best player in the world. What do you say?"

"I say that if you can keep your word and honestly commit to making the US the best team in the world then you and I are going to get along fine, and only then will I play under the US flag."

There was a pause on the other end of the phone. "Why else do you think I took this job? I am not simply committing to making this the best team in the world, I *will* make this the best team in the world, but in order to do that I need your leadership. If you're simply committing to that goal, don't join. If you completely believe in your heart and soul that it will happen then my offer still stands. It cannot happen without you."

The pause was now on my end. "Okay Coach D. Let's set the world on fire." The winning mentality that was spilling over from me was bubbling through the US national team. Coach D was also an inspiring presence.

He took special care in grooming the team from afar, staying in contact with all of us who played abroad, always offering words of advice and motivation with fiery passion.

In every conversation he said, "Remember, it always comes back to the United States. No matter what other jersey you have on it's the American blood. American soil that you grew up on and that's ingrained in your skin that matters most. It always comes back to the United States of America." I never got tired of hearing him say those words.

The pride in the US flag showed itself on the field any time we set foot on the pitch for our remaining qualifying matches. We scorched the competition with a tremendous balance of speed, skill, and competitive spirit that allowed us to dominate the CONCACAF region. The dream offensive triangle of Malcolm, Jalani, and I was reunited. We fell right back in sync although each of us had grown in our own way.

Jalani was playing in Milan. He continued to party hard, but it didn't affect his play. Malcolm was enjoying life in Germany. He was frustrated with the lack of black culture, but he was comfortable.

And I, I finally felt at home, comfortable in representing a country that holds so much pride in itself that it refuses to be seen as anything less than the best. I became the light that lead the way from the dark years of what the world considered to be dumb, sloppy feet and robotic motions.

It is the rhythm of the "Bebop Boys" that has transformed

the world's view of United States football. It is the culture of winning that has positioned the United States as the worldwide favorite to win the 2006 World Cup and lead to one of the most important days in my life.

Chapter Fifty-Nine

IT WAS NOVEMBER 2ND, the day of the world player of the year ceremony, and like many other years before I was in the running for the award. Given all that I had done that year, I didn't see how they would deny me but they surprised me so many times that I was prepared for disappointment.

Joanne and I walked the red carpet, dressed in our gala attire meeting and greeting both fans and media. She wore a beautiful, shimmering dress and I wore a fitted single breast black suit with a black shirt and tie.

My parents, Damian, and Jack came separately but took their seats next to us inside by the time the ceremony started. During the two hour event the committee gave trophies to individuals who achieved throughout the year.

Patrick, my friend and Chopper teammate from France, won for goal of the year. Coach LeClerc, won coach of the year for our flawless league season.

The closer they got to the end, where they would announce the world player of the year, my breathing became heavier. Joanne noticed and whispered in my ear. "It's okay baby. No matter what you're the best." I thanked her, but her words of comfort didn't quell my breathing.

The time had come. The host of the evening called The Coach out to the stage to announce the world player of the year. When I saw The Coach, my knee bounced rapidly. Joanne squeezed my hand.

Moms tapped my leg. Pops nodded in my direction, being a seat away from me. Both Jack and Damian tapped my shoulder from behind me.

As The Coach took his place behind the podium, the applause of the crowd died down and two of the World Committee leaders took their place on stage next to The Coach. Once they were in place, the host asked The Coach to do the honors. The Coach leaned towards the mic and said "gladly."

He began opening the rectangular envelope. We could hear the sound of the seal on the gold envelope tearing through the microphone. My knee continued to bounce up and down feverishly. A symphony played softly in the background.

Then The Coach pulled out a card from the envelope. A smile spread across his face. He looked up to the crowd then fixed his eyes to me.

The only other time I remember my heart pounding so hard was when I first met Dave and I thought he was going to kill me. The fear of both situations were the same but different. The Coach leaned towards the mic and said "The winner is, Japeth Walker."

I always thought that I would have jumped out of my seat when, or if, I ever heard those words but instead I sat frozen. Everyone around me lept to their feet and there was a happy hysteria in the building.

After a few long seconds, I got up hugged my family and walked to the stage. When I got to the stage The Coach hugged me tightly and said, "You deserve this more than anyone son. I'm so proud of you."

He passed me the golden football trophy. When I held the trophy, the tears started flowing. I took my place behind the podium. The audience continued to stand and applaud for nearly two minutes.

I looked out and saw my former and current teammates Breo, Oier, Malcolm, Jalani, and Patrick amongst the tearful room. The crowd slowly stopped clapping and took their seats after the host signaled for them to sit. I waited until it was quiet, then I spoke.

"I first want to thank God for everything. Without him none of this would be." There was a light round of applause. "I want thank my beautiful Moms and Pops today. I know that you sacrificed everything so that I could be standing here today. You guys went to a foreign land, leaving all that you knew and your family behind in St. Vincent so that your children could live their dreams. My brother, Damian, thank you for all of the support and love. I think that I can say that as of today, I'm now more famous than you." I laughed to myself then looked at Jack. I stared at the tattoo of a walking cane on his neck for a few seconds, then back at the trophy, then out towards the audience. I took a deep breath and continued.

"My boy Jack is here today and as I look over at him I can't help but think about all of the friends we've lost that should be here with him tonight. Two in particular – Mike Wilson and Landon Smith. I've wanted this trophy for most of my life and it's kind of surreal to finally hold it and know it's mine. I dedicate this trophy to their memories. Thank you to the beautiful island of St. Vincent and The Grenadines that allowed my talent to flourish. I want to thank Coach who believed in me when I didn't believe in myself and the same goes for Coach LeClerc. I want to thank the London Chopper organization and all the Choppers out there for their support. And finally…"

I paused, swallowed hard and bit my bottom lip. " My wife, Joanne. My personal angel. She was the key that unlocked me. She is the sunshine that blast away my storms. This woman is irreplaceable. I love you Joanne. So while I dedicate this award to Mike and Landon, I share it with all of my family and close friends who have all saved my life at some point. I love you all. Thank you."

Acknowledgments

IN LOVING MEMORY of the following: Victor Hendrickson, Pearl Dopwell, William and Sharon Waldon, Be Garrett, Rudolph Joshua.

First and foremost, I must thank God. He is the spirit that inspires and moves my pen.

My mom and dad for all of their sacrifices and hard work that have allowed me to become the man that I am today. Teneisha (Tonto Timun) and Darrian Story – Thank you for all the laughs and support during the creation of this project. Ja'Yana thank you for the enthusiasm.

To my family, who have made the largest sacrifices in the completion of this book. Erin and Carmen, my beautiful daughters, who continually accused me of "eating the cookies ALL up." I did, during the late nights of writing. Keren, my beautiful queen, thank you for your support, honest opinions and encouragement.

My editor, Megan McKeever. Thank you for your help in bringing this story to life. Yohanes Haile. Thank you for the incredible cover art. Miles Davis. Thank you for the great photos.

A big thank you to the following: Olive Hendrickson, Cam O'Garro, Joel O'Garro, Berles Desire, Kenrick Chambers, Vinceroy (Vin) Chambers, Holly Charles, Bruce Bryant, Gary Phillips, Marvaline Chambers, Brandon Ellis, Terrell Waggoner, Ezra Hendrickson, Matthew Smith, Heather Shotke, Chris Sanders, Corey Ealy, Reanna O'Garro, Larry Harris.

Photographer: Miles Davis

JOMO HENDRICKSON is influenced by many artists but especially the likes of Toni Morrison, Eduardo Galeano, Nas, Chinua Achebe, John Coltrane, Peter Tosh and Bob Marley. Although he now lives and works in Los Angeles, he originally hails from Kokomo, Indiana. He is also an avid hip hop and soccer fan.

www.ingramcontent.com/pod-product-compliance
Lightning Source LLC
Chambersburg PA
CBHW020235180626
46810CB00006B/2206